THE
CROWN
IN THE
HEATHER

Also by N. Gemini Sasson:

The Bruce Trilogy
The Crown in the Heather (Book I)
Worth Dying For (Book II)
The Honor Due a King (Book III)

The Isabella Books
Isabeau: A Novel of Queen Isabella and Sir Roger Mortimer
The King Must Die: A Novel of Edward III

Standalones
Uneasy Lies the Crown: A Novel of Owain Glyndwr
In the Time of Kings (14th century Time Travel Adventure)

The Faderville Novels
Say No More
Say That Again

Sam McNamee Mysteries
Memories and Matchsticks

THE
CROWN
IN THE
HEATHER

THE BRUCE TRILOGY:
BOOK I

N. GEMINI SASSON

cader idris
press

In memory of

Phyllis Jean Sasson

Historical Note

IN THE YEAR 1286, King Alexander III of Scotland was an aging man, whose two sons from a previous marriage had already died. His daughter, who had been married to King Erik of Norway, had also died two years prior, leaving behind an infant daughter named Margaret. The succession of his line was in peril and he vowed to waste no time producing another heir. And so on a storm-battered night, he left royal Edinburgh Castle, took the ferry across the Forth, and rode against caution from Inverkeithing toward Kinghorn, stirred by the need to cool his lust on his new French bride, Yolande. Forging anxiously ahead, blinded by a driving rain, Alexander became parted from his companions somewhere along the coastal road. His horse, startled by lightning, lost its footing. The next morning, the king's broken body was recovered at the foot of the ragged sea cliffs. Scotland mourned, not only for the loss of its king, keeper of peace and progenitor of prosperity, but for troubles yet to come.

Little Margaret, the Maid of Norway, was Alexander's only direct descendent. Her dowry would one day be the whole of Scotland. South of the border, King Edward of England, also known as Longshanks, whose firstborn son was but two at the time of Alexander's death, sniffed an opportunity. It was agreed between the Guardians of Scotland and Longshanks that Margaret of Norway should be put aboard a ship and brought forthwith to her ancestor's homeland. By grace of a papal dispensation, she would marry, in due time, Longshanks' oldest son, thus ensuring peace between Scotland and England. Cognizant of the advantages of such a union and yet prudently wary of its implications, the Guardians were, however, shrewd enough to force Longshanks to swear in writing that the two countries would remain separate.

But the little girl, on whose slight shoulders so much depended, had not yet reached its shores when she fell gravely ill. The Scottish escort that awaited her in Orkney to take her to Scone to be crowned was never able to complete its mission. On the 26th of September, 1290, she died.

Dozens put forth their claims to the crown. In the end, two powerful Scottish families possessed the strongest ties to royal blood: the Bruces and the Balliols. The late King Alexander had favored Robert Bruce, fourth of that name, also known as Robert the Competitor. But not everyone was convinced a Bruce should become King of Scots, including Longshanks.

If a Bruce wished to call himself 'king', he would have to fight for the right to do so.

PROLOGUE

<u>Robert the Bruce – Atholl, 1306</u>

EACH NIGHT WHEN I lie down, bathed in the rank sweat of a day's pressed march, I am so weary I neither stir nor dream in my sleep. For weeks, I have felt neither the cushion of a pillow beneath my cheek, nor the caress of a blanket upon my shoulders. Sometimes my bed is a pile of bracken. Sometimes a slab of stone. Come morning, I am soaked with dew. I feel the barely warm light of the sun upon my soiled face. Hear the familiar murmurs of wretchedness. Smell the ungodly stench of bodies and I am awake.

Now five hundred, we live off the land, taking only what we need. We stay far from the towns and main roads, keeping to the highland heather and dark forests. I had often looked upon the hungering poor as I passed through the cramped, stinking streets of London, but with nothing more than a fleeting twinge of pity and a wave of disgust. Now, I think, I am living a worse life than they, for I envy of them whatever little they possess: a place to sleep, a roof to shed the rain, a stolen loaf of bread. Arrows and spears be damned, I would sell my armor for a stew of peas and carrots or a handful of radishes and some salt.

This is the army of Scotland and I . . . am their king, Robert the Bruce, sixth by that name and grandson of Robert the Competitor.

Once, I was Longshanks' sworn man. Now I am his mortal enemy. Beaten to the hills, hiding in the forests of Atholl, clinging to existence.

What irony that in these months since I have been king, not for a day have I lived like one. A crude living it is, especially when we have no plan or provisions to begin with. The heather is a beautiful place, but when you are cold at night and hungry all day, beauty becomes nothing.

Our sick and wounded we are bringing with us. Although they slow us, to leave them behind is to offer them up as quarry. The days are long, the miles endless, our feet and backs weary and aching. It is the pinnacle of summer and hot as a blacksmith's forge. The rain so usual of Scotland is not to be seen. Every night when we halt, the foot soldiers pull off their shoes and nurse their raw, oozing blisters with poultices. The air reeks with the stink of moss and herbs boiled and mashed into a paste, or ointments made from whatever animal fat they can scavenge.

Often, I wonder if I will ever be able to shape this brawling, fractured group into one united army. My own men, those on foot from Carrick, limp from wounds not yet fully healed. I hear some of them say that maybe it was not so bad living alongside Englishmen and paying them taxes to keep the peace. The Highlanders, who would never entertain such a notion, squawk at the hobbling stragglers. Our noblemen complain of the company, including each other. Along the way we abandon many a lame horse, so that fewer and fewer of us have one. Most of the time, we allow our womenfolk to ride, but even they take to foot eventually, giving their mounts to those too battered or ill to keep pace.

I have kept my own horse, the sturdy, gentle gray I claimed at Methven, so I can ride the length of the column several times a day to encourage my men on. For reprieve, I often settle in beside Elizabeth and the other women in the middle of the column. Of them, only sweet Marjorie whimpers, sometimes, about the grinding in her empty belly. To placate my daughter, I send good James Douglas to her and he lets her ride in the saddle with him as he teaches her French to pass the time. Although only ten years of age, she is an apt pupil, enamored of his gentle manners, and in a matter of days she has learned enough to converse with him in French. I cannot hear most of their conversations, but whatever he says to her makes her laugh and for the kindness I am grateful to him. James is protective of her, like an older brother always watching over her—holding her hand when they cross a stream on foot, brushing the dirt and grass from her clothes when she falls, bringing her wild strawberries to eat, forget-me-nots to entwine in her hair, or brooms of bell heather to shoo away the flies. With a young girl's bright curiosity for adventure and pleasure in a newly found friendship, only Marjorie appears to flourish on this weary and dreadful Exodus. The rest of the women ride or walk in silence, eyes ever watchful, their shoulders forced downward by the constant strain of weariness, yet never complaining.

I have never seen the shadows so deep beneath Elizabeth's eyes. I talk to her of how we will go south to Kintyre and rest there a bit before going on to Ulster where we will be safe and wait out the winter, but it is as though she is a hundred miles from me. She gazes into the mirroring depths of the lochs we pass by—Errochty, Tummel and Tay—as if some other voice from there speaks to her more plainly than mine. At night I hold my wife—her small, fragile form aligned perfectly to my own. She is restless, starting at every tiny sound, irritable come morning. I cannot reach or comfort her. I cannot set free the troubles of her soul, for I know that because of my ambitions I have caused them. In making her my queen, I have delivered to her naught but a shattered kingdom caught up in despair. No more is she the Elizabeth I once knew—and it is my doing.

The morning mist lies heavy as a blanket of January snow across the valley below our camp. We all stir lazily and might have slept longer but for the midges diving at our ears and agitating the horses, which stomp and swish their tails. Fog chokes the road ahead and so we break fast and wait for it to lift.

Alone, Elizabeth claims a flat rock as her seat to avoid the damp ground. Around her, the junipers glisten with droplets of dew on a hundred spider webs. Hunched over her bowl of thin porridge, she sips slowly, perhaps trying to convince herself it is a meal worth having. Knowing her as I do, cold swill and stale bannocks are hardly a temptation to her, no matter how famished she is.

Silent as a stalking cat, James Douglas moves to stand some ten feet from her, his arms straight at his sides. Impatient for her attention, he drums his fingers on his legs until she lifts her eyes and nods at him. He sinks to his knees. I am tending to some of the horses, close enough to see them through the drifting mist, yet far enough away that I cannot hear them speak. Men cross in front of me and I drop the reins of the horse whose foreleg I have been inspecting.

James crouches before her, his dark hair glinting with the morning damp. He slides a letter from his shirt, then tucks it hastily back beneath. She shrugs, looks down and away. He creeps closer and says something more. An easy grin flickers across her lips. He reaches out to her. She extends her hand. Slowly, he leans forward to gaze at her with those haunting, pale eyes, smiling faintly. Then his lips brush her delicate fingers. He bends his neck, so his forehead rests on her knuckles.

The longer the touch between them lingers, the more my neck burns. At Kildrummy, I had seen Elizabeth glance down the table toward him, but never thought anything of it then. He is young.

Closer in age to her than me. Soft-spoken and gentle in manner.

"Sire," Boyd says, startling me, "the Abbot of Inchafray's come. With sacks stuffed full of bread. Can't you smell it? Fresh bread, I tell you. Not a spot of mold."

I beckon to an idle soldier and hand him the reins of the horse. "Give the abbot my thanks, Boyd. Pass the food out to the wounded first, then the women—they'll need their strength for the hills."

"He says we're close to Tyndrum. There by noon if we leave now. Says he can lead us there and on through the Pass of Dalry. Should I tell them all to make ready?"

As I look again toward James and Elizabeth, they are speaking in whispers, strangely intimate. Are they so enthralled with one another they cannot notice the rest of the world?

Boyd turns to see what has my attention so fully. He scratches his belly and grunts.

"I'll tell them to wait." He ambles off, thumbs hoisting his sagging belt.

I bound over a pile of rocks and send a stone scuttling to nick James in the knee. He leaps up and jerks in a bow, his cheeks flushed.

"James, go tell Boyd and the Abbot of Inchafray we'll move out within the hour, so long as the fog lifts. I'll not take any chances, having the womenfolk with us."

He leaves without protest, his hand pressed over the lump beneath his shirt.

Slowly, I turn toward Elizabeth. "The letter."

But she is still watching James, unaware of my words. "He'll make you a fine knight one day. His heart is true."

"Dare I ask what you mean by that? Or do I want to know?"

"What? Robert . . ." Her eyebrows weave together in perplexity.

A curse on my heart for being so near my tongue. I wanted the words back before they reached my own ears. I want to believe in their innocence, but . . .

"The letter, Elizabeth. What was in the letter?"

"Nothing that regarded you. This is not the time for petty jealousies, Robert."

"Then dispel them. Tell me—*what* was in it?"

She rises to her feet. The hem of her gown is tattered—torn away strip by strip for bandages to just above her calf. Her feet are bare and calloused, but she has taken care to wash away yesterday's road dust. The small oval of her chin works back and forth. "I haven't the will right now to argue with you over this. But since you must pry—it was from his brother Archibald. When James came to Lochmaben to find you, he asked me to deliver a letter to his brother. The reply eventually came to Kildrummy, where I was. It was one of the few things I brought with me when you sent for us to join you, because I knew he would be wherever you were. Just now he was thanking me. That's all, Robert. Don't make more of it." She crosses her arms over her breast and turns her back to me. "If you doubt me, ask him yourself."

Struck dumb, I shuffle my feet. "Elizabeth, I'm sorry. I . . . I didn't mean . . ."

Softly, she sighs. Her shoulders slump forward. "Perhaps I should not have come."

I reach out to trace the twining ridge of her braid where it lies against her neck and loops over her sunburned shoulder. Then I take her by the arms and turn her toward me, even though she resists. In those ever-changing eyes of pale greenish gray, I see the worries she yearns to share daily, but keeps to herself. I let go of her and gaze down at my empty hands. "In those weeks after I left you at Kildrummy in Nigel's care, I had no idea where you were . . . if they had taken you, if you had fled to safety or boarded ship. Thirty days may as well have been thirty years. Elizabeth, I should have told you . . . before I went to Scone, how hard this was all going to be. I knew, but I could never say, because . . . Ah, Christ . . . hard, aye, but God knows I never thought we would be running like this, not knowing where to go, who to trust, when to fight or hide . . . never thought I would talk of leaving Scotland altogether. What an awful mess I have stirred up in trying to put things aright." I meet her eyes again, and for the first time in months, see her tender and caring heart there just as I once had at every casual glance. "Before I can fight for what is ours—yours and mine, Scotland's—first, I must know you're safe."

She presses her small palm flat against the middle of my chest. "Do you say that for my ears, Robert . . . or your own?"

"I have thought of nothing but your safety since I left you at Kildrummy."

She shakes her head. "When you think of me, perhaps. What you think most of, though . . . what matters most to you . . . it *isn't* me."

Aye, one thing matters to me, above all else, and for so long a time I have fought it and pushed it away . . . and then it found me even while I denied it.

"And this about me," I say, "it frightens you, does it?"

"No, I'm not frightened of you, Robert. I'm frightened of what will happen to *us*."

I pull her to me, wanting to reassure her, tell her somehow, that all will be right in the end. She lays her head on my chest. Her ear is at the perfect height to hear my heart beating.

"Elizabeth, whatever you think, I'll not risk losing you. I swear it to both you and Our Lord. But I'm not ready to fight again. Not after Methven. Not yet. It's too soon. We've lost too many men and have neither the weapons nor the strength to defend ourselves."

"But you will fight. You'll have to. You . . . we . . . we can't keep running forever."

She draws back, gazes at me softly as her lips part, then quickly buries her head against my chest again.

"What, my love? Something else?" I say.

"'Tis a small thing," she murmurs. "It can wait."

"You'll tell me tonight then?"

"Aye, tonight," she whispers. "When we have more time."

I tuck my whiskered cheek against the gentle slope of her shoulder. I don't want to think about it—only about her and this moment, wishing it would go on forever.

"My lord?" James trots toward us. "The abbot says we should move out soon. Our scouts have word that the English passed close by not two days ago."

"Thank you, James. I'll join him shortly and we'll be on our way. But first . . . first ask the abbot to take us by St. Fillan's shrine, so I may ask God's forgiveness. In the meanwhile, I shall beg for my wife's, if she will give it?"

Elizabeth's arms tighten around me and in that rare moment, I know I have never loved anyone or anything more.

Perhaps, though, that isn't true. For if I loved her more . . . I would not be who I am. I would not be king.

And we would not be here, in the wilds, running for our lives, hurting and hungry.

Make her believe it is so, Robert. Make her believe she is your world and reason for being. Ah, but she knows, she knows better. She knows you and you cannot fool her into believing otherwise.

I hold her, not wanting to let go. As I lay a kiss on the crown of her head, I hear my grandfather's voice, as clear and strong as if he were standing here beside me:

"Reach out your hand, Robert. Touch the horizon."

Aye, Grandfather, I know. I barely heard you then, but now your voice echoes like the thunder over the moors. 'Tis a grievous burden you have left to me. Many are the days when I wish that I could hand it back and follow you instead.

"Up with you," Boyd says to a pair of soldiers, who were lazing beneath the low-hanging boughs of a pine. He is used to bellowing, but under orders to keep his voice low, he resorts to prodding and kicking to get them on their feet. "On our way now. If you can't walk, crawl. Unless, that is, you want to stay and let those bastard English bleed the misery out of you."

Groans and grunts, then weary silence. They stagger to their feet and melt into the bedraggled column as it forms along the trail. The creak of leather as riders shift in their saddles. The weary plod of horses' hooves. Marjorie leads a black pony. She strokes its muzzle and speaks gentle words of reassurance. My sisters Mary and Christina lean upon each other, their eyes roving broadly, like a pair of hens who've caught wind of the fox.

The sun, already, is high and hot. We've as many miles yet to go as we've put behind us. South through the pass, then on to the coast and over the sea. Tomorrow morning we'll rise again, more tired and hungry than we are today, but God willing still alive and whole.

1

Robert the Bruce – Lochmaben, 1290

THE AUTUMN WIND WAS murderous cold. Small gray clouds raced like mountain hares above a drab and muddy billowing of land. Leafless limbs clattered in complaint against the onslaught of wind. My grandfather and I rode to the highest hill around, me muttering under my breath at the rude awakening while my insides churned with every bounce and him sitting stiff-mouthed, but steaming, on his mount.

On the crest of the hill, we stopped. For a long while, he did nothing but gaze across the land, pensive, agitated. Then he said, "Look around you, Robbie. What do you see?"

I hesitated to speak. My mouth tasted of vomit and stale drink. Late last night I had downed four tankards of first ale, followed by a dose of cider strong enough to knock me from my stool. My cause for celebration had been a private one—wildly, delightfully private. I scraped my tongue beneath the edge of my front teeth and spat, but the taste remained. Lochmaben, from which we'd ridden out less than an hour ago after he'd tossed me from my bed, was hidden beyond a stand of trees. Against the glare of morning sun, I squinted and twisted around, my eyes finally stopping to rest on the long, endless, shifting ribbon of blue in the valley beyond. "I see the River Annan."

I thought it a fitting observation. Grandfather was the Lord of Annandale. Fourth by the name of Robert Bruce—and I the sixth.

"And where does it lead?" He snapped his hood over his thinning silver-black hair and tugged it forward to shield his face from the relentless wind.

"To the Solway Firth, then on to the sea." I tasted bile again and held my breath until the wave passed. I would give him any bloody answer he asked for right then. All I wanted was to go back to bed and think of what it would be like to have Aithne there beside me for a whole night. A quick frolic in the stall yesterday had left me not only with a whetted appetite for my sister's new handmaiden, but smelling faintly of manure and plucking bits of straw from my hair and clothing at dinner while my father glared at me reproachfully. I had smiled at him as I thought of her—not so much her, really, but the physical thrill of her. I was well beyond boyhood now. I could drink as heartily as any of the older knights and I'd had a woman. I'd have her again if Grandfather would just get this over with, whatever it was about. As much as I admired and cared for him, I resented this intrusion on my daydreams.

"Beyond that?" he said.

"Ireland lies beyond. But they say there is more land even further off than that. Places where the Norsemen have been and come back from."

"Look the other way now, lad. What do you see?"

I yawned. "The forest. More land." My thoughts drifted back to Aithne. Damn, I wanted her again, even as tired and wretched as I felt just then.

"Beyond that?"

I shrugged, vague as to the point of this all. "England?"

Within the thousand folds of his leathered countenance, he smiled, although it appeared not so much a smile as a crumpling of stiff cloth. "Reach out your hand, Robert. Touch the horizon."

Feeblemindedness, I was certain, had nested in his skull and woven a cocoon there. Soon enough he would imagine himself a child.

"Reach!" he bellowed.

I extended my arm to placate him. The wind brushed at my bare fingertips. "But Grandfather, how can I touch what is so far away? How can any man?"

"Just move your feet, lad. There's far more out there than what is here, within your sight. More tomorrows than yesterdays. More men in the world than just you. Knowing that is the difference between being an ordinary bore, forgotten before you're dead, and being remembered."

"What has all this to do with why we're here right now? I need to get back. My fingers are slowly freezing and I've someone to—"

"Hear me out!" I thought for a moment he would strike me for my insolence, but he merely squinted at me. "There are things beyond your ken right now, Robbie. Things that, in time, will come to mean more to you." He looked down at his gloved palms and flexed his stiff, old fingers, nodding to himself. "We'll go back, then. But gather your belongings with haste. You'll accompany me to Perth. We leave at noon."

My whole young, giddily blissful world shattered. Leave Aithne and go to Perth? I clenched my knees against my mount's ribs. My pony nickered and flicked its ears, eager to move off the windy promontory and into some sheltered glen. "No, I won't. I can't."

"You will. It's time you begin the work you were bred for. Forget her for now. There will be other lasses willing to bed with a comely young nobleman like you, Robbie."

Others? Perhaps, but none like Aithne.

"Aye, I know who she is," he said with a nod. "All of sixteen and you think your whole bloody world exists under a lass's skirts. Men your age have sired sons upon their wives, ruled over entire kingdoms . . . killed men in battle, conquered complete armies, even. Being a man is not about gulping down ale until you pass out. And any dullard with a stiff pole can shove it into a knothole for pleasure. Time you woke up, Robbie, and realize what it means to be a Bruce. Council is convening at Perth this very moment. The nobles have been gathering there in anticipation of a coronation. As it happens, our infant queen, the little Margaret of Norway, is dead. You and I have a claim to remind them of. The Balliol kin will be there fighting for theirs."

Council? Claims? The Balliols? I had no care for any of those things.

Grandfather gathered his reins and nudged his horse in the flanks. It started with a jolt and he began to ride on down the slope, cautiously, as his old bones did not yield to forces like they once did. He raised his voice above the wind. "Your father need not know you're that coming with me, though I doubt he'll care."

I shook my head and shouted after him, "But why not Father? Why me? Why can't I stay here? What have I to do with any of this?"

He halted partway down the hill and slammed his fist onto his hip. His blue lips twisted into a ragged snarl. "*You* have everything to do with this. Don't you understand, lad? We're talking about who will be king one day—whether it should be a Bruce or a Balliol." He wagged a crooked finger at me. "As far as your father goes, I have wearied of trying to push a rope. You're different, young Rob. You can't see it yourself, but in time, you'll know it."

Who will be king one day . . .

Stunned, I watched him ride ahead of me back toward the castle. He didn't stop to wait for me. He knew I would follow.

<u>Perth, 1290</u>

THE WIND HAD CEASED for a time. The rain stayed away. Under a crisp, clear sky, our journey from Lochmaben to Perth went quickly. All along the road, men came out to join us. By the time we arrived, over four hundred rode behind my grandfather. The nobles and clerics there took notice. A full eighty years of age, he asserted his claim to the throne of Scotland in the middle of the council hall with all the eloquence and acuity of Plato or Socrates. As a son of the Earl of Carrick, I stood toward the front of the hall with other great lords and prelates. The tables and benches had been cleared away to allow as many representatives of Scotland's noblest blood and holiest orders to fill it as could be packed into it. Toward the rear, lesser barons jostled elbows and stood on their toes for a view. On a short dais at the head of the hall sat the four Guardians of Scotland: Bishop Wishart of Glasgow, Bishop Fraser of St. Andrews, James Stewart and John, the Red, Comyn of Badenoch.

In a voice strong and clear, Grandfather said, "It was the wish of our own gracious and noble Alexander that I should—"

"Decades ago, Bruce," Comyn interrupted. "The succession has changed since."

Something about Comyn disturbed me in a way I could not shape into words. Brother-in-law to John Balliol, he railed against my grandfather—against any Bruce—at every opportunity. That alone was reason enough to loathe him. But more, there was nothing about the man to admire. He seethed with anger and contempt. In looks he resembled a goat, with his tapered rusty beard and wiry hair. Even toward his own kinsmen he was gruff and demanding, showing neither respect nor tolerance. I had as yet to hear an intelligent word dribble from his sour mouth. Grandfather disregarded

Comyn's surliness, never indicating he was the slightest bit ruffled by him. I knew differently, however, having spent the entire ride from Lochmaben to Perth with my ears being filled by his curses for the Balliols and the Comyns.

Bishop Wishart raised his cheerful voice. "Ah, it was indeed long ago, my lords. But on the succession . . . in that view you and I, and others here, may differ. That is why we have come together now, is it not? The matter is not entirely plain, as you both bear evidence to." Publicly the mediator, privately he was an intensely passionate man.

At the other end of the dais, James Stewart sat rigid and impassive, his eyebrows barely twitching as he studied each speaker in turn.

"I thank you, your grace. What you say is very true," Grandfather said. "Now, let us go on, good men, and get straight to the point of this all. We come together, here today, because we all care to know who will wear Scotland's crown. If we all believed this was not about blood or power, who would rise and rule and who would wither into obscurity, we would all have come here with open minds, and open hearts, and abundant love for our fellow Scots. But I see not embraces and well wishes. I see in your glances suspicion, envy, and mistrust . . . old affronts resurrected, as if the ghosts of our grandfathers were here beside us, inciting us all to right the wrongs of spilled blood long since turned to dust. Each of you count up your relations and you weigh how heavily you lie on one side or the other and reckon which side will benefit you more, do you not? And some among you would hand the crown, our crown, to the King of England and allow him to decide? Come now . . . where is the sense in that?" He was now speaking not to the Guardians, but to all those assembled in the hall behind him. "When, I ask, do we each thrust aside our own ambitions and think not 'What is best for me or my kin?' but 'What is best for Scotland?'"

"A Bruce!" someone cried out. More shouts rumbled off the rafters.

At that, the patriotism Grandfather had elicited was just as quickly swept away. He shook his head and waved his arms up high. "No! No! You speak too soon, man. And from your heart, not your head."

Bishop Fraser, an ardent supporter of John Balliol, rose from his seat. He held up open palms to push back the ardent stream of Grandfather's words. "Your arguments are persuasive, Lord Annandale. But the law is as it is, and for sound reason. In the absence of a male heir, the crown shall follow down through the eldest daughter to her eldest son."

"By that logic," my grandfather argued, standing alone but resolute between the agitated mass of nobles and the eclectic tribunal of Guardians, "Scotland should be ruled by Count Florence of Holland, your grace, being descended from the eldest daughter of King David's son. Yet, I see not a man here upholding *his* right. The count himself did not even bother to come to stake his claim. For that matter, where is John Balliol? Not here. So, a pox on your reasoning, I respectfully say. My grandfather was—"

"Grandson to King David," Red Comyn finished for him, leaning forward with one elbow planted on his knee and his head hunkered down between his rounded shoulders. "We all know. Why not spare us the rhetoric and state your case? There are others besides you waiting to be heard from today."

"Fair." Grandfather ambled toward the crowd of nobles, catching eyes with his supporters and nodding respectfully toward his adversaries. As he reached my side and took my arm for support, he scratched at his bulbous nose and said, in an unmistakable taunt, "But with John Balliol as your brother-in-law, may we assume you argue for his cause and spare ourselves that weary bluster? I'm eighty, my lord, and wish this resolved before they put the nails to my coffin."

Grumbles of resentment and ripples of laughter collided. Comyn gnashed his teeth. He dug his fingernails into the arm of his chair. Only a swift glare from Bishop Fraser subdued him.

In the end, logic presided over nothing. They had all come to uphold the interest that best promised to advance them and their own, as in Comyn's case. But of those who held no familial connections with either a Bruce or a Balliol, those men leaned toward my grandfather. They admired and venerated him and pledged their support to him, including the earls of Atholl and Mar.

I learned something that day, something that I would never forget: that when men give their loyalty willingly, they give it with conviction.

Lochmaben, 1295

BEFORE BEGETTING HIS OWN sons, King Alexander had named my grandfather as his heir. Grandfather would have made a passionate king, brusque perhaps, to the point of provoking annoyance, but always fair in his honest way. In that year of 1290 at Perth, he was already an old man and not well. His body had begun to fail him. For the next five years he fought with his rotting teeth for the throne that was his. Longshanks' contrived courts decided against him at Norham, against my family. Balliol took the throne. My father, complacent, accepted various offices doled out by Longshanks to requite his loyalty, among them the governorship of Carlisle.

Although my father never contested the coronation, for in truth he never yearned to be king because to him the crown only invited trouble to whomever wore it, neither would he pay homage to Balliol. Conveniently, he sailed for Norway, where he married my older sister, Isobel, off to the King of Norway himself. If he would not risk his head for a crown, he at least knew how to ply opportunity through diplomacy. He had not yet returned when in the early spring of 1295, Grandfather was struck by apoplexy. I arrived at Lochmaben and rushed to my grandfather's chambers, where I found him propped up stiffly in his favorite window seat, sagging heavily to one side. The shutters were open and a chill breeze enveloped the room. A storm had passed over earlier that morning, soaking the air in a dampness that I could feel in my clothes.

"Grandfather?" I snatched a blanket from the bed and crossed the room in four strides. He stared blankly out the window. His right shoulder slumped and the arm below dangled limply across his lap. His eyelid on that side hung so far down that I could barely see the blue of his eye beneath the drooping flap of skin. I laid the blanket across his legs and right arm and even as I did so he gave no recognition that he was aware there was anyone with him. Then I slid onto the seat across from him, placing a hand upon his knee. "Grandfather, it's me—Robbie."

He tried to turn his head, to smile, to reach out with his hand, but the palsy, which had troubled him the past few years only to the point of embarrassment, now was uncontrollable. How difficult it was to see this once proud man, esteemed by so many, laid low by infirmity.

"Robbie? Is that you?"

"Aye, 'tis me." I took his trembling hand. It was stone cold.

"Where the bloody hell have you been?"

His words were slow and slurred, but they made me laugh. "Up north, in Kildrummy. With my new wife, Isabella."

"Mar's daughter? You devil." He half-smiled and chortled. A choking sound gurgled from his throat. I started forward, but just as quick he went quiet. He tried to swallow, but it was an effort for him and a thick line of spittle ran from the corner of his mouth. I wiped it away.

"Happy?" he asked.

"Very. We've been wed a month now."

"Gave up your lass? The pretty redhead?"

I sighed. "Ah, Aithne . . ." When I returned from Perth with him five years ago, she was the first person I sought out. I couldn't do without her. I even thought to marry her, if only to keep her to myself. But my father would not hear of it—'not worthy of a man who would one day be the Earl of Carrick', he said—and I was often gone with Grandfather then. I'd found her attentions hard to keep. My brother Edward, two years younger, lunged at the opportunity during one of my absences. He flattered her. Gave her gifts. And in the end, he took her to bed, tired of her, then moved on to another conquest. I begrudged Aithne nothing, for our romance had long since faded and Edward was quickly becoming notorious for his fleeting trysts. He already had three bastards to his tally—and not yet nineteen years old. I leaned deeper into the window. The first rays of sun in several days pried through the clouds to brighten the land below. After a winter of long, cold nights, the hills were flushed with a splendid green where not three days before they had been the color dun. I almost remarked on the sight to Grandfather, but I doubt he could have seen. "Married a man named Gilbert. Lives on Loch Doon. They have a son, I hear."

"You?"

"None yet."

"Yet." He nodded faintly and closed his eyes. "B-b-balliol?"

"A pathetic king, just as we all knew he would be. But he's in trouble with Longshanks already. Chafed too much at being yanked about. Finally spoke his mind and was promptly chastised for it, to put it lightly. Then the French—God bless King Phillip—declared war on England when Longshanks refused to pay homage for his lands there. He was set to sail for France when the Welsh were gnawing at his backside and he rushed there instead. They'll keep him busy awhile. As for Balliol . . . I'd cheer him on if I didn't real-ize all he did was invite Longshanks to march here and trample on us again. Bloody fool. If he thinks . . ."

He slept peacefully. His breath was faint. The tremors gone. His skin the color of cold ashes.

I gazed out the window, smelled the rain and earth mingling on the cool breeze. For a long time, I sat there with him, holding his hand, wishing for one more hour, one more day to be with him, to talk, to tell him of Isabella and so many more of the things that filled my life.

When I looked again, he was no longer breathing.

Grandfather, pray I may one day have but a speck of your courage in the presence of my enemies, a sliver of your grace toward my fellow men. You carried me as far as you could and because of that I shall never stand alone.

2

<u>Robert the Bruce – Turnberry, 1296</u>

T HE WIND GUSTED, HOWLED as it blasted into the mouth of the sea cave above which Turnberry Castle perched, and then quickly fell away to a plaintive moan.

I traced a numb finger along the feather and felt the prick of its stiff edge. Lifting the arrow, I stared down its shaft: dead straight and crafted from the finest ash. The leather wrist brace, stiff from the winter cold, crinkled as I curled my palm inward and nocked the arrow. Wind roared in my ears. My hands stung. I raised the bow and pulled back hard on the string until it cut down the length of my cheek. Squinting one eye, I aimed slightly to the left of my mark. The pale gold light of a winter sunset reflected off the sea in broken flashes. I blinked away momentary blindness and focused again on the target: a sack of grain propped against an overturned rowing boat. Corn had spilled from a rip in the sack when my first arrow— the only one to come close—snagged its cloth. A scattering of yellow grain flecked the dark gray shingle of the ragged shoreline around it.

I let out a sigh. Half a clutch of arrows already dispatched and not one had yet found its mark.

Beyond the abandoned boat and the torn sack, the black mouth of the sea cave gaped. Clamorous kittiwakes dipped beneath its high opening and claimed refuge from the weather in scattered nooks within. The hulking fortress of Turnberry sat on a long arm of land that reached out into the sea. When it was built a hundred years ago, a tunnel had been hewn through the rocky earth beneath it down to the cave, so if the castle was ever laid siege to supplies could be brought in by sea. In all that time, it had not fallen from my family's possession, to either rivals or foreigners. Likely, it never would.

How many times as a lad had I scrambled up and down these cliffs, hunted among the tidal pools for shells curved like rams' horns, or plied these relentless waters in a sailing boat with Grand-father barking at my shoulder? Although remote, Turnberry was a fine place: a safe haven where I and my many brothers and sisters had grown up. Soon, my first child would be born here in the very same bed in which my mother, Marjorie of Carrick, had given birth to me. God willing, Isabella and I would have many more. But childbirth . . . there was danger in it for the unborn child as well as the woman.

A rusty brown crab skittered from beneath a flattened branch of seaweed and I pulled a foot back to allow it past. Hours ago, noon perhaps, I had descended a trail further south along the shore and come to this small, secluded cove to wait out the arrival of our child. For two days now, Isabella had suffered through this labor. In between tides of pain, the air punctuated by her screams, she succumbed to bouts of exhaustion. As if I could somehow protect or help her, I had stood guard outside her door. Then, a faint groan leaked from the room.

I had bolted upright and gripped the door latch. The inhuman sound rose sharply to a keening. I burst in, fearing the worst. But

Isabella, merely frustrated at the fruitlessness of her efforts, turned her tearful face from me. The midwife flailed her arms and ordered me gone, saying that my fretting was of no help. For another hour I leaned with my back against the door, but every wail or mumble from within only distressed me more.

So finally, I had come here, away from servants' eyes filled with nervous pity, with a borrowed bow and a handful of arrows to distract myself. With a weapon in my hands I felt some control. Or perhaps it was purpose? But the comfort such objects usually provided were useless to me now. However strong or skilled I thought myself, I was utterly powerless to ease the torment of my beloved Isabella.

I took aim again and eased the bowstring back further. Its tension against my bloodless fingers sang out for release. I pulled frigid air into my lungs and held it. My heart pounded against my ribs. *This time* . . .

"Lord Robert! Lord Robert!"

Startled, I exhaled sharply. My fingers loosed their grip on the string. The arrow hissed across the stave, curving right, and smacked into a rock at the cliff's base, not ten paces from me. The splintered shaft plunged into a shallow tidal pool with a tiny 'plop'. Still clutching my bow, I looked skyward, toward the screeching voice, where terns cut through a sullen sky, their tails streaming behind like double-pointed pennons.

A face, eyes wide with panic, and then a small, beckoning hand appeared at the top of the sea cliff. More calmly, the girl said, "You must come at once, my lord."

I could barely hear her above the wind whistling through the crevices of rock and the waves slapping against the shore. "The child?" I shouted.

Isabella's chambermaid—a reed of a lass of twelve or thirteen whose name I could never recall—went down on her knees and, clinging to a clump of yellowed grass, dangled over the edge to peer at me beseechingly. A thick, black rope of hair swung from over her shoulder. "A girl."

"Is she hale?"

She nodded, a feeble smile flitting over her mouth. "Aye. Loud and hungry, as well."

I nodded, feeling the buoyancy of relief. *God be blessed.* A healthy daughter. That was good. Very good. "And my wife?"

The girl frowned. "The Lady Isabella . . . she . . ." Her voice thinned to the strained pitch of one fraught with concern. "You must hasten, my lord."

For a moment I stared at her, my mind suddenly gone empty. A strange heaviness filled my heart and trickled into the pit of my stomach, anchoring me where I stood.

"My lord," the girl begged again, "*please*, hasten."

I did not ask why the urgency. Some things need not be asked. Some things are better left unknown. Some . . . should never happen at all.

A stiff breeze tore at my woolen cloak. From where I stood, there was no way to the cave except by boat. To go back to the trail which had brought me here would take too long. I would have to go up, through the staggered footholds of the cliffs. I pushed my stave away, letting it fall to the ground with a clatter, and leapt onto a boulder, from which I began the precarious climb upward.

THE DOOR OF ISABELLA'S chamber swung open to darkness. A murmur of instruction came from somewhere inside. Isabella's chambermaid nodded and flew back down the stairs. I reached for the doorframe, but a splinter pricked my fingertip and I drew my hand back. Gradually, shapes took form. Thin slats of light shone duskily through closed shutters. My eyes fell first on a milk-skinned young Orkney woman: Ljot, the wet nurse. Married to a local fisherman, she had already birthed six, each little more than a year apart and all girls—the last of which had died in the cradle a fortnight ago.

The wide neck of Ljot's tunic gaped, exposing a plump, ivory breast. At her teat an infant fed greedily, a downy tuft of yellow hair crowning her tiny head. *My daughter.* Ljot smiled at me, seductively almost, then shifted the babe to her other breast, taking time before she reached to cover herself.

My eyes swept toward the great four-postered bed across the room. On the far side, the old midwife, Alice, wiped delicately at Isabella's white brow with a cloth. And nearer to me, at the foot of her bed, Father Malachi . . . performing last rites.

"Dear God in heaven," I uttered. "No, please, no."

The priest daubed the soles of Isabella's feet with holy oil as he blessed her soul to heaven's keeping. I drifted past him, the iron tang of blood filling my nose and mouth. A great blotch of red-brown stained the sheets on which she lay. Over her bloated belly and bare legs someone had draped a blanket in modesty. Her shift, wet with the slickness of birth, clung to her full breasts in dark, sodden wrinkles.

Stunned, I knelt beside her and took her hand, still warm, in mine. Sweat glistened like a fine sheen of hoarfrost upon her cheeks. The only color in her face was a mask of red encircling closed eyes. Her waist-length hair, once fair and shining, lay across her pillow in twisted, lackluster strands. I stroked her fingers, even as I sensed them stiffening, and bent my head to my forearm.

My Isabella, she cannot be . . . No, no, it isn't possible. This is not right. Did her eyelids not flutter just now? Her chest rise in the slightest of breaths? Was that twitch beneath my fingertips not the faint pulse of blood streaming through her veins?

A wail of lament ripped from my gut, but I clenched my jaw

fiercely, trapping the knife of pain in my throat. My hands began to tremble, then my arms and shoulders, until soon my whole body shook uncontrollably.

"Marjorie," came a hoarse whisper.

A long moment later, I swallowed back the hard knot in my throat and looked up through bleary eyes. "What?"

"Marjorie, my lord," Alice murmured, a sorrowful smile on her thin lips. "Lady Isabella's last wish was that you should name the child Marjorie—after your mother."

With quivering fingers, I pushed away tears. But like a fresh cut doused with vinegar, their sting remained.

"If . . ." My voice cracked with grief. "If that was her wish." I glanced at the tiny babe swaddled tightly in the curve of Ljot's arms.

Father Malachi touched my shoulder. "The godparents should be summoned, my lord. If I remember, you chose your oldest brother, Edward. And your sister . . . Mary, was it? I will send to Lochmaben for them. We can perform the christening as soon as they arrive."

Christening? How could I take joy in the baptism of a child in the same week I was to bury my wife? More often, it was the mother who lived and the child who died, as Ljot's did. If only this babe had—

God forgive me. How can I even think such wickedness?

Then I heard the slurp and grunt of my daughter's vigorous suckling and soon her bittersweet cries rent the air.

"Marjorie," I repeated.

3

James Douglas – Berwick, 1296

"A FRAID, JAMES?" MY FATHER asked.

I gazed up at him through the veil of mist that clung to my eyelashes. He was not tall, but I had to crane my neck to look up at him, for I was small for my ten years. A stiff March wind scoured my cheeks and tangled my hair into a hopeless knot. I shook my head and looked back at the long horde snaking its way along the Tweed toward frantic Berwick. Above, leaden clouds scudded on winter's final winds.

"Perhaps you should be." Father kneaded stiffly at my bone-thin shoulder and braced his other hand, the knuckles crisscrossed with jagged white scars, against the rough stone of the battlements. As he turned to survey the chaos erupting below the castle walls, the metal chape of his scabbard scraped the stones.

Father's dark eyes reflected a brooding sky. The two crevices that cut across his forehead furrowed themselves even deeper. Usually, he said whatever was on his mind, frankly, sometimes brutally, but this time he held his tongue.

With a tattered sleeve, I wiped at the endless trickle that ran from my nose. "Are you?" I softly pried.

His lips twisted into a wry half-smile. He leaned against me, the links of his mail chafing me through my linen shirt, and put his mouth close to my ear, breathing cold words into the cold air.

"A little fear is a good thing. Without it, a man will meet the devil all too soon."

He lifted a finger, the tip of it missing from some long ago skirmish. "King Edward's standard. See it yon? He crushed the Welsh under his heel and means to do the same with us. What say you, James? Shall we throw open our gates and fall to our knees before him? Behold the mighty Longshanks!" He swept his hand across the horizon, his voice growing louder. "Master of man and all living creatures. What a fool the sun is not to shine on his glory. Ah, there! A breach in the clouds."

I could see nothing but gray sky above and below it, sprawling out over the gaping valley, the world to come.

Father had said the English king would come. England alone was not enough for a man like Longshanks—he would have France and Scotland, too. But what a man of his riches would want of us Scots, wretched lot that we were, was beyond mystery.

Along the sluggish Tweed, the black column crawled . . . closer, ever closer. Longshanks rode at their front—thirty-five thousand men in all, I later heard. There were so many. So very many. By midmorning they had surrounded Berwick, where my father, Sir William Douglas, was governor. Berwick, a port town on the Scottish border, became that day a sinking island amidst a sea of glimmering blades and polished armor.

To my left on the battlements an archer counted his clutch, then counted it again and pressed a quivering arrow to the waxed string of his bow. Sweat poured from his hairline in spite of the chill air. He held his breath and declared, "Mother of God . . . we're dead. All of us."

The look he gave me was one I shall never forget, for all my days. A look of hope destroyed. Of memories given up to ashes. You learn to know that look—the soulless pupils cast heavenward, the clenched jaw, the tendons on the neck stretched taut. It touched a raw place inside of me, as if my heart had been carved from my chest and laid bare to the biting wind of winter. I looked away. I was not strong enough, not yet, to turn my fear into anger and my anger into purpose.

The wide eyes of the archer bored into my soul and peeled away my false courage. I realized then, as I know full well now, what the English had come for. What they would take from us was not measured in gold coin, but in hopes and dreams . . . and lives.

How suddenly everything can change. In a day or a moment, all innocence can be swept away like dust motes banished into oblivion by a straw broom.

"To your room, James. Hasten," my father urged as he beckoned one of his lieutenants close. He pulled from his belt the small hunting knife he always kept there. "May heaven preserve at least one of us to remember this day."

He ruffled my hair. I looked down at the worn leather binding of the handle and closed my fingers around it as archers brushed past and scurried to their positions along the wall. When I looked up again, Father was gone, his voice tangled in the terrible din with a thousand others.

I did not go as I was bid to. Fright and curiosity kept me on the battlements. Around me, grown men made the sign of the cross, clamped their eyelids shut and muttered their prayers. On the road just outside town, the countryfolk shrieked and cried out for God's mercy. They poured through the gates, seeking sanctuary from the approaching swarm. Our soldiers poked at them with spear tips and struggled to clear the way to close the only entrance to town. Then the gates groaned shut, leaving unfortunate dozens hammering at them with bare hands until their fingers were bloody with splinters.

The citizens of Berwick dangled from the timber palisades, taunting the English. Inside the walls, womenfolk hooked their wailing bairns by the sleeve and dragged them inside their homes. The boom of bolted doors echoed like thunder across an open valley. Baskets, bundles and pots were dropped in the streets as the people fled for safety. A mother called to her fair-haired son from a doorway. He ran toward her. The sky began to rain with arrows, whistling in warning before they pierced their mortal marks with a twang. A shaft struck the boy in the skull with such force that his feet flew out from under him.

I crouched behind one of the crenels, shaking like a birch limb in a strong wind. Some time passed before I could call upon my courage to peer over the wall again.

Orange flames with tails of smoke arced through the sky. If not for the mist that had dampened roofs earlier that day, the whole town would have erupted like tinder. It went on for hours like that—the screams and moans, the smell of smoke and blood, my father pacing the wall walk then flying down the stairs into the castle and emerging above again to bark orders.

A merciful siege was not to be. Longshanks knew his strength. He knew our weakness. He raced back and forth along the length of our paltry ditch on his powerful steed while Scottish arrows fell fecklessly around him. Then he reined hard and rode away some distance. Cheers erupted from Berwick . . . but died just as abruptly when he thrust his sword above the waving plume of his helmet and charged, alone.

His great warhorse leapt over the ditch, landed on the thin lip of earth abutting the stockade and then crashed through. A host of English soldiers, knights and footmen alike, poured over the ditch, wading up to their waists in reeking muck, and clambered over the collapsing palisades. Swords and axes glinted in the pewter light of the smoky, cloud-choked day.

The Flemings of Berwick, who had sworn on their lives to protect the town, holed themselves up in the Red Hall. They died there, in smoke and flames, while the rest of the town perished by the sword. Somehow, amidst the butchery, my father had me retrieved from my post by the very archer who had foretold our doom. Brusquely, he shoved me along through the dim corridors and threw me into the room where my stepmother, Eleanor de Ferres, was soothing my two younger brothers, Hugh and Archibald. Having not seen what I had, they were oblivious to the events occurring beyond the castle walls. Hugh, four years younger than me, rattled a pair of bone dice in a wooden cup, apparently for no other reason than to hear the clatter they made. Eleanor sang a lullaby to Archibald, although her voice cracked with strain, while she rocked him softly in the cradle of her arms.

She brushed away the ringlets from little Archibald's forehead, then laid him gently in the middle of her bed as if he were an egg she were afraid might crack. Then she ordered Hugh to bed. As she tended to them, I crept toward the door and when my hand touched the latch, I heard her soft but sure voice.

"James, you are needed here. There are dozens to defend the walls. We have only you." She extended an ivory hand toward me.

I closed my fingers around hers and let her lead me to the bed. As I burrowed beneath the down coverings, she swept stray locks of hair away from my forehead. A smile, genuine and yet tentative, graced her mouth.

"You will have a brother or sister come autumn . . . if all goes as it should," she revealed. Then her smile vanished as quickly as it had come.

"A sister this time, if you please. No more wee brothers." I squeezed her trembling hand in reassurance.

"We will consider ourselves blessed with whatever God sees fit to give us." Awkwardly, she pulled the coverings up and tucked us all in. "And it will be your duty, as the bigger brother, to make sure they are all safe. You understand?"

"Aye." I rolled over and laid my arm across Archibald's small chest. For hours I listened to the steady rhythm of his breathing before I fell into a fitful sleep where I knew not nightmare from memory.

AS BERWICK SMOLDERED AND the screams of the dying cut inside our ears, my brothers and I kept company in that room, the shutters drawn tight and a solitary peat brazier glowing meagerly. Every now and then, we heard a sound like thunder rattling the walls. It was not thunder, high up in the sky, but stones flung from the powerful arm of a trebuchet. We always knew when another one was coming. First came the shouts of warning from our own, as they watched the great machine being loaded; then came the groaning of the windlass and the dull thump and twang as the engineer pulled the pin and the arm arced skyward. Most of the time it fell either short or wide of its mark. *Most* of the time.

Our bellies roared for food. The town had fallen within hours, but my father was not so quick to surrender the castle. I was old enough to know that he would, in time, have to yield. The soldiers brought us dark bread and watered wine to sustain us, but Archibald was not happy with such fare and flung his scrap of bread at the wall in a tantrum. Hugh stuffed chunks into his cheeks, as if he feared he'd get no more. The smell of food, or perhaps it was the smoke or the stench of something as yet unknown to me, made me retch, even though I was never more famished in all my short life.

Eleanor read to us in a calming voice that put my rampant heart at ease of one William Marshall, a knight of England no less, who served five kings. I always admired that of her, for not all womenfolk could read. We clustered at the base of a small folding table tucked against the wall, carved by the careful hands of some of the very Flemings who had since perished together brutally in their refuge of companionship. Atop it sat the one symbol of comfort we possessed—a cross of silver-gilt two hands high. In its center, a single, vermilion jewel glittered. I was more intrigued by the light playing off its facets than the significance of the crucifix itself or the purport of recited verses. Every now and then my stepmother would pause, reread a passage and gaze at me sincerely, as if to break the spell the jewel had cast upon me and note the special importance of the words so meticulously penned on the ocher pages pressed beneath her fingertips. My father had stolen her away from her English parents while they were staying in Scotland. Against their wishes, he made her his wife and my brother Archibald was born within the year. My own mother, Elizabeth, sister of James the Stewart, had died when Hugh was born. My memory of her was but a fleeting shadow and it seemed my stepmother had always been there in the fore.

For three long days and three even longer nights, we huddled together, our hearts racing in unison, our eyes fixed upon the door, our voices hushed so we could hear above our own words any sound from without. Minutes seemed more like hours. A day like a week. Hugh was content to stare into the glow of the peat brazier and hum nonsense, but wee Archibald yearned to exercise his legs. Within a few hours of our first day of seclusion he had inspected every inch of the room, including whatever piles of dust he could gather in his hands from beneath the bed or strands of cobwebs from behind the furniture. He was too much like me in his energies and tenfold more vocal. When Archibald at last wept himself into utter exhaustion, to pass the time I scratched letters onto the bottom side of an overturned stool with the knife Father had given me and pointed to each as Hugh repeated them. He was a dull lad. No matter how many times his tutor, Eleanor or I patiently sat with him, marking letters into a clay tablet and then letting him trace them again with a stylus, he could not remember the proper way to write them.

I dug my knife into the wood, but Hugh paid no heed.

He tugged at his lip with a thumb and forefinger. "Edward," he muttered. "Edward, son of Henry, son of John, son of Henry, son of—"

"No, Hugh," I corrected, as I grabbed at his hand and guided his finger over the letters. He had a penchant for memorizing lineage, even that of English kings, though I doubted he knew of whom he spoke. "This is your name: H—U—G—"

The clang of metal on metal erupted in the corridor. I lowered my knife and watched the door. Eleanor snatched up sleeping little Archibald from the bed and retreated into the furthest corner of the room. My little brother thrust his bottom lip out and began to wail. Eleanor buried his face against her breast to muffle his betrayal, but he only cried louder. I heard the thud and rattle of weapons falling to the floor. I tucked my meager blade up into the loose folds of my sleeve and then pulled a wide-eyed Hugh into my arms. When the door burst open, tottering on its rusty hinges, it was not my father's guards before us, but soldiers of England, harbingers of Longshanks.

4

James Douglas – Berwick, 1296

THE FIRST THROUGH THE door was tall and gaunt of cheek. Over his hauberk was a coat of vibrant red quartered by purest white. He was too young yet to be a lord of any influence, but clearly he held himself in some esteem. Not an earl or a lord, pos-sibly the bastard of one or the other, but more likely the son of an English baron. His piercing dark eyes swept the room. I noticed the faintest smile of satisfaction as his gaze fell upon Eleanor.

"The door," he murmured, gesturing at it as he strutted toward Eleanor. Four others closed in behind him, grinning with superiority. The door groaned shut. His heels clicked with each haunting stride. He halted a few feet from her and removed his conical helmet, dropping it to the floor. Then he peeled his coif of mail from his head with rehearsed precision. He went to the window and threw open the shutters. I blinked away blinding sunlight. His tight ringlets of blue-black fell from crown to collar and glistened with oil in the afternoon light.

Eleanor tucked her fitful bairn tight against her breast, even though he struggled to free himself of her protective grip. As the soldier reached a long arm toward Archibald, Eleanor lunged toward the folding table. With Archibald clamped beneath her left arm, she snatched up the silver-gilt cross and swung it at the man. His head bobbed to dodge the blow. White teeth gleaming, he snarled and ripped Archibald from her as easily as if he were plucking petals from a daisy. Archibald tumbled into the legs of another soldier, with a beard halfway down his chest, who laughed and then kicked my wee brother for sheer sport. The laughter ended when Archibald bit him in the calf. A moment later he had Archibald hanging in the air by his shirt.

"Don't harm that one," the red-coated leader barked, jabbing a finger toward Archibald.

"Christ, Neville, the pup deserves a lesson," the bearded one begged. "Shouldn't go 'round doing that to his elders. Least of all me. I've no tolerance for brats."

"*Douglas's* brats, mind you, so leave him be. The king will want them all in one piece."

Then he turned his eyes, as dark and cold as a January night, back on Eleanor. Her trembling hands crept over her belly, where her child was growing.

As he hovered closer, she brought the cross back to strike another blow. He swept it from her grasp and sent it clattering across the floor, then pinned her to the wall beside the table.

He chuckled with amusement as she flailed her fists at him. "First—let us reap our harvest."

Neville slammed her down on the table. She winced as her head snapped back and struck its unforgiving surface.

"Quiet now. Close your eyes, sweet one. It will be over . . . soon enough."

"Our turn then?" the youngest and greenest of them piped. Panting, he pressed closer.

"Shut up, you fool," Neville growled. "Hold her for me."

The youth flew forward and clamped her wrists between his long, grimy fingers as he trembled with excitement.

Undaunted, the filth flipped up my stepmother's skirts and then fumbled beneath the bottom of his heavy hauberk for the cord on the flap of his hose.

I was a boy yet, but not blind. I had seen the older pages and handmaidens coupling in the buttery and in the bushes behind the mews. The stallion mounting the mare. The ram covering a ewe. But I knew the difference in what I was bearing witness to. I saw the tears cold as sleet against Eleanor's cheek, the plea for mercy in her gentle eyes.

Neville had wedged his knee in between her clamped legs and even as she fought to writhe from him he probed recklessly with his hips. The tendons in Eleanor's neck went taut like the chords on a harp. Neville tried to kiss Eleanor's quivering mouth, but she jerked her head to the side. He locked his hands on both sides of her jaw, wrenched her face around and pressed his foul mouth onto hers even as a scream rose and died in her throat.

Then suddenly, Neville howled—his ecstasy turned to agony. Eleanor's teeth were latched onto his lower lip. He ripped himself from her and shoved her onto the floor, where she landed face down with a resounding thud. One hand holding up his leggings, he pulled the back of his other hand across a blood-soaked chin and stepped toward her. Heaving with sobs of pain, Eleanor clutched protectively at her belly.

I do not remember letting go of Hugh . . . or drawing out the knife I had kept concealed. Only that I found myself on the violator's back, my blade up high and then arcing down toward his neck.

He reeled around and whipped his arm back just enough to deflect my blade. Its sharp edge glanced cleanly across his cheek.

I fell to the floor and rolled away. As I did so, the knife slipped from my grasp. A red river poured from the gash on the side of

Neville's face. His eyes blazed at me with abomination.

My palm burned. I locked my fingers in a fist. As I glanced again at Eleanor—she who had held me when a young boy's nightmares stole away sleep, taught me my letters, told me tales of fairies and smiled with patience whenever she tended to my bruises and scrapes—I knew I would do it again. For her. For Hugh or Archibald. For anyone.

And deep, deep inside me, while the blood streamed red from Neville's gaping flesh, I held no shame for my newfound hatred.

"What here?" boomed a voice from the doorway.

The pimple-faced one stuttered, "N-n-nothing, Sir Marmaduke. We were only—"

A mailed knight walked into the room. Older, authoritative, he admonished them all with a glance. Most of all Neville.

Eleanor, shaking with tears, retreated into the corner. Archibald dove into her trembling arms and stroked away her tears with tiny hands.

The soldiers drew back from Sir Marmaduke as he approached Eleanor, his well-worn face soft with concern. For a moment, he studied her, though she would not meet his gaze. Then he tilted his head and turned back toward his charges. Hands behind his back, he approached Neville.

"Humph," he grunted. "I would ask, but knowing what trouble you have evoked time and again . . . Bother having you about sometimes, Neville. Not the pretty 'peacock' today, are you? Wipe the blood off your face. I shall deal with you afterward."

Sir Marmaduke lifted my heavy chin with a thumb and forefinger. "Take this one . . . no, take all of them. To the hall. Let King Edward decide what's to become of them."

Then I felt the back of my shirt twisted into a wad. I was hoisted to my feet, thrust out the door—Hugh behind me, Eleanor and Archibald before—and escorted to the great hall by four grumbling guards, who swung their swords at their sides with each damning stride.

IN THE GREAT HALL of Berwick, before the dais, my father was down on both knees, the soot of the burning town on his surcoat and the blood of Englishmen speckling him from head to foot. His hands were bound at the base of his spine, his wrists so raw they oozed.

"Father!" I cried, rushing forward.

I had not made it within twenty feet of him before the butt end of a pike belonging to one of the king's guard jammed into the soft of my belly. Winded, I crumpled to the floor in a heap. Only the pile of rushes there, decaying and littered with dirt shaken from muddy boots, softened the blow to my head. The room spun around me in a whirl of color, the threads of the tapestries on the walls blending with the riot of scarlet, green and azure adorning the coats of the English intruders. While I struggled to push myself up, a plaintive voice filled up the hall.

"My beloved nephew, Richard of Cornwall, is dead," the king lamented. "Smote down by a ragged army of butchers and fish-mongers . . . sliced to pieces like boar for Christmas dinner. When they brought him to me there was nothing of his once comely face to recognize. It was only by the ring I had given him that he was identified."

Longshanks paced the length of the dais in front of the head table, his hands clasped behind his back. He paused at one end, raised his chin and drew a long breath. His flaxen beard, streaked with white at the corners of his mouth, was meticulously trimmed. Every hair on his head lay precisely in place. The scarlet cloak that flared from his angular shoulders was fringed with pristine ermine. Kingliness imbued even the air he breathed. He was absolute power. But he was neither a gentle nor a forgiving king. If ever a trace of either existed in his soul, they had long since given way to grimmer traits.

"You are to blame for this, Douglas," he accused, turning his long, pinched, severe face toward my father. "My nephew's death lies on your head. As does that of every corpse littering the streets of Berwick and the fields beyond it."

The king's left eyebrow drew far up onto his forehead until it touched the gold circlet he wore. He slipped from the dais and walked toward my father.

Father met his accusing stare with unwavering certainty. "I differ, *my king.*" The last two words dripped from his tongue like burning oil. He straightened his shoulders. "I would not have murdered women and children as they ran from me."

Longshanks drew his sword from his scabbard. With a gasp, I shot up from the floor and dove at the king's legs to topple him. My cheek smacked against one of his long fine-edged shinbones. As I jerked at his leg fiercely, he brought his other leg back and levied a kick forceful enough to propel me toward the side tables. The side of my face collided with the stout legs of a bench and as I skidded beneath the table the bench landed on top of me. I shoved it away and clutched a throbbing jaw. I swallowed back a pool of blood. My tongue found something loose and floating. Scurrying from beneath in indignant fury, I held out my palm and spat a tooth into it. I was beyond angry just then, and my father knew it. A smirk of satisfaction passed over his lips when I clamped the tooth tightly in my fist and spat blood onto the floor. The blood that pulsed from the empty place in my mouth had the sharp, obsessive taste of revenge to it.

Tugging at his lower lip, Hugh whimpered. Eleanor tucked his head against her ribs and shushed blubbering little Archibald. She swayed slightly, still reeling from the shock of the past hour, as though trying hard to stay on her feet.

"Quiet your bastard," Longshanks drawled, leering at her, "or I will have his tongue."

Sir Marmaduke strode toward the king from the far end of the hall, knelt hastily and then whispered into Longshanks' ear.

"He lives?" the king queried, glancing sideways at me with icy regard.

"Very much." The knight nodded, then stood aside.

"Pity," he muttered. Then to my father the king remarked, "I see your whelps come by their impudence honestly."

He strolled back toward the head table, certain I was too humiliated to be of any further threat. With his head held high in royal arrogance, he dragged the tip of his sword through the rushes, then jammed the point into a crack and pivoted to face my father.

"John Comyn, the Earl of Buchan's son, attacked Carlisle barely one week past. The day after dozens of your nobles freely offered their oaths of fealty to me at Wark. If not for the loyalty of the Bruces who knows in whose filthy hands that stronghold might now rest? You should have followed the Earl of Carrick's example. You yourself could have saved the bloodshed of thousands. You! But instead you chose to defy me. Pray tell, governor, what false thinking led you thus?"

Father clenched his fingers around an imaginary hilt, a gesture unseen by the king. "I followed the command of my liege, King John."

Longshanks laughed hollowly. "John Balliol is a country squire. I stripped him of his crown for all his deception and impertinence not half as fast as I will strip the skin from your very bones. What blatant ignorance to believe he could pay lip service to me as overlord while courting the King of France. A union between his son and Philip's niece? The absurdity of it is beyond gall. You are my vassal now, William Douglas. Mine alone. You and your ilk are not fit to govern yourselves. You cannot breed a proper king; therefore, I will serve that end. And I will take the quarrel from you if I have to plunge my own hand into the chest of each and every Scotsman and squeeze it from his beating heart."

Father bristled beneath his shirt of mail. He closed his eyes momentarily and swallowed back the bellicose words that must have pushed at his tongue. He nodded as his chin dropped.

"Forgive us our pride . . ." Father muttered into his chest, "and our savagery. At times, we must be reminded of our place."

Had I not known my father half as well I would have thought him a base, unsavory coward for prostrating himself thus. He had never given weight to what others thought of him, never censored his words to soften their blow, never kept secret which side of an argument he was on. But as we shared a fleeting glance, I read there in his pupils the words he did not speak: that a day would come when he would make Longshanks pay.

Longshanks' fingers shot out and grabbed a handful of Father's black hair, matted by wind and rain. He jerked Father's head back and stared down at him as his other hand clenched the hilt of his long sword. "What are the lives of your wife and sons worth, Douglas? Are you prepared to swear to me? If you are false . . . help me, but I will not show mercy. Not only will I bury your head and your body in separate graves, but your boys will inherit nothing but their own pile of dung."

"Free my hands and I will swear, upon my life, whatever you wish."

A smile opened up the king's narrow face. He let go of Father's hair. With a snap of his fingers, one of the king's men sawed away the ropes that bound Father's hands.

Grimacing, Father rubbed them together to return the blood. Then, he touched his hands to his forehead briefly and extended them, palms pressed flat together, to rest between the king's outstretched fingers. The oath of fealty passed his lips, but what was in his heart was surely otherwise.

As soon as Father had sworn himself as Edward's man, his hands were bound again and he was whisked away to the dungeons. The next morning we were given brusque escort to the edge of town and sent on our way on a cart drawn by a plow horse with not a year left to its natural life. Two of our garrison served as our guard on the long, bloody road to Douglas Castle. Thousands upon thousands of dead bodies lay strewn from every doorway of the smoking town out to the strangely tranquil, stubbled fields of the Tweed valley. Eleanor kept her head down, stroking Archibald's hair as he wailed from hunger still. Her face was blanched from loss of blood. The shove Neville had given her . . . it killed the babe within her. She grieved alone, in gray silence. Father did not know and my younger brothers—they couldn't understand how a child not yet born can die.

Mute, Hugh gazed around him, almost looking intrigued, as our cart rumbled over a stream where the bloated and bruised body of a young woman, violated in unspeakable ways, floated face-up. Her bulging eyes stared up at a cloudless sky while a golden sun blazed furiously overhead, drawing out the first flies of the season to feast on the rotting offal of Berwick's citizens.

5

James – Douglas Castle, 1297

ELEANOR, MY BROTHERS AND I returned to Douglas Castle, overlooking the indolent Douglas Water—more a home to me than Berwick had ever been. My dog, Fingal, greeted me on the road half a mile from the castle. He seemed less the giant than I remembered, but far more grizzled around the mouth. I wondered whether he had waited for me every day since our parting a year earlier, or if he had somehow sensed I would return on that particular day. As I ran the last stretch home alongside the wagon, his tail thrashed against my knees.

When autumn's turning leaves gilded the hills of Lanarkshire, Father came home. Longshanks, certain the insolent Scots had been subdued, went to Gascony to settle matters there and so he had finally set my father free. I was never happier to see him, but he had little time and less concern than ever for my brothers and me. Lady Eleanor, whom he had wooed so abruptly and resolutely, became naught but a nursemaid to his issue.

Men of every sort came and went, as did Father. We were never quite sure when or if he would come back. Some of those who came to Douglas were young, with hardly a whisker; some were old and wizened, their jowls loose and flapping beneath snow-white beards. Some were familiar, some strangers. There were noblemen of high rank, with their many-colored coats; wind-burnt Islanders who spoke in strange tongues; faceless townspeople, wealthy merchants, carpenters and masons; bearish Highlanders lugging spears; and farmers with bronzed skin and bulging arms. They came alone and in small clutches of three or four, never in larger groups, arriving at dusk and parting before dawn. Our courtyard rang with the clatter of hoof beats and the rhythmic chink of metal bits. Ale and wine flowed in our hall like rain in springtime. All wore the look of perpetual suspicion and spoke little of ordinary things. They whispered and they hurried and each walked with his hand close to the hilt of his weapon.

Father still bore the purple scars on his wrists and ankles where they had shackled him. Once, as he changed shirts, I glimpsed the festering welt marks on his back. Eleanor applied a hot poultice, which made him grimace. I wondered how many lashings he had suffered and what he had finally said to make them stop. His black mood infected us all—but whether that darkness was due to the wounding of his pride or because of what had happened to Eleanor . . . I often wondered if she had ever even told him that she carried his child, let alone that she had lost it.

Throughout winter, a restive wind howled from the deep, dark forests of wild Galloway, like a host of banshees awaiting their claim. Archibald was ill until spring with a cough that would not be banished. Lady Eleanor tended to her ailing bairn day and night and grew terse with father for every wee thing.

When the clouds were few, which was seldom during the course of that bleak Scottish spring plagued by sleet and ice, I took Hugh on my pony and we rode toward the southern hills. There, we watched the wind ripple the grass over the land and the buzzards glide above, if only because there was no pleasure in being home. In the short gray hours of day, I taught Hugh how to throw a spear and use a sling. I brought down a swan in midair with a stone from my sling. With its feathers, I fletched my first arrows under the patient tutelage of my father's man, Ranulf. The shafts were made of ash and the heads of finest steel. Father gave us each a bow, short enough to shoot with from horseback and easy enough for a young boy to flex his muscles on as we learned to pull it. I had all but given up on teaching Hugh to read, preferring to leave that futile task to our tutor. If he was not keen of mind, he was at least strong of arm and that, I prayed, would someday be his salvation. So we kept at our spears and bows, playing in the today, but practicing for the tomorrows ahead.

But the peace forced upon us was unsteady and short-lived. The following year a man named William Wallace, whom until then few among us had heard anything of, killed the Sheriff of Lanark. His growing insurrection drew not only the commonfolk to him, but also one of higher station—a man whose scars would not let him forget the rage of seeing thousands helplessly slaughtered and then the heat of humiliation for being wrongly blamed. By late spring, my father joined Wallace at Perth. Together, they chased the king's justiciar, William Ormesby, from Scone. He fled in such haste that he had only enough time to gather his documents and so abandoned his valuables.

My father, a richer man than when last he left, returned along the road from Dumfries while the thistle was in its first splendor. I dropped from the sunny window where, like a fledgling eagle, I had kept vigil for weeks, eternity to a lad of my vigor. Down the stairs I raced, into the courtyard, through the gates and along the rocky road to greet him. For a quarter mile, I pumped my arms, running hard until my legs burned and my lungs blazed. I did not halt until I came close enough to see my father's face clearly.

I stood there in the roadway, my chest heaving, my hands upon my knees.

Beside Father rode a gruff, golden-maned man, whom I guessed to be Wallace. Indeed, he was the very giant tales had portrayed him to be: the tallest man I had ever seen, with shoulders as broad as a mountain and bulging arms that could have heaved a stout timber end over end. They said he could hew a man in half—sideways or lengthwise—with one flail of his sword. I believed it.

Close behind them were ten others: rugged creatures with bare legs and wolfish scowls, and clutching long spears.

Father acknowledged me with a glance, but he did not stop to scoop me up and let me ride on the back of his fleet horse as he had always done when he returned home. The band of riders parted around me as though I were a rock in a stream and continued on to the castle.

I turned around and gazed at them through a cloud of dust. The round shields slung over their backs grew smaller and smaller. Then, wheezing, I drew the deepest breath I could and raced after them.

When I caught up, they had dismounted and were waiting for my father's instructions. The smells of sweat and leather were overpowering. The grit of dust in my mouth was nothing in comparison. Their mumbling fell away as I stepped through them and tugged at my father's shirttail.

With a frayed sleeve, Father wiped at the grime of road dust and sweat covering his face. Then he reached up, untied a clanking sack from his saddle and yanked it down.

"Water, James. The horses need tending."

My smile slipped away and my shoulders sank. I hesitated, hoping he would reach inside the sack and toss me a gift, but then he hoisted it over his shoulder and headed inside. I watched his back and waited for him to turn back to me. Only Wallace lingered.

"Do as your father bids, lad. It will build your strength. After that there are field stones to move and logs to be hauled to the top of that hill you just came from." Wallace cuffed me on the upper arm and ruffled my hair.

A curious gesture, I thought, for a man as savage as him. Then he winked and grinned. An easy, huge grin. His lightheartedness, however, rankled me. I had been slighted by my own father, treated like a stable boy and not his heir, and was in no mood for jesting.

Wallace turned to follow the other men into the hall. As soon as his back was to me—that great long sword slung over his back—I launched both feet at the back of his knees. He stumbled, only slightly, and spun around. My ill-planned attack had landed me on my rump . . . my arse soaking in a puddle, no less.

Blue eyes sparkling with mirth, Wallace laughed.

I stayed where I was, muddy water seeping into my breeches, until the doors closed behind Wallace. My tongue found the hole in my teeth—a perpetual reminder that I had yet much to learn. Hugh strolled out from the shadows where he had been watching and held out a hand to help me up. He did not care for strangers and never spoke in their presence.

"Hurt?" Hugh asked. The over-sized shirt he wore hung to one side, baring a shoulder, but as ever, he took no notice. His leggings bagged so enormously at the crotch that it looked as if he might lose them at any moment.

I struggled up, shaking my head, even as I rubbed at the place where the bruise would later appear. We fetched the water in stiff silence. While I stopped to rest and knead my sore back, Hugh continued to lug the sloshing buckets without complaint. Afterwards, we brought the horses hay and grain. Banished from the hall and whatever talk went on there, we were sent to our room for supper.

That night as I lay in bed, I ached every inch—more from the tumble I had taken than the task I had been commanded to do. I turned on my side to see Hugh fast asleep beside me, as blissful in his ignorance as he was in slumber. The faint light of lingering twilight shone yellow upon his face. Hugh did not understand the closed doors, the shifting eyes, the sharpening of weapons. But I was disturbingly preoccupied with it. I was too old to be oblivious to it all, yet too young to be privy to great secrets.

FOR DAYS I WAS told to keep away and consigned to the drudgery of lessons. Today, sent on a menial errand to fetch my father's spurs, I felt I had finally been elevated in the order of things. I turned the two silver pennies over in my clammy palm, then tucked them into the purse beneath my shirt. Fingal whined and sniffed at my fingers. I stroked the coarse fur along his spine, his back the same height as my lowest rib. Father had given me the money that morning and dispatched me on a mission. My chest had swelled with a feeling of importance. But as I stood at the door to the smith's shop, the sign creaking overhead, the gaping silence within put me ill at ease. The streets of the town were quiet, for it was not market day, but even so the alleys gaped vacantly. The weaver's and the potter's shops were shut up tight. Across the street, the nailmaker's shop was busy enough, but it was the fat wife whose voice I heard and not her husband's. The talk sounded more like gossip than trade. I tethered my pony to a broken wagon just outside the shop, for he was prone to wander, and ventured inside. Fingal, never in a great hurry except when he was chasing hare, loped behind.

The coals in the furnace were cold, the bellows propped idly in a corner, the ingots of iron neatly stacked, and the anvil clean of any sign of work. As I investigated, Ralph, the smith's apprentice, ambled into the front of the shop, wiping his hands upon his smudged apron. He startled at the initial sight of my huge, furry companion, then reached up onto a high shelf, digging his fingers into a bowl from which he produced a long shank bone that he tossed to Fingal.

"Been saving that for a week," Ralph informed me. "Where've you been?"

"Around." Thoroughly absorbed with his treasure, my dog's teeth were grinding against the bone as he lay beneath one of the worktables.

"Doing what?"

"I've come for my father's new spurs." I probed the lump beneath my shirt.

"Och, a bit too soon, aren't you? He only asked for them yesterday." Ralph, a very worn fourteen years, snatched up a bucket of water and dumped it into the trough. "Besides, they won't be done until Eachann gets back."

"Back . . . from where?" I bunched my eyebrows, perplexed. A laborer as skilled and in demand as Eachann the blacksmith did not leave his duties undone.

"You haven't heard? They've all gone north. To Irvine."

My heart hastened in its rhythm. "Why?"

"A meeting of some kind."

"With whom?"

Ralph shrugged. "Didn't say. And I don't care to know."

I could not run home fast enough. I found what I expected, but had hoped would not be. Father and Wallace had gone . . . to Irvine. The task I had been entrusted with was merely a diversion, meant to keep me from loitering underfoot while my father prepared to leave.

I barricaded myself in my room, leaving Fingal in the corridor to scratch and whine until I could bear his insistence no more and let him in. With reckless fury, I beat at my pillow until the feathers exploded around my head and plowed my fist into the wall. Then I wept in bitter pain as my fingers plumped up like a sausage. Fingal licked the salty tears from my cheeks. I clamped my arms around his massive frame and buried my face in his fur to muffle the sobs of a young boy hungering for adventure, but left forgotten.

MY FINGERS THROBBED WITH every sullen heartbeat. I refused my supper and Lady Eleanor at last gave up her attempts to console me. When the lavender light of gloaming yielded to overwhelming blackness, a soft rap came at my door. I opened it quick enough to allow Hugh in. In rehearsed silence, he took off his shirt and leggings and pulled his nightshirt over his head, then crawled into bed. Fingal did not even stir from his post on the floor next to my side of the bed. Hugh fell asleep as fast as his eyelids closed. The peace of sleep that night to me was like some elusive bird—a thing I could not hold or own, no matter how I might covet or need it.

An hour later, still seething, I went and leaned from my high window. The lights of the village flickered lazily from opened shutters in the expanse just beyond Douglas Castle, just as they had done night after night, year after year. I closed my eyes for a time and imagined myself a soldier of great stealth, fighting bravely beside my father, smiting my enemies with a single fierce blow. I hoped beyond hope that I would hear the distant clatter of hooves and my father would come back for me. The night breeze whispered coolly in my ears. The old smell of peat fires filled my nose. The scattered and distant sounds of nighttime grew stronger and more frequent. The scent that wafted on the air—stranger . . . sharper.

I opened my eyes to my nightmare. Upon the thatched roof of a home on the edge of town, amber sparks of fire danced elfishly. Riders, torches held aloft, wove in streams of smoking yellow through the streets, but they were not my father's men.

Soon, another roof erupted in flames. And then another. Dark forms scattered from the town in chaos, their screams edged with hysteria. Shouts went up from the skeleton garrison my father had left behind. In the castle, soldiers bolted from dead sleep and scurried to their posts.

As the town burned, a ring of torchlights gathered just beyond the castle wall. The sounds and smells and images of bloody Berwick rushed through my head. I retreated from the window and sank down in a corner of the room, my right elbow propped upon my knees to ease the pounding in my hand. On silent paws, Fingal joined me. There, in dark, cavernous solitude, I waited for whatever might come.

And I prayed for father to come home.

6

<u>Robert the Bruce – Douglas Castle, 1297</u>

THE ROAD TO DOUGLAS stretched lazily before us. Dust billowed from beneath the hooves of our laggard horses. Late afternoon June sun seared into their dark hides.

I looked at my squire, his round face puckered in thought. "Aye, Gerald?"

"M'lord?" His bushy, dark red eyebrows danced above his round eyes in feigned innocence.

"You think I was wrong, don't you? Confess."

Blushing crimson, Gerald's head sank with a shrug. He glanced over his shoulder at the men trailing behind us. "Ahhh . . . not wrong, no."

The rest of my company, markedly diminished since we left Carlisle, swayed from boredom in their saddles. A scouring with hot water and soap would make their company more bearable. I had smelled sweeter swine than the lot of them.

"Premature?" I prodded. "Foolish, then?"

He grunted, as was his habit when he preferred not to speak. It was all the answer I needed.

For several years now, my father had been withdrawn from the public eye. The curse of rotting flesh had begun to reveal itself—a result of his time spent in the Holy Land—and he wanted no one to know of it. So when Longshanks ordered him to take the castle of Sir William Douglas, who was known to be conspiring with rebels, he sent me in his stead. Too often, my father and I had quarreled and always I had bent to his will. This time, however, I deigned to be my own man, for all it might cost me. Perhaps it was brash youth that made me feel so invincible. Twenty-three short years was scarcely enough time to be dealt a proper dose of humility.

When we passed through Annandale, I had offered my small army a choice: follow me, join Douglas and stand for Scotland—or leave, go back to Carlisle, and do the King of England's bidding. The offer had left me with not a single knight. They had protested their loyalty to my father, Lord of Annandale, and wanted nothing of rebellion. Only a few dozen footsoldiers from Carrick, those who had fought beside me and knew me best, those who had the least to lose and the most to gain, had chosen to follow me.

"Whichever way it goes," I said, shielding my eyes with a cupped hand while I peered ahead, "I will have men of true hearts behind me. Men who can be bought will yield to the highest bidder. Even our nobles bear evidence to that."

I opened up my flask and took a drink to wash the dust down, then offered it to Gerald.

Gerald waved it off and cast another glance behind him. "You'll need more than this motley herd."

"The mightiest castle is begun with a single stone."

"And is built by an army of skilled masons, not by a handful of farmers wearied of turning soil." He shifted in his saddle. One shaggy red eyebrow arched upward. "What of Longshanks? And your father? They'll hear of this."

"As if I ever doubted you would come 'round to that. Aye,

they will brand me a traitor. But I have already been a traitor to my own, Gerald, and I do not like the fit of it. Wallace, Douglas, Moray . . . they at least have their honor and that is something nearly lost to all Scotsmen. King Edward has dangled his glittering promises far too long. Let him make good of them and put a Bruce on the throne."

As I said that, however, I was not thinking of my father. He was as withered of limb as he was of virtue. I had long since wearied of his drivel. I secretly prayed his leprosy would rot his tongue.

As the road crested over a ridge, the stark lines of the tower of Douglas Castle were silhouetted against a purple sky before us. I raised a hand to halt my company and told them, "Ride through the town. Make yourselves known. But split not a hair on any man's head or else you'll answer to my blade, understood?"

They nodded their agreement. Then we spurred our horses and rode toward slumbering Douglas.

A BLANKET SNUG AROUND my shoulders, I shivered against the night chill. A faint plume of smoke from a hearthfire in the castle streaked across a starry sky. On either side of the road leading over the ditch to the gatehouse, our small camp was spread across a stubbled field of oat. The garrison of Douglas Castle observed our every move, no doubt counting our numbers and straining their eyes in the endless dark to uncover more of us hidden in the hills beyond. Every now and then we glimpsed the glint of a blade between the merlons. Murmurs of instruction were followed by the faint clack of boots on the stones of the wall walk as the guard changed.

In the town huddled below the castle, I had ordered a few houses put to the torch as a clarion to our coming, with ample warning given to the inhabitants so none might come to harm. The smoking thatch had been quickly doused. But aside from upsetting a few carts and toppling some barrels, my men had done little damage—only enough mischief to leave their mark. Enough that reports would flow back to Carlisle and trickle on down to London. We met with little resistance—doors slammed before us, mostly. Menfolk were blatantly lacking in the town, which told me we had come to the right place.

When day broke, we could see there were too few to defend Douglas Castle for any length. Quietly and patiently, I waited. The sun was still stretching its pale, golden fingers across the fields when one of Douglas's men rode out with word that I would be granted an audience with Lady Douglas.

I left the bulk of my soldiers outside the gatehouse and took only Gerald and a handful of others. Gerald chastised me for my lack of prudence, fearing an ambush, but if I was to bargain for information then I knew I must come on the premise of absolute trust. As we rode beneath the portcullis, it became evident that although we were few, they were even fewer. The whole place echoed with vacancy. The garrison had been recently depleted, with little thought employed as to how it would hold out if attacked. Just inside the gate, an aging soldier with a stooped spine leaned against his spear for support. A scant three archers stood at their posts along the wall, each with an arrow caressing a bowstring. Two men posing as guards, most likely the cook and steward, judging by their attire, flanked the door to the hall. Both held a sword in hand, although in more peaceful and less desperate times those same hands would have been grasping a pot handle and a quill.

Lady Eleanor received us in the great hall. The lady had been not long a widow when Sir William Douglas, an ungracious and reckless sort, absconded with her from beneath her English parents' noses one long winter night a few years ago. Her parents protested that she was forcibly taken and her honor ruined. Thus, she was shamed into becoming Douglas's wife. I doubted the verity of that tale. Her only shame had been in becoming enraptured with a Scotsman of rough repute.

At her skirt was a boy, somewhere between two and three in years, pale of complexion and eyes rimmed in red from recent tears. As Gerald and I strode toward the head table, before which Lady Eleanor stood, she yanked the boy behind her. Over to the side of the hall where tapestries colored an otherwise drab wall, an older lad studied our every move through cool blue eyes. His hair was as black as a raven's feathers and his limbs long and thin in that awkward age. Two guards, their fingers curled about the hilts of implements probably unfamiliar to them, flanked the lady, but I could see they faltered in their courage. The lady and her guards were placing great trust that we had come on peaceable terms, just as I had that I would be received the same.

Lady Douglas bent her knee hastily and cast her eyes downward. I took a few steps closer, but as I did so, she stiffened. Her young son peeked with curiosity from behind her skirts. I reached out and tousled his hair.

"Your husband," I began softly, lifting the boy's plump chin in my fingers as he inched forward and grinned at me, "where is he?"

"He will . . ." She pulled her son back to her side. "He will be back soon."

"Ah, then he has not gone far." I let go of the boy's chin and turned my gaze on the older one. There was intensity in his stare and defiance in the hard line of his chiseled jaw. No doubt he was Sir William's oldest son. "We will not inconvenience you greatly, then, while we await his return."

I strode over to one of the side tables, pulled out the bench and took a seat. I patted the bench beside me. "Gerald, please, rest your legs. My lady, might my men have some drink? And bread, perhaps?"

Although she tried to hide it, she had the look of a doe staring down the shaft of a hunter's arrow. She raised her small chin as if defiant of my request. "I have nothing to give you."

An awkward lie. Had I been ill-intentioned, the refusal might have served as an invitation to a ransacking. There was, however, a noble strength about her, a depth to her. Undeniably, it was brave of her to receive us without the protection of her husband close at hand. She gambled on my honor.

"Forgive me, Lady Eleanor. I would not take anything from you that was not freely given."

Gerald chortled. His ruddy face took on a deeper hue. I jabbed him with an elbow for his obvious lack of manners. Ever since Isabella, the fleeting and tender love of my youth, had died in childbirth, Gerald had exhorted me to get on with living, as a man ought. Indeed, I loved women, loved the way a quick smile or lingering glance from me could make them weak at the knees, but I did not care to love any one woman again—not with all my heart as once I did. I had suffered enough sorrow for a man three times my years. Little Marjorie, my daughter, whose beauty rivaled the angels, was an ever-painful reminder of what I had lost. Time was the only salve to my wounds, not bedmates.

I laced my fingers together and gazed at her. "Please, I want nothing from you. Only to know where Sir William is."

The dark haired lad stirred with discomfort.

"Why should we tell you?" He strode boldly forward to stand between his stepmother and me.

"What is your name, lad?"

He pulled his shoulders back and stood straight as a post. "James. You?"

"Robert Bruce, Earl of Carrick."

Squinting, James tightened his fists. He wore his thoughts as plainly as his father was prone to speak his.

"You do not trust me, aye," I said. "What blame can I lay on you for that? But, you see, I am no longer King Edward's man. I have heard of William Wallace and your father. I wish to join them."

"Why?"

"James," Lady Eleanor interrupted. "Enough!"

"No, no," I said, rising. "I welcome the inquiry. I have no wish to keep anything from you."

Parched, I reached for a pitcher on the table, then remembered my promise and drew my hand back. "John Balliol is in the Tower. In due time, he will be escorted back to his lands in Picardy where a life of comfort awaits him. He has worn his crown around his neck like a collar. Whenever Edward is not leading him about, it is our own council of nobles telling him what words to say and on which documents to put his seal. Meanwhile, Scotsmen have flocked to William Wallace like the Messiah, because he says what they thirst to hear. He gives voice to the thoughts and beliefs no one else dares to. Something to be admired." Some might have believed that to be nonsense, coming from me. I crouched in front of the boy, so as not to tower over him. "James? Do you want to be like your father?"

His eyes narrowed even further. He shot a brief glance at Lady Eleanor. "Aye, I do."

"And why is that?"

James chewed on his lip, then shrugged. "Because he is strong . . . and brave. Brave enough to fight the English."

"Aye, brave he is." I touched him on the arm and nodded. "And that is why I wish to join him."

Gently, I pulled him closer and to my surprise he did not resist. I lowered my voice to a whisper, so only he could hear. "Can you tell me where he is? I cannot join him if I do not know. I trust you to not lead me astray. And you must trust me, James. You must."

He leaned in closer yet. "Do you hate the English, too?"

There was something about the lad that foretold promise—something in the manner of his stance, the flicker of mischief and determination behind his pupils, and the measured care of his words that told me not to dismiss him for wont of years so readily. I winked at James. "Not all of them, but . . . I hate anyone who comes and takes what is not theirs."

"If you fight them I will tell you," he whispered back.

I lowered my eyes for a moment. I no more wanted it to come to that than I desired my own demise. But I had chosen a path and would never know to where it might lead unless I followed it to the end. Finally, I nodded and looked back up.

"Irvine," he said.

"Irvine." I patted his shoulder firmly. "Thank you, James. Someday I shall heap a rich reward upon you."

The cloud lifted from his sky-blue eyes and they twinkled with the starry hope of adventure. "Will you take me with you?"

I could feel Lady Eleanor's burning gaze—felt it as sure as if I had waved my own hand over a candle flame. She believed me to be one of *them*. Feared for her sons' safety and her own.

"No, I . . . I cannot," I answered regretfully.

Then I rose and approached the lady. I plucked up her hand and placed a soft kiss upon her knuckles. Her arm stiffened from fingertips to shoulder. Something in her past had cultivated a distrust of strangers—she was not to be easily won. Clumsily, I attempted to charm her with a smile. "Sir William's boys will bring honor to the name of Douglas one day."

She jerked her hand back and buried it in her skirts.

"If your men will leave their weapons at the door"—Lady Eleanor gazed sternly at my men—"and if they do not mind the wait overmuch, the cook can manage enough to satisfy them. But the wine will be generously watered. Drunkenness is not looked upon pleasantly here."

"As you wish, fair lady." I motioned to Gerald and moved to withdraw.

"My lord earl?" she said.

"Aye?"

"Make promises sparingly. As I tell my boys,"—she wound her fingers in the curls of the youngest—"words are soon lost to the wind."

My lips parted, but words resisted. All the promises I could conjure just then, to aid her husband, to protect her son, to stand by Scotland, I realized were worthless if my actions did not bear them out. I bowed, as much out of decency as thankfulness, for it was all I could do.

That night we were permitted the comfort of her roof. A timely blessing, for the rain came and with it a strong wind. Late the next morning, our bellies satisfied, we departed for Irvine.

We rode along the rugged road toward Irvine. The horses' hooves slapped mud up high. In the puddles pocking the road, chattering sparrows gathered to bathe. Gerald leaned from his horse and tapped me on the arm, then pointed ahead.

On a bare hill overlooking the long stretch of road northward, James sat on a dark, shaggy pony. In one hand he clutched a short spear. Over his back was slung a boy's short bow.

"It is as well he is too young to come with us," Gerald remarked. "There is bound to be bloodshed."

"You forget, Gerald. He was at Berwick." I shook my head at the tales I had heard and the horror of them. "He has seen more dead than you and I in ten lifetimes put together."

7

Robert the Bruce – Irvine, 1297

FROM DOUGLAS, WE RODE north, swinging wide of Loch Doon, and crossed the River Ayr far to the east, closer to Cumnock than Ayr itself, where the English were reported to be. At last, the broad hills dipped seaward. There, they flattened out and opened up to a rolling expanse of wind-battered tussocks of grass. A rising westerly wind drove grains of sand from the scattered dunes and tossed them into our eyes. The horses tucked their heads down and snorted. I gazed to the west, over the sea. On a fair day you could see the mountaintops of Arran, but today low gray clouds obscured the horizon.

In the distance, half a mile inland from the shore, a modest collection of one-story buildings hugged a small river. A bustling encampment sprawled just south of it. Our destination. With the recent gathering of Scottish discontents, Irvine had erupted into a town ten times its former size.

By the time we arrived, I had collected a respectable number of recruits from Carrick, although I was soon to discover that those who had gathered there had all come for pure quarrel, not for cause. Word had spread of James Stewart's summons for his knights to gather at Irvine to stand against the English. Stewart, the brother of William Douglas's first wife Elizabeth, held lands from Bute to Teviotdale and it was clear his wishes meant something to Scotsmen—even men like Wallace and Douglas, who were not beyond disagreeing with their own or disavowing authority. Unlike me, Stewart did not hold any lands in England, so no one could question on which side of the border his loyalties might lie.

At a comfortable distance from the main encampment, I ordered my men, but for Gerald, to wait. Breath held, back straight, I rode my horse to the very brink of the Scottish camp and dismounted. Someone murmured my name. Men sprang to their feet and came toward me—I thought to offer greetings, but on their faces were scowls rather than smiles. My way was barred with spears held firm. I dodged to the right, only to find the glimmering point of a long sword aimed at my belly. *Ah, devil.*

"Let me pass," I commanded, donning an air of authority. "I wish to speak with the Stewart."

Sir Alexander Lindsay, with his thick head of silver hair bobbing above all others like a seagull riding the waves, made his way through the rumbling crowd. He had known my grandfather well and although Lindsay was but a vague memory of my childhood, I sighed inwardly with relief to see a familiar face.

"Lindsay, I wish to speak with the Stewart. I have brought men . . . to join you."

Lindsay's eyebrows wove together and he folded his arms across his chest. "You're not welcome here, Robert, and I don't think the Stewart will care to see you. So be off . . . while you still have your skin."

"Then let me see Bishop Wishart." I knew that Robert Wishart, the Bishop of Glasgow, was involved in this and had no doubt he, if no one else, would speak with me. "Tell him that I come on church business."

Hostile eyes glared at me from every angle. Scotsmen hungry for a fight pressed closer. A tribe of wild-eyed Scotsmen is enough to make any man hesitate to cross the line they have drawn. I saw fingers flex on dagger hilts and began to wonder if I might have to turn around and go all the way back to Carlisle . . . something I would avoid at all costs.

"I think it's unlikely you do," Lindsay said loud and clear. Then he sauntered close, glanced about him and, with a wink, added low-ly, "But I will give him the message anyway."

A few minutes later, Gerald and I were led to a tent, unmarked by any standard, but bigger than any of the others. I left Gerald out-side and entered between the open flaps. Sir William Douglas was seated at a table, one fist braced against his cheek and the other tapping his knuckles on the table. To his right stood a tall, broad shouldered man, with his wild, sun-golden hair gathered loosely at the neck: William Wallace. He slammed his hand down on the table and argued his point. Opposite Wallace were a few other nobles, shaking their heads vehemently. At the table's head, James Stewart in his fine attire sat straight and silent, regarding the others coolly. And at the far end was old Bishop Wishart, snug in his clerical robes.

Bishop Wishart squinted his right eye at me. Indeed, I do not think his other eye ever moved. His face drooped heavily on the left: the effect of too many years and too many burdens. He nudged back his stool, but even as he stood he was hardly any taller than those who were seated. The right side of his mouth curled up into a lopsided smile.

"Robert?" The bishop waddled around the table, arms wide. I felt the soft paunch of his belly as he embraced me. "Ah Robert, Robert. I was greatly aggrieved when I heard of your wife. Your daughter is well, I trust?"

A deep pang stabbed at my chest. "Very," I replied softly. That single word resounded like a shout in the now gaping silence as the others there stared at me with obvious repulsion. I returned his embrace, and then stepped back. There was no point in hiding the reason for my coming. "I have brought men from Carrick."

They looked at me blankly.

"For what purpose?" Stewart asked, as if unsure of whether I would fight beside or against them.

I circled the table. "Stewart, you have known me for a long time. You know I have no reason to lie. I have come to fight the English. To fight for Scotland."

"No reason to lie?" Sir William Douglas scoffed, the disgust written on his swarthy face as plainly as shadows in the noonday sun. "You and your father . . . You have come to the wrong camp, Bruce. The English are at Ayr."

"You misunderstand. I am not on the side of the English. I am with you, Sir William. And you, William Wallace. Though I have one boon to ask of you."

Wallace sank down to his stool. "Tell us first—did you come here of your own will . . . or at Longshanks' bidding?"

"A fair question," I said, "and one I would have asked as well, were I you. But I come of my own accord and purpose and I ask you to abandon Balliol's cause. Forsake all the oaths you uttered under duress at Carlisle, at Berwick and foremost at Norham."

Stewart traced a finger along his jaw and leaned back. "Support the Bruce claim. Is that what you ask?"

"What reason to fight for a Balliol, when a Balliol will not fight for you, let alone himself?" I questioned, sure that single point would strike an undeniable truth. But I was regarded with only low grumbling, the shuffling of feet and eyes downcast. William Wallace alone met my gaze.

He swept away all contention with a mere glance and rose to

tower above everyone, including me—and I was far taller than most men. He strode around the table, stopped an arm's reach from me and squinted. "What would you have us do then, Lord Robert?"

Thus far he was the only one to address me with respect. I pulled him aside and lowered my voice. "I know you stand by Balliol's claim to the throne. There are many here who do. But you have seen the results of his kingship. Are we any better off than we were before? Worse, I venture. If we are to shed our suffering, Scotland needs a strong king."

Wallace cocked his head and grinned. "And who would that 'strong' king be, Lord Robert? Yourself? Your father? Stewart? Me? There are too many Scots, even here, who trade sides whenever the wind shifts."

The implication struck deep within me. "I know there are many here who question why I have come."

"Why *have* you come?" Wallace asked with a doubtful shrug. "Why now?"

"Why not? I might have joined you years ago, but a son does not so easily go against his father's wishes. I have tired of Longshanks' empty promises and manipulations. He confessed to my father and grandfather that it was a mistake to place the scepter in Balliol's hands, that a Bruce—"

"Ah!" Wallace pushed back the stream of my words with his huge palm. He raised his voice so those around us could hear. "Say no more. We shall ride out to the English and say it is for the Lord of Annandale that we fight now, eh? That he should be our king? He who sits this moment in Carlisle, taking orders from Longshanks? That would please the English well, I reckon."

"No, that's not—"

"Then if you propose that we muster behind you, give us good reason." He went to the half-open tent flap and pointed outside. "Otherwise, you are no different from all those other bloodless, begging nobles who wait to see on which side of the table the scraps might fall." Then Wallace stooped and plucked a handful of grass from the ground. He held it out and let it fall, blade by blade. "The wind blows to the south today, earl. Toward Ayr."

He returned to his stool and the bickering huddle commenced with their doubts and differences. I had been dismissed offhandedly. Given no regard, ignored. My blood was a river of fire in my veins. What profit to pledge myself when none would open their ears?

"I am no cur to English masters!" I cried. "And I do not beg for scraps."

"Aye, you've no need to beg," Douglas muttered. "I would say you are well fed." He and Wallace laughed.

I had turned my back on generations of convention, tossed aside privilege and gain to stand by my countrymen and all for what—for this? Grandfather could have swayed them with words powerful enough to peel the skin from their bones, but I . . . I was too insulted just then, or perhaps too unsure of myself, to find such potent words within me.

With measured control, I approached the table and said, not so much to Wallace or any one man in particular, but more so to myself, "I was born unto Scotland . . . and by Scotland I shall stand and serve her with all my heart. *You* are my flesh and blood, my brothers. So have me or not, but I am home and here will stay, without hatred for any of you, however vain your judgment."

Bishop Wishart alone met my eyes. The drooping folds of his fleshy face melted with benevolence toward me, but I received it like a gesture of pity, as Wallace had barely paused to allow my words space and then continued his arguments with Douglas. I had too much to prove and no way of doing so without the opportunity to speak and be heard.

I left them then. To have stayed any longer would have raised my ire to a point of indelible regret. I returned to my men and instructed them to make camp.

They would not be so easily rid of me.

IN THE GROWING GLOOM of evening, Gerald and I took supper together. My plate of beef and turnips was growing colder by the minute as I pushed them around with my knife. The tent we shared was east of the town, far from the main encampment. Not feeling welcome there, I had decided to keep my distance.

Gerald cleared his throat. "Should I light a candle? No doubt your eyes are better than mine, but I've nearly cut off the tip of my own finger twice now."

I nodded glumly and tried to turn my mind from the day's disappointment, without success. Stewart and the others did not trust me. They thought me a traitor to my own people—and rightly so. Convincing them otherwise would be a difficult, if not impossible, task.

I barely noticed Gerald fumbling in the darkness and the sharp scent of flint being struck, followed by the meager glow of candlelight, when a strange voice interrupted my thoughts.

"My lord?"

I glanced up to see a messenger, brown with road dust, standing at the tent opening. "What is it?" I asked.

The messenger wiped at the dirt on his forehead with a bare arm. He shuffled forward and thrust a tattered letter at me. "From Rothesay."

Without rising from my stool, I took it from him.

I thanked him, held the letter to the light and began to read it. Without prompting from me, Gerald scrounged for a few pieces of silver and gave it to the man, who disappeared as quietly as he had come.

I must have read it ten times over before Gerald said, "Well? Who is it from?"

"Someone named Elizabeth. Elizabeth de Burgh. She is the niece of James Stewart's wife, I believe. She says my daughter, Marjorie, is doing well." I let slip a tiny smile. "My lass not only walks now, Gerald, she runs like a deer."

The last time I had seen Marjorie she was barely able to sit upright. Although I had not wanted to part from her, to keep her safe I had sent her away, to Rothesay Castle on the remote Isle of Bute.

Hot tears scoured my eyes. My grief was yet fresh and raw. Two years past I had wed Isabella, the Earl of Mar's daughter. A year later she had given me a child, only to give her own life in the doing.

I laid the letter aside and tended to the sadness that crept upon me. I feared wee Marjorie would grow up without me there to watch. That one day, in a strange place, I would happen upon a young lady of exceeding beauty with ringlets of gold that cascaded down her back and not know it was my own daughter.

8

Robert the Bruce – Irvine, 1297

P RIDE RUNS DEEP IN Scottish veins, along with obstinacy. Myself, I do not claim to be free of the flaw. The squabbling of the so-called Scottish leaders did not come to an end. It went on and on, even as the English advanced up the coastline from Ayr.

A clean tunic draped over his forearm, Gerald emerged from the tent. "Five days since we came here and you haven't changed shirts once."

"Six." I took the tunic from him, put it on and pointed.

He squinted into the low morning sun to take in the sight unfolding at the edge of the main encampment. There, in the distance, Wallace climbed onto the back of his stout pony. The shaggy beast snapped its head up and tapped a hoof on the packed earth. With a shout, Wallace thrust his arm high and two hundred men, many of them mounted, started forward with a rumble.

"D'you suppose he's leaving for good?" Gerald said.

"It would appear so." Not even the unceasing sea wind blew today. Already, hot air lay stagnant and suffocating over the land like a pile of woolen blankets. Sweat trickled from my temples, over my cheekbones and down my neck. I wiped it away and then flicked a sopping palm at the ground. "Last night Bishop Wishart told me that Wallace had demanded command over the entire army. Stewart would not take sides, but the other nobles, including Douglas, refused to give over a right that should belong to one of them."

It was one more disagreement among many, but a divisive one. Bishop Wishart had urged compromise, a plea which fell on deaf ears. The nobles, in response, grumbled that Wallace was vainglorious and would lead them all to ruin if placed at the head of a Scots army. In truth, they envied the adulation Wallace inspired in the soldiers.

"So that's why he's leaving?" Gerald asked.

"No."

"Then why? I thought Wallace, more than anyone, wanted to fight."

"Fight the English, you mean? He does . . . or did, rather." My men were gathering on the slope below our outcasts' camp to ogle at the unfortunate turn of events. They grumbled and shook their heads. A few cursed. "It's the nobles who don't think we can win. Reports are that the English outnumber us four to one."

"Four Englishmen to every Scot?" Gerald dropped his chin, an impish grin tugging at his mouth. "Sounds like a fair fight to me."

"If we had more men like Wallace and fewer inconstant nobles, perhaps."

As he ducked back inside the tent, Gerald gave a faint grunt. He returned with my sword and belt, an unconvincing look of innocence on his face.

"Aye, I know," I said, snatching my belt from him and slinging it around my hips to fasten it. "I was one of them not so long ago."

Whenever we want something, we must weigh the cost of getting it. A farthing is a fair price for a loaf of bread. Two shillings for a yard of wool. But what price will a man pay to be his own master?

I think Wallace had already decided that, but the others . . .

Gerald held out my sword and I took it, my arm dropping with the burden of its weight. Wallace and his gruff band filed over the bridge at the edge of town and headed north.

Word came to us before the sun set that same day. The English would arrive at Irvine on the morrow. We could go off in our different directions, as Wallace had done, or face them as one. We chose to stay.

THE ENGLISH HORDE POURED over the horizon. Sunlight flashed harshly on polished blades. The barest of breezes lifted the tails of their banners into a faint flutter. Across the grassy plain they faced the Scots. It was a moment of grave reckoning.

Realizing they were vastly outnumbered, Stewart and Douglas rode out to meet the English commanders, Sir Henry Percy and Robert Clifford, to ask for the terms of surrender. When they returned, Stewart's face was ashen. Sir William Douglas dropped from his horse and came straight to me. The moment itself took me unprepared, for I had much expected to learn the outcome of their consultation the same as every other soldier standing by, sword in hand, wondering whether today he would lay down his life or walk away unscathed.

"My lord?" Douglas glanced down at the trampled grass, spat and swallowed. "I must tell you what was spoken of. It concerns you."

I nodded, even though I hesitated to hear what he had to say. Wallace had not returned and there was still disagreement among us.

"Percy and Clifford . . . they will let us walk from here, but they ask one thing of us in good faith: hostages. They want my son, James. They have also asked for your daughter."

My heart went cold and still. I willed it to go on beating. "No," I protested. "I would rather fight and die, knowing she would live freely."

"You fight to live. You don't fight to die. But if you do fight and you die, I guarantee she will *not* know freedom."

"No, no, I—"

"Don't be daft. Listen!" Douglas's voice went suddenly low, his words pouring out rapidly. "The Stewart and I have no intentions of giving them what they want, but we'll promise them as much . . . if only to buy ourselves time. I can speak from both sides of my mouth just as well as you, Lord Robert. And without remorse. I'll tell them what they want to hear. Right now we're in no condition to put up a fight. We need Wallace and Moray just as we need our right hands. Otherwise, like fat squealing pigs in the butcher's pen, we may as well line up for the slaughter."

"Lie outright?"

Douglas smirked at the question. "Does that bother your conscience? Did you think I would give them what they want as easy as that? With luck, they will not find your daughter. She is as safe at Rothesay as anywhere. For the time being."

"Your wife? Your sons? What of them? You will but utter the word and—"

"Already on their way elsewhere . . . if the message I sent makes it to them."

Like the first shaft of light above the mountaintops at dawn, I understood. My foot was firmly in the snare. "It was you . . . you who proposed this, not them. You planned for it. How? How can you barter the lives of children? You did this as much as a test of me as to worm your way out of a fight. You knew I would not give up my daughter, for if I refuse . . . if I refuse to take part in this sham I am false to all of you—a betrayer of Scotland."

"You are as free to refuse as any among us."

In the blink of an eye I had Douglas's surcoat clenched in both my hands. He clamped his fingers around my wrists in reflex. As sorely as I wanted to shove him to the hard, dusty ground, I thought of all the soldiers, my own men from Carrick among them, watching to see if I would strike him or let him go. Then, it was Bishop Wishart's words that prevailed upon my senses.

"Robert . . . Robert," the bishop begged, his plump hand upon my back, "a moment to speak with you."

Slowly, I let Douglas go, but not without a glare of warning. The bishop drew me aside and walked me over to a stand of pines a hundred feet away.

"My son." Bishop Wishart granted me his quaint, slanted smile as he faced me. Douglas had now joined with Stewart and the other nobles in a circle before the army of Scotland, some shaking their heads, some nodding, others shrugging their slumping shoulders. It looked something akin to twelve cooks standing over a pot of stew. The bishop took my hand and pinched the back of it like one would a small child whose attention is needed but not quite had. "Your grandfather would have bristled with pride to see you this day. But he would also advise patience, something youth is disinclined to embrace, at least from what my fading memory serves."

I rubbed at my forehead. "Aye, but my father would as soon disown me for those same actions. Your grace . . ." I glanced toward heaven, desperate for guidance, "everything I envisioned when I left Carlisle has far from come to pass."

"And this surprises you how?" His eyebrow curled upward in amusement. "You need to awaken from your dreams, son. Robert, these men"—he wagged a finger at the thousands of Scottish faces staring out over the sea of parched, yellowing grass—"I regret to say they did not come here, but for a few, to serve you. That is a mighty assumption on your behalf. And do not wonder why then the nobles keep you at arm's length, for you wear your ambition as plainly as you do your sword. You must win their loyalty through sweat and blood, not by words alone . . . and certainly not within a week's scant time. Even Moses had to perform a miracle or two before he led the Hebrews out of Egypt."

"My father would wait until the end of eternity for the throne that Longshanks dangles before him. I am not so patient a man. Tell me, bishop, how long is long enough?"

"Ah, Robert, you are hardly your father, are you? You tell me, son—is today the day? Or tomorrow? Or ten years from now? You are wise enough to weigh it all out. Opportunity comes at its own pace. You want to lead, but they turn from you. They do not trust you. The good Lord knows they do not trust each other. Set aside your own visions for now and join with them in theirs.

"There is strife between King Edward and his barons over taxes imposed on the church. Percy and Clifford have every wish to avoid battle, for they are all there is of Longshanks' army now, but still they know they stand before us with as many mounted knights and archers as we have paltry footsoldiers. Bide your time. Lay your plans. Keep them engrossed in negotiations . . . and Wallace is allotted precious time to do his work elsewhere. Quibble over details. Is that not what nobles do?"

"But hostages? My own flesh?" I begged.

"Heed Douglas on the matter, my son." He sighed heavily. "It is done and you must decide what to do from here."

"If I knew, do you think I would be in this state of vexation?" I peered at the ragged lines of men, their plain faces painted with grime, their heads bowed as smocked priests floated by, chanting their blessings. By now, the circle of nobles had broken and Stewart was walking toward the bishop and me.

"Robert, I know where your heart lies and in time others, perhaps, will come to see that. But don't curse them for wanting to save themselves. They all have sons and daughters to go home to, as well. A farmer is not one whit different from an earl, in that respect. I can arrange safekeeping for your daughter with the Abbot of Inchafray if Bute is threatened at all. As for the young Douglas . . . Bishop Lamberton knows a schoolmaster in Paris who will take him in. They will be far from King Edward's long reach."

Silence overcame me as Stewart closed the last few strides to us. His face long and austere, he looked at the bishop and then at me.

"Douglas and I," Stewart began plainly, "are riding out now. To discuss terms."

"Surrender? Is it my blessing you want? Or have you come to escort me to the other side?" My sarcasm failed to pierce his stoicism, however. I knew the bishop was right, but my heart cried for a fight, if only to prove myself.

"Lord Robert," the Stewart said, "Scotland is indeed in want of a good king. Much stands in your way . . . your father being first. Although I would not say this in front of the others, I would much prefer a Bruce to a Balliol."

I smiled briefly at so small and yet so huge a victory. Stewart was not one to flippantly cast his lot.

"Will you ride with us?" Stewart asked.

"If you would dare ask me that then you do not know me well enough. It would be better if I did not." Even as the words passed my lips, my thoughts were in two places: in Rothesay, where my daughter lived and grew with each passing day, and in Carlisle, where the man resided who from that day forward was sure to renounce me as his son. "Go. Do as you must."

Stewart extended his hand and I clasped it firmly.

Despair replaced hope as I watched Stewart ride back out with Douglas to meet Percy and Clifford. For me, it was not enough that I had come. I burned with shame as I witnessed the relief on the faces of the ragged warriors who turned to go home and at once began to talk of their crops and their livestock. They had been as quick to muster to a fight as they had been to give it up.

Wishart was right, though: I was no different.

Selkirk Forest, 1298

NOW AN OUTLAW WITHOUT a shilling to my name, I acted as an outlaw does: burning crops far and wide in my own Carrick, for I wanted to leave nothing behind for our enemies to take. While I fed the coals of my temper, Moray and Wallace joined forces. They took Inverness, Aberdeen and Dundee with such ferocity that the aged Earl of Surrey, Longshanks' appointed viceroy of Scotland, moved toward Stirling to seize and defend that vital gateway to the north of all Scotland.

With a valiant Scottish army at his back, Wallace faced the English at Stirling across the Forth. He did not retreat; he did not parley. He refused their offer to yield, telling them he was there to do battle and free Scotland. The English never doubted for one moment they would win. The first clash, they thought, would be merely a formality. Ever arrogant, the English began to file across the narrow bridge over the Forth to assemble on the other side, while the Scots waited and watched from Abbey Crag for hours. Until finally . . . Wallace gave the order. While the Scots attacked along the English front, others destroyed the bridge, cutting off not only a route of escape for the English, but half their army, as well.

In the year 1297, on the 11th day of September, Scotland claimed the greatest victory it had ever been known. Hope lived again.

One month later, Andrew Moray died of the wounds he received at Stirling. But Wallace rode on, ravaging the north of England to bring food to his starving countrymen. Commoners, clergy and nobles alike rallied behind him.

In the spring of the following year, my men and I rode to Selkirk Forest to attend a meeting that was to take place there.

Tight buds of palest green tipped the branches above, letting mottled sunlight filter through and fall upon the forest floor. Ahead, in a glen sheltered by low cliffs, light morning mist drifted between moss-covered tree trunks, partially shrouding the host of fighting men gathered there. Our guide, one of Lindsay's men, rode before me along the thinning trail. Smoke from a smoldering cooking fire permeated the damp air. From a stout limb, a deer carcass dangled, blood staining the dried leaves beneath. Nearby, its scraped hide was stretched over a felled log. I pressed my eyes shut, imagining the dark taste of roasted venison on my tongue. Behind me, Gerald and a dozen more of my men groaned at the emptiness in their bellies.

As we entered the clearing, men scuttled back to allow us through and bowed. It had not been easy to gain their trust—and it had cost me dearly.

"Lord Robert!" hailed a familiar voice.

I slipped down from my mount, my thighs burning with the soreness of too many hours spent in the saddle. Gerald took the reins of my horse and led it off the trail to tether it to a bush.

"Lindsay . . . I think you may dispense with titles for now. According to Longshanks, I have none."

Sir Alexander Lindsay strode forward and clasped my hand. His blue eyes crinkled with a smile of irony. "He gives and takes as he pleases. His word means nothing here. Your father is living off his estates in Essex, I hear."

"Aye, with my brothers and sisters. And mad as a honeybee robbed of its hive. Even though he denounced me, Longshanks would not permit him to oversee a post as critical and precarious as Carlisle."

He motioned me toward the clearing, where hundreds of men gathered. Many had the gaunt, unshaven look of someone who had been far from home for many months and lived off the land. "Your daughter?"

"Still at Rothesay." When the day had come by which we were to produce the sworn hostages, I had let it pass, as if it were of no accord. I would not give my sweet little Marjorie over to the English, not for any price, and I would gladly gamble my freedom and life for hers.

"And the young Douglas?" Lindsay asked.

"Bishop Lamberton saw to it that James Douglas was put on a ship carrying furs and wool to Calais. From there, he was supposed to have been escorted by a servant of Lamberton's to a school in Paris. I pray he made it and that whoever delivers to him the news of his father does so kindly."

Lindsay stopped so abruptly I nearly collided with him. He turned around slowly, puzzlement obvious beneath the shadowy hood of his thick white brows. "News?"

"You don't know?" We were at the edge of the circle, ringed by those who had joined openly in the cause to stand against the English. Alone, in its center, stood William Wallace, a silver-gray wolfskin draped from his shoulders and his thick crown of golden hair neatly swept back from his face. He stooped at the waist in acknowledgement. I nodded to him.

"We heard rumor," Lindsay said, "he was hunted down and taken in chains to Berwick. Is that what you mean?"

I shook my head. "They took him on to the Tower of London. He died there not ten days ago."

A stunned hush fell upon the gathering. Lindsay's chin sank to his chest. "We didn't know," he mumbled.

"Then a prayer for Bishop Wishart," Wallace said as he approached us, "that he'll come home soon . . . and well."

I, too, feared for the bishop's health. He was past fifty and suffered from the rheum. A dank cell and a hard bed would offer no comfort for his aching bones. Unlike the rest of us, Bishop Wishart could not take to the forest for refuge. To appease Longshanks, he had given himself up. He was the only one who had done so willingly.

"William Wallace," I said, "your sword?"

Wallace reached over his shoulder and drew his long sword. He held it out to me, its edges nicked with use, the leather binding of the hilt worn smooth by the grip of his hands. Head bowed, he went down on his knees before me.

I held the great sword aloft for all to see, my arms spread wide to bear its onerous weight. A priest in a black cassock with a sheathed knife at his belt stepped from the circle, incanting a blessing upon the occasion. Someone sank to their knees and soon, like the pulse of the tide upon the shore, others knelt, until none but the priest and I were standing.

Taking the hilt in both hands, I lowered the blade slowly, glancing one of Wallace's broad shoulders and then the other.

"I, Robert Bruce, Earl of Carrick, proclaim thee, William Wallace: Guardian of the Kingdom of Scotland!" My voice echoed ominously in the glen, each word overlapping the one before until only the word 'Scotland' resounded, finally fading away—not like a dying breath, but like the whisper of a wind soon to rise in force.

9

Robert the Bruce – Rutherglen, 1300

ALAS, HOW WICKEDLY CLOSE fortune may loom, brushing the fingertips, only to slip beyond the grasp. Late in that summer of 1298, not quite a full year after his victory at Stirling, Wallace gazed down upon mighty Longshanks' army from the slopes of Slamman Moor near Falkirk. The English cavalry thundered across the open ground, while Scottish arrows sputtered innocuously against their plates of armor. In the first impact, the English knights shattered the ranks of Wallace's spearmen. Then, that terror of Longshanks' genius, the Welsh archers, ripped through the Scottish schiltrons. Wallace escaped with his life, but the veneration he so deserved died that bloody day among the mountains of Scottish dead at Falkirk.

Flushed with conquest, Longshanks swung west toward Ayr, my headquarters since Irvine. I was gone before he ever got there. In my stead, I left him a smoking town and a castle in ruin. No one can take anything from you if you leave nothing behind.

In May of 1300, a Scottish parliament was called to convene at Rutherglen. If not for the coaxing of my friend, Bishop William

Lamberton of St. Andrews, I might have stayed away.

A scowling John Comyn, the one they called the Red Comyn for his fiery hair, sat on the other side of the long table, directly across from me. The man had but to part his lips and at the first hiss of his drawn breath I was imbued with loathing for him. Every other moment, he fidgeted like a lad wearied of his lessons. Sometimes he looked askance and stifled a yawn; other times he leaned his elbows upon the table and spewed his dissonance; and all too often he leapt to his feet and sermonized at whoever dared disagree with him. I writhed at every syllable.

At the end of the table, James Stewart ruled the parliamentary gathering at Rutherglen Castle with a stiff spine, his hands folded loosely in his lap and his countenance clear of judgment. Comyn, Bishop Lamberton and I were the appointed Guardians of Scotland—an awkward triumvirate. William Wallace had abandoned the post after Falkirk. After retreating to the Highlands briefly, he had since made his way to the continent. Some said that shame was his reason, but I knew otherwise. Besides, a man like Wallace never knows shame. How could he, when he lived by his heart and had nothing to regret?

By mid morning, nobles hungry for an argument crowded the great hall. Those of highest importance were seated at the oversized table in the center of the room; the rest lined the benches along either of the side walls. A strong May sun flaunted its brilliance through high glazed windows. The outer door stood open, but no breeze stirred the sultry air. Tempers, already simmering, quickly rose to a boil in that cauldron of discord.

Sir David Graham stood before his chair, hands clamped upon his hips. His gray-streaked beard bobbed above a bulging chest as he spoke. "Wallace has been abroad more than at home, negligent of his promises. Possessions granted to him in faith of those oaths should be forfeit."

The hall rumbled with both accord and dissent. The Earl of Atholl, never an ally of Balliol, kept his peace, but Sir Ingram de Umfraville, a kinsman of Balliol himself, urged Graham on. Common sense would have led one to believe the Balliol supporters would have stood faithfully behind Wallace, who had fought their battles for them. But he had lost, and in so doing, he had relinquished what little shred of faith they did have in him. A commoner and a failure, he was nothing to them.

Graham rattled his bulbous fists on the table. "Forfeit, I say!"

To my right, Bishop Lamberton nurtured his composure and tossed me a stern glance—imploring me to hold my tongue. I was finding it beyond difficult to bite back my words of protest. Even as Lamberton clenched my forearm, I slid my chair back and stood.

The rumble fell away slowly, like boulders tumbling down a long hill before coming to rest in a valley.

"Abroad on the business of this kingdom," I reminded them, "not hidden away in fear on a French estate with casks of wine and silk cushions surrounding him . . . like John Balliol."

In one succinct sentence I had uttered too much. They muttered and shouted and pounded their fists on the table. All eyes shifted to Comyn, awaiting the next move. The Red Comyn's wife was John Balliol's sister. He would defend Balliol to his dying breath.

Comyn wiped away a smirk above his scraggly red beard. With a heavy sigh, he leaned his full weight back in his chair and tossed his boots up on the table, dust rising in a small cloud. "Abroad on whose orders? This council never granted leave for him to go anywhere."

"Why should he have ever taken orders from a contrary lot like you?" I countered. "You argued with him at Irvine, abandoned him at Stirling and ignored him at Falkirk, even as you cheered his victories. You prodded him to action and yet criticized his decisions the moment he was beyond earshot. And you dare ask why he would not bow to you or why he is not here now? A hundredfold more able than any of you at bringing the English to heel and *still* you doubt him! What have any of you done to equal his courage?" I could not hide my contempt then as I looked from face to face. A few looked away in disgrace; others glared back defiantly. "You are too arrogant to defer to him and too ignorant to acknowledge all that he has done. As I stand before you, I know how he must have felt at Irvine and why it is he walked from there. Reasoning with you is like trying to teach hogs to crow."

"Hogs are we?" Comyn cocked his jaw sideways, his face reddening. "Well, perhaps you could impart to this fat, snorting boar why it is that Wallace dallies in France? Word has it he takes coin as a mercenary now."

"Mercenary?" I echoed, incredulous. "Wallace will fight for none but Scotland, I tell you, and in the accursed name of Balliol, if that is who you would all bow to as your king, whether he be sitting at the head of this parliament or exiled in a foreign land. In that, Wallace is truer of heart than me or anyone here. He has gone to France at Bishop Lamberton's urging. Longshanks has shoved a treaty before King Philip and Wallace means to convince him not to sign it. It is a treaty which is as good as Scotland's death sentence if it comes to pass. And if Wallace is persuasive enough, an audience with the pope may be forthcoming. This very moment, Pope Boniface is contemplating a bull directed at Longshanks that would admonish him for trespassing upon Scottish soil and plundering that which is not his."

"Treaties? Death sentences? Papal bulls?" Comyn mocked. "*Wallace* pulling the strings of Paris and Rome? Hah. More likely our Lamberton stirring the furtive pot of politics."

Lamberton drew breath and, eyes downcast, curled his fingers back beneath the hem of his loose sleeves. There were too many sympathizers with Comyn there, circling like buzzards, waiting for the first sign of weakness. The bishop was cool enough to censor his thoughts, but he must have felt as I did—that even blatant lies may plant seeds of doubt.

I clenched my fists until the blood left them and then slammed them on the table. "How dare you question the intentions of His Grace? He is your fellow Guardian. Do you turn from the face of unity to fling baseless accusations?"

"I dare as I may," Comyn replied snidely. "Armor, vestments or hemp-shirts. Traitors wear sundry clothing. Some genuflect to an English king and when—"

I sprang upon the table and dove at Comyn. His chair toppled backward with his corpulent frame beneath me. We rolled onto the floor and the back of his head struck the flagstones. I pulled back my fist to aim at his scarlet face. But with amazing strength, he threw me off and shot to his feet. On my knees, I spun around to face him, but before I could stand he gripped my neck and throttled hard.

Unable to escape, I felt my windpipe being crushed. I battled to draw air. His grip tightened. The edges of my vision went gray and blurred.

It took five men to pry his fingers away and yank him from me. They dragged him away as Stewart rose to his feet and strode the length of the meeting table to stand as a barrier between us. I gulped in air, my ribs aching with each rattling breath. Comyn, cursing, strained violently against the men who held him back.

Stewart raised a long finger at me. "Robert, do not force me to do this, but . . . you will harness your anger or . . . or go from here."

Slowly, I gathered myself and staggered to my feet. I rubbed tenderly at a sore neck and hacked raggedly in between hard-won breaths. "I will not . . . idle while others . . . hurl false inventions at honest men. Have you all heard nothing? Has honor so fallen from regard you retreat from rising in defense of it?" I shook my head at all of them, at their quibbling and complacency. Heaven help us, they were all either deaf or daft. I searched the faces there and wondered where lay Scotland's hope.

"Command John Comyn to harness his wagging tongue," I warned, "or I will cure the problem in brutal fashion."

Stewart gave Comyn a lingering glance of warning.

Comyn scowled at the men still holding him. "Let go of me." His shoulders relaxed and with a curt nod from Stewart they released him. He tugged the hem of his shirt down and wiped the sweat from his brow. "A temper, Bruce. You've your grandfather's vices and not a whit of his virtues."

In a more secluded place I would have, in turn, robbed the vile breath from him.

Ignoring Comyn's jeer, Stewart moved closer to me. He inclined his head, his voice now low and calm. "I remind you, we have not convened here to levy harm upon one anoth—"

"Share that sentiment with the Comyns, Stewart, not me," I interrupted. "I have exhausted more of my time and men in trying to keep him and his kin from marauding my lands in Carrick than I ever have of turning back English intruders. *That* is the bloody truth!"

Stewart turned, took a few steps away and faced me again. "Weighty accusations, Lord Robert."

I held out my hand toward Lamberton. He stood and drew from beneath his robes a letter, the seal broken. He handed it to Stewart, who then read it carefully. When he was finished, Stewart slid the letter into the middle of the table. A dozen men gathered round, those who could read well, and soon others pressed against their shoulders to listen as the Earl of Atholl read it aloud.

"John Comyn," Stewart began, shaking his silvered head in exasperation, "your own brother Sir Alexander has recently burned and plundered lands not his, Scottish lands, in Annandale." His gray eyebrows knitted together as he glanced about the room. "We will lay it at your door to correct the matter and to make certain that if he has profited by this action he will make due recompense. Any crime he may own shall be called upon as well. See to it."

Comyn threw his arms wide. "Am I to be my brother's jailor then?"

"You are to uphold the laws of this land," Lamberton said.

"And what laws does a traitor answer to?" Comyn spat.

Lamberton kept his arms stiff at his sides, his jaw held firm in that ever-saintly tranquility he possessed. "The laws of this land as well of those of Our Lord God are clear. We do not inflict suffering on mankind, least of all our own."

Comyn strode toward the table and spat squarely in the middle of Lamberton's brocaded collar. "Your piety galls me. How can any of us come near to it? You do as you please and say it is for Scotland alone that you act. I cannot serve as Guardian with one as almighty as you . . . or with one as arrogant as the Bruce."

"Then let me unburden you of half your troubles," I said. "I resign as a Guardian of the Realm."

Lamberton's eyes flew wide, a look of shocked abandonment imprinted on his countenance.

"Your grace," I said to Lamberton, my chin sinking to my chest with regret, "you will endure better than I in matters of"—I glanced sideways at Comyn, then down at the floor—"diplomacy. For now, I am needed more at home than here."

As I went from the room, the silence was so great that my every footfall was amplified. Even though I was the son of a traitor, I had been entrusted by my peers with a station of high honor. But I could no longer bear the strife of it. Best to go, then and there, before the want for retribution overtook me.

"Lord Robert," Stewart called out.

I paused before the door.

"We have yet to discuss plans to prepare against Longshanks," he said. "The king of England has issued writs to summon his levies at Carlisle by midsummer. You cannot walk from here. Not now."

"With regret, I do." Slowly, I turned to face him. "Was it not you who proposed I should go from here? I turn my back not on Scotland, my lords, but on disorder. One devil at a time is all any of us can manage."

The problem, I reckoned, was figuring out who the devil was.

That night I nursed my burgeoning sorrows over wine. How I had failed in every way. My temper, as always, had prevailed over my senses. Had I any chance at redemption? My grandfather would have turned from me had he witnessed what I had done. I would have given my every tooth to beseech his guidance that day.

They were misguided, errant. They could not comprehend beyond the here and now or outside their own welfare. How could I make the blind see? I had tried. God knows how hard I had tried.

10

Edward, Prince of Wales – Lichfield, 1300

WHEREVER PIERS DE GAVESTON stood, he cast no shadow. He was the sun. Brilliant. Glorious. Above all others in wit, exceeding them in feats of arms. Piers, or Brother Perrot as I endearingly called him, had arrived in England as a boy on the dusty heels of his penniless father, Arnold de Gaveston, who had escaped from a French prison. My sire the king, moved by pity for his former Gascon retainer, took his son Piers on as a squire.

None ever had a face more fair or eyes as bright as Piers'. His hair was straight and tawny and in every light it shone like shafts of sunlight reaching down through broken clouds. Always, he was attired in the finest cloth from Flanders, Venice or the East. He bathed in a bathwater of olive oil sprinkled with lavender and sandalwood and chewed on coriander seeds to sweeten his breath. In all these rituals, there was not so much frivolity, but more of an attention to detail. He was impressive in every manner and for this I was in undeniable awe of him from first sight.

One damp spring morning when I was but sixteen and he two years more, we rode from Kenilworth and through Longforest. We had been up and on our merry way well before dawn. Gilbert de Clare, the Earl of Gloucester and son of my older sister Joanna, yawned incessantly. We stopped in a clearing to make water. Wat, my flute player, caught Gilbert as he swayed sideways on his horse, having fallen asleep. Together with Robin, who had his lute tightly strapped to his back in anticipation of a spontaneous burst of musical inspiration, they propped the groggy Gilbert against the trunk of an ash tree.

I made my way through the mist toward a more private spot, spear in hand to serve as a walking stick. But before I could relieve myself, I heard the telltale crack of a twig. A small, young doe bounded from the newly-leafed underbrush. Her red hide shimmered with dew. Deftly, I shifted my grasp on my spear and brought my arm back. Her eyes, pools of endless innocence, caught with mine. She twitched her ears but did not move otherwise, as if offering me the choice. I lowered my spear and kicked up fallen twigs to startle her to action, then watched her sprint away into the gray tangle of forest.

"Why didn't you take her?" Piers panted at my shoulder as he ripped his bow from over his back and fumbled to nock the arrow.

"A roe deer. Hardly more than a fawn. Not worth the trouble, really. Besides, she was a few strides too far for my spear aim. If I had my bow ready . . . maybe then."

"Are these the king's lands?" Piers asked. The quarry now out of sight, he plucked at the bowstring and squinted into the drifting mists.

I glanced behind me to see my nephew, Gilbert, rubbing at his eyes as he tiptoed through the nodding daffodils toward us, his own bow forgotten. "Bishop Langton of Lichfield's," I said, stroking my spear with my thumb, "and thriving with every manner of fur and feather you can imagine. He never touches it."

"Then it wouldn't bother him to share it with us, eh?" Gilbert leaned against the nearest tree, slid down and drew back the hood of his cloak for a moment to glance about, then pulled it back over his eyes and wrapped himself more tightly as if to bed down for the duration. A year younger than me, Gilbert enjoyed gambling and music and was known for slurping from the forgotten tankards of others after he finished off his own. Little wonder that after last night, given the two casks of ale he'd downed, he wasn't puking up his breakfast.

"Unwise, Gilbert," I warned. "He is parsimonious beyond belief. Keeps his collection box nailed shut."

"Edward." Resting the bottom of his bowstave on the muddy ground, Piers clucked his tongue and planted a fist on his cocked hip. "Afraid of a holy man? What is he going to do? Cudgel you with a gilded altar cup?" Flipping away his bow, he raised his two clutched hands above him, as if lofting an imaginary cup. Then he feigned an angry grimace and flung it at me. A waft of air stirred my hair and I flinched instinctively. Wat and Robin joined us.

"Oh, what have I done? Heaven forgive," Piers jested in an old man's crackling voice, hobbling to me and clasping my head in his hands. "You bleed, you bleed. Oh, I meant it not. My prince, my prince, please . . . take all you want. What's mine is yours, for I have no need of it. I am a man of God and need live on faith alone."

A mocking frown tugged his lip downward. Cradling his face in his hands, he pretended to sob and plunged to his knees. "I beg your forgiveness, merciful lord. I have committed the carnal sins of avarice, gluttony and fornication with unwilling virgins. What is one deer? Take them all, my fair and gracious prince. Take them . . . all." He flung himself at my feet and kissed them profusely.

"Spare his head," Wat said, elbowing Robin in the ribs. "I fancy his clothes and if'n you would hang him instead, avoid a bloody mess and all, I could have 'em for m'self."

I laughed as I slapped Piers on top of his head. My sire

frowned upon the company I kept, but they were vastly more amusing than a council chamber stuffed full of barons and bishops, clawing at one's tolerance.

"Indeed." I lifted Piers by the puffed sleeves of his upper arms. "You're soiling your hose. And . . ." I patted him twice on his flushed cheek, "you're too pretty to be a cleric, Brother Perrot. Temptation would overwhelm you like a fly in a field full of cow shit."

"Proper rot, Edward." He winked at me. "But *so* true. Now, what say we bring down a stag or two? Langton will never know he's missing any."

How could I ever resist Piers' charm? I walked over to Gilbert and kicked him in the gut.

"Jeeeesus!" he wailed into a muddy pile of leaves as he rolled over. "What are you doing?"

"Arise, nephew." I loped to my horse and sprang into the saddle. "The day is wasting and the forest is teeming with game. So up, Gilbert. Up and away! Ready your knife, your spear and bow. Wat, Robin, keen your ears. And gentle Brother Perrot, lead the chase. You've the best eyes of all of us. Wherever you go, I and the whole world will follow."

Windsor, 1300

I DRAGGED MY FEET as I entered the room where my father, King of all England and more, was taking his supper at a small round table. Bishop Langton sat across from him. I cringed inwardly, but kept a level chin and square shoulders. I knew, without being told, why I had been summoned to Windsor. Behind them, the chill air of a dimming sunset poured in through an open window, so they were but dark silhouettes before it. Black-robed judges ready to levy their sentence on me, with or without a trial.

Ignoring me as one would a menial servant, the king finished off his meal to the very last pea and chased it down with half a cup of wine from a jeweled goblet. The bishop's stern eyes never left me. He leered at me like a nagging mother who stares down a disobedient boy before she can get across the room to tweak him by the ear and drag him outside for a beating. I so wanted to prance over to him, knock the bloody miter right off his fat, bald head and then strike him senseless with the gold crucifix that swung from his short, little neck. By Babylon, it must have been heavy enough to anchor a ship. I glared back at him, rolled my eyes and sighed with annoyance.

When your time comes, your grace, God will judge you, too, by your legion of vices. I hear your steward's niece birthed your bastard not a year ago and her belly is already swelling again.

"What is it," my father began, as he dabbed at his hands on a square of white linen, "about the word 'property' that you fail to understand?" With a flip of his slim fingers, he tossed a chicken bone to the floor. His lazing brindle greyhound snatched it up, growled as it passed me with its tail tight between its legs and then lay down across the doorway, as if to block my escape.

"*Mea culpa*," I muttered, bowing low in Langton's direction. "It will not happen again."

"Indeed, it will not." My sire dipped his fingers in a bowl of rose water and then wiped them dry on his lap. "You behave *infra dignitatem*, perhaps because of those you surround yourself with. You are confined to Windsor for six months. Your 'friends' may not come within sight of you during that time. That should provide you with ample time for reflection." Beneath cold, gray eyes, he smiled smugly.

My heart froze in its rhythm. Six months? Six *months?* "But, sire . . . Brother Perrot? You placed him in my household at King's

Langley. You cannot send him away because of one little escapade. What harm was done that cannot be undone?"

"Much. You both suffer from poor judgment. You knew you were on Bishop Langton's lands and yet you failed to seek his permission. You killed more deer than you could bring back and left a dozen carcasses in the forest to rot, spread disease, breed flies and stink whenever the wind blows. You have been a nuisance, a wastrel and a common thief. The bishop here urged me to be more lenient with you, but I think I have been far too lax until now. Punishment is overdue. It is time to alter your ways. You are a man now and should begin to act like one."

With a sweep of his hand he dismissed me from his royal presence. I lowered my eyes and backed away, turning sharply about as I reached the door. The greyhound let out a yelp, jumped up and snapped at my shins. I had stepped on its tail—not by accident.

Turnberry, 1301

I ENDURED THAT SUMMER in dull solitude, fed by smuggled letters, and when autumn came Piers and I embraced as if six years, not months, had divided us. My mirth, however, was short-lived. The next spring my sire commanded me to join him on a campaign against the Scots. He sent me up the western shore while he drove through the eastern parts. We were to conquer and lay waste to both coasts and then meet where the land narrowed, thereby dividing north from south.

When I discovered that the Bruce was en route to Turnberry Castle, I pursued him there like a fox gone to ground. Sooner or later, he would have to emerge from his hole.

But with each passing day, anticipation slowly turned to frustration.

Gilbert, who had arrived only that morning straight from Gloucester, plucked up a flat stone at his feet and flung it in the direction of Turnberry Castle. It arced across a luminous summer sky, hurtling end over end, before it fell from view and clattered downward over the sea cliffs. He searched the trampled grass for another stone. "Did you attempt to gain access by the sea cave yet?"

I waited until he looked at me before I imparted a sneer. "We've been here nearly twenty days, Gilbert. What do you think we have been doing? Hunting grouse with slings and stones to pass the time? Of course we have."

"And?" His hands empty, he straightened.

"That devil-spawn killed twenty of my men."

He scratched at his head, ambled toward the cliff's edge and peered down at the sea gate, its opening obstructed by the massive iron portcullis. "Don't you think that was too obvious? Sending twenty at once?"

Had I not known Gilbert for his naïve honesty, I would have accused him of mocking me in my father's stead. "Twice we tried. But there's no way to it, not without being seen and murdered in our tracks. No, I haven't enough men to overwhelm the castle on both fronts. Not nearly enough. Even the land route is too narrow for an assault."

Gilbert's mouth gaped in a drawn-out yawn. "So where's the king now?"

I shrugged and glanced at my army, encamped further inland. "Hammering Lothian to a pulp. He's set upon Bothwell Castle, I hear. We're to join up in Linlithgow by mid September."

"And what there?"

"I presume he'll gloat, what else? Only now do I see why he sent me here. Bloody Christ—he knew all along. Knew how this would go for me." I gripped the hilt of the long knife at my waist, wishing for something to slash at in my mounting fury, but there was nothing around us except sun-gilded swells of grass underlain with sand. "Bruce is firmly ensconced on his rock and I haven't the siege machinery to topple him from it. Meanwhile, his pack-mate Soulis gnashes at our calves from behind every time the sun goes down. Cowards!" I shouted at the castle as I drew my knife and flashed it before me. A rising wind swallowed my words. Spinning on my heel to face Gilbert, I slammed my knife back into its sheath and paced past him. "They refuse to come out into the open to do battle. Instead, they lurk in the hollows and woods of this God-forgotten wasteland, then attack while our backs are turned. What my sire thinks to gain by squandering his resources in this stinking latrine of humanity, I fail to understand. It would be better to forget the savages altogether and leave them to cross swords against each other."

"They do that sometimes already, don't they?"

"Not nearly enough."

Sinking to his haunches, Gilbert dug a rock from the gritty earth and thumbed its smooth surface. "Edward, do you know for certain Bruce is in there? In the castle?"

"Do I know for certain?" I stopped before him to stare at Turnberry's elusive towers. In one of those, the Bruce slept soundly every night, confident he would outlast me. His avoidance, though, was merely a delay of the inevitable. "Before you arrived yesterday, he came out onto the parapets himself, just to insult me personally. I swear I'll bring that bastard low one day. Not this time, perhaps. But one day . . ."

WHEN I REJOINED THE king at Linlithgow, the reception was a tepid occasion. He could say little in chastisement, though, for success had eluded him equally. The formidable warrior had been foiled. Instead of returning home to the comforts of London, my sire forced me to remain in desolate Linlithgow over winter. He took cruel delight in tormenting me. The gloomy loch reflected my melancholy at again being parted from jovial companions—most of all Piers. For that fellowship, I was to suffer persecution at every step.

Just as the sun must give way to night and even at times to clouds of gray, so did Brother Perrot come and go to banish or bow to the darkness in my wretched life. When I was with Brother Perrot, there was always joy. When I was not, misery consumed me. In the high days of our youth, when we kept company at King's Langley, I would often delight him with my fiddle-playing. As the last note danced from my bow he would clap and shower me with praise and beg for more. My music, he said, was like a wine to the soul that would have roused the jealousy of Bacchus himself. Indeed though, it was Piers who roused the jealousy of others for courting perfection. Envy breeds such insatiable evil in men.

11

Robert the Bruce – Isle of Bute, 1300

FROM AYR, GERALD AND I sailed up the coast into the Firth of Clyde, chased by a darkening storm. As arrows of sleet from steel December skies drove through us, we landed on the wind-assaulted Isle of Bute.

The reins of our ponies clenched between stiff fingers, we traveled on in wretched silence over crooked streets, brown with mud and filth, and then through the squat gate of Rothesay Castle. A thickset, gray curtain wall encircled the inner ward and embedded within the wall were four round towers equidistant from one another. Barely able to straighten our legs, we dismounted and, shivering, waited beneath the narrow pentice connecting the kitchen and great hall, while a garrison soldier with a hacking cough went to fetch a groom for our horses. Soon, a lad scurried forth from the stables. Behind him, a hooded figure approached us, his dark surcoat slapping heavily against his shins with each lengthy stride.

James Stewart swept back his hood and squinted against the sleet. "Welcome to Rothesay, Lord Robert." Then he motioned for us to follow. We dragged our rigid bodies across the ward and through a double door.

Icicles dripped from the hem of my cloak. I stood temporarily frozen in place, despite the blazing hearth that beckoned on the far side of the hall. Twenty or so folk clustered next to it, quaffing ale and making merry. Their laughter tinkled like fairies' talk in a distant glen. Had I been in a more presentable state, I would have called for drink and joined them, but I wished only to climb out of my wet clothes and into a dry bed. The doors swung shut behind us, banishing the winter draft that had invaded on our tails. Every face turned to survey us.

"Father! Father!" my Marjorie squealed. Gay as a wren on fluttering wings, she skipped and twirled across the floor on tiny feet. Yellow curls bounced at her shoulders. She leapt into my arms and I caught her, mindless of my drenched clothes.

"You're wet!" Her pale brow puckered. Then twice as quick, she smiled and pecked me on the cheek. "I'm so *happy* to see you."

I forgot the fire in the hearth. My heart had been warmed from the core. "And I you." I squeezed her tight and then set her down to admire her.

She held onto my hands and danced gaily. I had left her in the Stewart household for safekeeping. Had I thought for a moment she was ever in danger . . . Oh, banish the thought to purgatory. She was hale and hearty. Her mother's perfect image. Four years old now. And she still remembered me, though six months had fled by since I last held her in my arms, kissed her ivory forehead and wished her pleasant dreams.

"James and Egidia have kept you healthy as well. You're half a foot taller and look there . . ."—I brushed her ruddy cheeks— "roses."

She giggled with delight, then tugged at my hand and yanked me across the floor.

"Elizabeth teaches me how to sew." She pointed somewhere to

the middle of the crowd gathered about the hearth. "And how to read and dance and so many things."

The minstrel had set aside his harp. A bemused hush was followed by murmurs of excitement. Bodies bent at the waist to me. There must have been ten ladies or more clustered around the hearth. I strained to recognize any of them. Truthfully, I was so weary it was difficult to keep my eyes open long enough to focus on any single face. I saw only a flock of skirts in varying colors, smooth faces framed by stiff veils, the occasional gleam of a gold clasp, hands that fluttered about laughing mouths . . .

Slowly, my head began to clear. Near them were as many men: James Stewart, Bishop Lamberton and—aye, it was—Bishop Wishart, liberated at last from Longshanks' dungeons.

"Is that indeed you, young Rob?" Wishart squinted at me with one beady eye and waddled across the floor. He enfolded me in his arms and pounded me severely between the shoulder blades. Then he thrust me back, his face ebullient. "How good it is to see you! You are none the worse for your rebel ways, I see."

"And you in good spirits, in spite of all. How long a time was it, your grace?"

"Almost three years," he said with an uneven frown. "One would have expected a willing hostage to receive far better treatment. My wine—it was vinegar. Ach, putrid. My window—too high up to see anything but gray sky. How gloomy. My bedfellows were fleas and the rats, they had names by the time I departed. I called one Mungo, after our beloved saint."

"That bad, truly? But tell me, are you well?"

"As well as a man of my . . . my *vast* experience can be, my dear Robert." He rubbed at his bald, shining head and winked with mirth. Wishart was well over seventy years, but what he lacked in youth's vigor, he compensated for in spirit and humor. He lifted his palms to mere inches from his nose and lowered his voice. "But my

eyes . . . not as good as they once were. This is how close I have to
hold a book to read."

"Surely by now you have the scriptures memorized?"

"I can recite them backward, lad. But official documents—
writs and records, sealed letters—those, they are a different matter.
At least I was free of politics while I rotted in my Tower cell. Now
there's an overdue blessing. William, come, come," he said as he
raised a hand and beckoned to Bishop William Lamberton. "Do
greet Robert properly."

Where I easily tossed aside formality in regards to my old family friend Bishop Wishart, for he himself thought them ridiculous, I
would never have adopted the same slack manners with the Bishop
of St. Andrews. Lamberton, with his crimson silk girdle and gold-
embroidered collar, was as much diplomat as prelate, shaping the
disjointed, intricate affairs of state with one jeweled hand while he
shepherded his roving priests, often depraved, with his crosier
clasped in the other. Wishart, I cherished. Lamberton . . . I revered.

I knelt before him and kissed his ring.

"Rise, Lord Robert. You've need of dry clothes."

James Stewart's wife, Egidia, flitted forward and bubbled with a
mother's doting concern. Everything about her was matronly: from
her broad hips, to her plump cheeks, to her full bosom, which
heaved above a tightly belted waistline as she drew breath. Though
she equaled her husband in decades, she did not show it in the still
smooth skin of her face.

"No fever," she declared, both palms pressed firmly against my
cold cheeks. "Let my woman, Oonagh, escort you to your quarters." She took cursory inventory of Gerald's condition. A puddle
had collected at his feet. He shivered visibly and sneezed, empha-
sizing his misery. Egidia clucked her tongue, frowning in sympathy.
"We'll have you both properly dressed and stuffed to your collars in
no time at all. Now off with you. Time for idle talk later."

"M'lady," Gerald bewailed through chattering teeth, "I would be content with a sack cloth as my tunic and a wool blanket for a cloak. Anything at all, as long as it's dry and warm. I ask nothing more."

"Rubbish," I said aside. "You'll beg for a heel of bread and then eat the place empty."

"You'll drink it dry," he muttered back.

"With your help." I clapped him on the back as we followed Egidia's handmaiden, the limping Oonagh, to our rooms.

WE WERE QUICKLY FITTED with clean clothes and escorted back to the bustling hall. Warm and dry at last, I could not satisfy my bottomless stomach. My manners forgotten, I reached across Bishop Lamberton's trencher to steal a fat, dripping goose leg from an abandoned serving tray. If this fare was merely a prelude to Christmas dinner, I could not even imagine the gluttony ahead.

"Egidia,"—I sucked the grease from my fingers in between words—"tell your cook . . . he is the finest in Scotland. And is that your son Walter . . . next to you there? I vow he favors you. He did not get those good looks from his father."

She smiled at me through a wavering glow of rushlight. Music whirled around my head dizzily. The boy next to her, only a couple years older than my Marjorie, slumped over his food with disinterest. Blanched as a bank of snow, he had his mother's large, dark eyes and thick, auburn hair, but the lanky, gaunt frame was that of his father. He sniffed and rubbed at a raw, red nose.

A heady riot of pipe and tabor music swirled around the hall. I tapped my foot on the floor to the intoxicating rhythm. The cupbearer drifted past my shoulder and I soon found myself staring into another brimming cup of ale of the first water. Strong stuff and something I didn't get much of when I was living off the back of my horse, wondering what I'd have for supper that night . . . or even *if* I'd have supper at all. Another serving or two and I would fall asleep with my face in my custard tart. I drank my cup down halfway, then braced my elbow on the table and leaned my swimming head on my fist.

Marjorie wriggled under my arm and squirmed onto my lap.

"Dance, father," she commanded. Her small teeth glimmered like pearls.

"Och." I rubbed at my forehead. "A bit too weary, myself . . . and getting well past your bedtime anyway, sweet lass."

"Not with me, silly goose." She pinched my nose playfully, then pointed. "With Elizabeth."

My eyes followed her finger. A circle of dancers had formed in the middle of the hall. With hands clasped, they wove in a serpentine beneath the arched handholds of the other dancers, skirts flying and laughter high. The music became more frenzied, the drumbeat quicker, challenging the dancers to keep pace.

"And which one is Elizabeth?" I asked.

"There, there. The pretty one. In the blue."

Bodies whirled past in a flare of color, but one young woman stood out. Pretty indeed, I thought to myself as I caught sight of her. Long of neck and slender of waist, Elizabeth de Burgh was hardly more than nineteen, I reckoned. Aside from the river of auburn hair flowing over her shoulders, which indicated she was not yet married, she shared little of the looks of her more sturdily built Aunt Egidia or her broad-framed father, the Earl of Ulster. When the music ended, she laughed and clapped. A smile flitted across her mouth as her eyes swept the room. I forgot my meal entirely then, rather imagining myself kissing those apple red lips of hers.

"Caution, Robert." Stewart waved his knife before me to get my attention. "Her father, Ulster, is loyal to Longshanks."

Nonchalant, I arched a brow at him and shrugged. "And yet he has allowed her to come here and live under your roof."

"She is my niece by marriage."

"Then it would be impolite of me not to be cordial with her, since we're both your guests."

He glared at me, the knife dangling, point down, from his long, thin fingers. "Nothing more, Robert."

"Of course—nothing more."

In a burst of joviality, Wishart leaned forward to engage Stewart in conversation. Soon, talk drifted from the abysmal weather to popes and wool taxes. Unwittingly, I found myself searching the crowd for the enchanting Elizabeth again. How was it that I did not notice Marjorie had slipped to the floor and run around the table to embrace her? My daughter cupped her hand and whispered in Elizabeth's ear. When her eyes met mine, I blinked and looked away, as if I had been discovered pilfering forbidden fruit.

"Robert, are you listening?" Bishop Wishart laid a stubby-fingered hand on my right wrist. "William asked if you've had any trouble recently with the Comyns or Gallovidians."

"Ah, no . . . it's been rather quiet, in truth."

"Spring will bring them out again," Stewart mused.

"Sure as it rains in Scotland," I added.

"I have wondered of late,"—Stewart turned a dried date over in his palm, then replaced it on his plate in favor of a drink—"if you might entertain the thought of a match between Walter and Marjorie? They have quite taken to each other. Your daughter is a lively spirit and catches the eye of everyone who comes here. The lad struggles at arms, but he is insatiable when it comes to his studies. He speaks French, Latin, German, English, as well as the tongue of the locals, as you do Robert. He even reads a bit of Greek."

Greek was a dying language and of use to no one but Greeks. I eyed the boy, sucking the snot back up his nose as he evidently nursed a cold. On paper it was a fine pair, but in person Stewart's son was hardly impressive. "Perhaps we can discuss it later." By 'later', I meant years from then. I would give the boy time. He might improve. As I teased the last shred of meat off the bone of the goose leg, a thought struck me. "You are speaking of a union, my lord, yes? Marriages are pacts. I could, at some point, be swayed by an exchange of favors. My daughter in return for your support of my hereditary claims. If you agree, I will *consider* the proposal."

The music was at a lull. The only noise in the hall was the prattle and wry wit flying at the side tables. Everyone nearby had attuned to our bargaining.

"I am not a man who gambles with my future," Stewart declared, "or my son's. My holdings are in jeopardy even now and have been ever since Irvine."

"So you won't, then?"

"Publicly? No, it would be suicide. But if you're ever in need, I'll answer you. Just remember this talk we had. Sworn?" It was his way of saying he, for now, agreed, but without making a public declaration of it.

I rolled my head back and gave it consideration. "Aye, sworn."

The music struck up again and for a while there was more talk of a dismal harvest, the early onset of winter and seas too stormy to sail upon. From time to time, I stole quick glimpses at Elizabeth de Burgh, though she never once looked at me.

"Lord Robert," Lamberton said, leaning forward, "the three of us—Stewart, Wishart and myself—think you should rejoin the council, take a more active part again in the laying out of policies. Help steer the ship, as it were."

"Comyn still on there?" I asked bluntly.

Lamberton sighed. "Unfortunately, yes, along with Umfraville. Although I'm giving thought to leaving the guardianship myself."

"Then I'm doubly not interested. I have sat in the middle of that endless circle before, my friends."

"But Robert," Wishart begged as he wrung my wrist, "Longshanks will be back again, come summer. Another invasion is in the works. Wallace prefers to act on his own now, raiding and lying in ambush, and you are the only one we can rely on to—"

"Told you," I said brusquely. "Not interested." I rose from the table and nodded to them all as they stared back with grave disappointment. "Now, I'm going to pluck up my daughter, if you don't mind overmuch, and tell her a story or two before I put her to bed. It's what I came here for."

I moved to the other end of the hall, but before I retrieved my daughter from her social rounds, I stopped before the bench where Elizabeth de Burgh sat. She did not notice me at first, despite my shuffling feet and throat clearing. Finally, the young female friend with whom she was engaged in conversation squeezed her knee, cast a glance at me and blushed.

"I wanted to . . . to um . . . my daughter, she . . ." *Sweet Savior of mine, could I be any clumsier with my words?* I shook my head and started over, trying to salvage a morsel of dignity. "Thank you, my lady."

Elizabeth stared at me blankly through eyes the color of spring's first tender shoots of grass. "For what, my lord?"

"Looking after my Marjorie." I clasped my trembling hands behind my back to hide them. What did it matter what beauty I saw in her? I was a decade older than her, not to mention a runagate whose only home was wherever his horse was. "And for sending me that letter . . . to Irvine, although it was awhile ago. I regret I never replied."

"I didn't expect you to, my lord," she returned with a polite smile. "I merely wanted to put your mind at ease. It was Aunt Egidia's idea for me to look after your daughter. Delightful, she is. A ray of sunshine on this ever gloomy island."

"I would hardly call it that from where I stand now."

She looked down, her cheeks flushed scarlet. Awkward seconds later, she stood and rearranged her skirts. "I should see Marjorie to bed now. She's frightfully tired and bound to be a beast about it. If you'll pardon me, my lord."

I touched her arm as she turned to go. "May I . . . escort you? It's just that . . . I don't know how long I'll be able to stay here. Every moment with her is sacred."

Elizabeth tilted her head in consideration, then nodded demurely. She parted Marjorie from her playmates and draped a cloak around my daughter. I lifted Marjorie in my arms and cradled her close. With a cherubic grin, she clasped her little hands around my neck and closed her eyes, seemingly content. We crossed the courtyard through a freezing mist and entered the far tower. Once inside, Elizabeth took a lit candle from its place on the wall and led the way up the narrow, winding stairs. Her footsteps brushed lightly over the stones in a soothing rhythm.

When we reached the second landing, Marjorie was already teetering on the verge of sleep. She peeked at me through barely parted eyelashes and yawned. Elizabeth nudged the chamber door open and placed the sputtering taper on a spiked candlestick on the bedside table. She peeled back the covers. Tenderly, I laid Marjorie in the middle of the high, goose-feather mattress. In a ritualistic manner, Elizabeth pulled off my daughter's shoes and tucked her legs under the covers. As I reached out to push a curl from Marjorie's forehead, Elizabeth took my arm. On tiptoe, she walked me to the door.

"You must leave now," she whispered.

I slid her hand from my arm and turned to look upon my sleeping daughter. "God in heaven, how sweet and innocent and beyond beautiful she is lying there. Would that I could look at her every night like that."

"Shhh." Elizabeth pressed a slender finger to her lips. "We share this room. It keeps her from having nightmares . . . or at least that is what she says."

Suddenly, I felt like an intruder. Elizabeth had become more of a mother to her than I had proven to be a father. I hung my head, rife with guilt and regret. "Your pardon, Lady Elizabeth. I *should* leave."

"Until morning, my good lord."

"Until morning." I retreated backward, but before I reached behind me for the latch on the door, I paused to savor another glimpse of my daughter. My heart surged with thankfulness that I had not followed through on the hollow, slippery deal I had doled out at Irvine to give her up. As I stood there in speechless fondness, Elizabeth floated across the room, plucked a silver comb from the table and raked it through the ends of her long, ruddy waves.

"Until morning," she said again to urge me out the door.

Pity the winter nights in Scotland were so long and I would have to endure it to see my Marjorie—and her—again.

12

Robert the Bruce – Isle of Bute, 1300-1301

I BURIED MY HEAD beneath my pillow to muffle the pounding in my brain.

Tat-tat, tat-tat. Tat-tat, tat-tat. Boom-boom-boom.

If I could have dug myself a hole to retreat into just then, I would have. Perhaps, if I ignored the rapping for a minute . . . *Ah, devil. It will not stop.* I lifted the edge of my pillow. Shafts of weak, gray morning light crept in through the single window of my room, intensifying the ache in my head.

"We knocked. Didn't you hear?" Elizabeth peered around the edge of the door.

Marjorie scrambled over me and bounced on the bed.

"Please, stop, dearest," I pled. But she continued on, higher and harder, my stomach doing flips along with her. Between clenched teeth, I said more sternly, "*Stop.*"

Up and down, she jumped, giggling. I pulled myself over to the side of the bed and dangled there, feeling the urge to vomit up last night's ale.

"Marjorie," Elizabeth said to my rambunctious daughter with

barely an edge to her voice.

Immediately, Marjorie stopped. A pout dragged her lower lip downward.

"Thank you," I mumbled, barely able to lift my head.

"Would you like me to call for a servant?" Elizabeth asked. "Your fire wasn't properly banked last night. It will need rekindling. You must be dreadfully cold without a shirt on."

A draft stirred the hair on my chest. I yanked my blankets up to my shoulders. Not only had I neglected the fire that had been made for me, I had left my clothes in a trail on the floor from the doorway to the bed. Indeed, I must have looked a fine mess that morning—and undoubtedly green in the face. Hardly impressive. More likely repulsive.

"We brought you breakfast, Father." Marjorie snatched a small bowl of curds and whey from Elizabeth and waved it under my nose.

I held my breath. "Later, later. Set it on that table over there. Aye, there. That's a good lass."

"You have to see my pup, Father." Marjorie twirled her way from the table to my bed. "Egidia gave him to me."

"I have a grand idea. Why don't you sneak him up here?" That would buy me enough time to collect myself. Besides, the pup would lap up the breakfast she had brought and what harm in that? I winked at Elizabeth as my daughter raced off, howling with excitement. "Ah, I've missed so much of her growing up."

Elizabeth suppressed a grin. She plucked up my shirt, snapped the wrinkles out of it and handed it to me. "Give me an hour, my lord, and I can tell you more than you care to hear."

"I've nowhere to go. Tell me."

"Very well. She rises before dawn. Stays up until the candles have burnt themselves out. It seems she never eats and yet she grows and grows and grows." As she talked, Elizabeth plucked up my dirty clothes and tossed them in a pile. "She cherishes a doll that she calls Marjorie, after her grandmother, so she says. Despite her inability to sit in one place for more than a minute, she has already begun to teach herself letters by listening to Egidia recite them to the older girls. When she is not combing the horses' manes or tails in the stable, she pesters the cooks for the name of every herb and dish known to mankind. Her curiosity will be the death of her. Three times I have fished her from the well's edge and once found her climbing up the portcullis."

"She has kept you occupied, then?"

"You could say that." Her skirts swished as she walked toward the door. "But if I could have ten of my own just like her someday, in a breath, I would."

AN EBBING TIDE PULSED against the shoreline of Rothesay's broad-mouthed bay. Elizabeth and I walked side by side, my fingers brushing her forearm, pebbles crunching beneath our feet. A pair of tracks stretched in an erratic trail before us: one set the loping paw prints of a young, long-legged dog in full stride and the other Marjorie's small, closely spaced footprints where she scampered after him. Seagulls, picking over spilled catch, exploded in a cloud of fulmination, then dove menacingly at the exuberant hound pup. Marjorie covered her head with her arms and let out a screech of terror. At once, Coll bounded in her direction and leapt into the air, his teeth gnashing at the clap of beating wings. Rolling in laughter, Marjorie sought out another petulant flock and repeated the game.

In the distance, fishing boats cluttered the sloping shore. There, fishermen were busily unloading the workday's yield before darkness descended over the island. The day, although sharply cold, had been unusually calm and sunny for January. Above the silver-black waters of the bay, the peaked rooflines of Rothesay crowded against a deepening blue sky. Inland, snow-topped domes contrasted with the vermilion hues of a sinking sun.

Elizabeth stumbled and I grabbed her by the arm to steady her.

"Careful of your step, Lady Elizabeth." I tucked her hand within the fold of my left elbow, the fingers of my other hand gently clasping hers. "Perhaps you would prefer to walk on my right, away from the water . . . before you fall in?"

She raised her oval chin, her lips pursed tight as if feigning indignity, and drew her shoulders back. "You presume I'm clumsy, my lord."

"No, I—"

"Well, I'm not, I assure you. I was merely watching Marjorie and her dog playing. Otherwise, I'm quite surefooted." She winked at me. "As nimble as a cat."

I fought a grin. "And when you tumbled to the floor last night during the dance?"

She slapped the back of my hand playfully. "Are you mocking me, Lord Robert? Perhaps I should stay closer to you, like this,"— she swung herself around to stand before me—"so you may catch me in your arms next time? Would you?"

For a moment, I forgot myself. Forgot it was past supper and we were overdue at table. Our absence would raise brows. I hardly cared. It was rare we were ever together like this without a crowd of onlookers ogling our every gesture and eavesdropping on every innocent word.

Her fingers wandered up my arms teasingly. "Would you?"

"Would I what?"

"Catch me . . . if I fell?"

A movement distracted me and I glanced up to see Oonagh hobbling toward Marjorie, who stood near the boats waving her arms at the seagulls. In all likelihood, Oonagh had been sent to beckon us back to the castle for the evening meal. In time. I was neither hungry yet nor willing to join the crowd in the hall. I gazed down at Elizabeth, fascinated by the way one of her rounded brows was set higher than the other and the spattering of freckles across her slender nose. I slid my hands around her waist and drew her to me until I felt the slight pressure of her hips against my thighs.

"Like this?" With a sudden heave, I swept her off the ground, one arm snug around her back and the other cradling her legs.

I expected a shriek of protest and an upbraiding; instead, she tossed her head back, laughter bubbling from her throat, and kicked her feet in the air. She reached an arm around my neck and I swung her in a circle: sky and sea and mountains blurring into a streak of shadowy blue and steel gray around us. Not until the ground pitched beneath me did I stop. My knees wobbling, I planted my feet wide and clutched Elizabeth closer to my chest to keep from dropping her.

"Shall I put you down now?" I asked.

Breathless, she shook her head and a reddish brown tendril sprung from the plait of her hair and tumbled across her cheek. When she raised a hand to push it away, I noticed she had been laughing so hard her eyes had welled with tears. Her smile melted away as she tilted her head opposite mine. My mouth drifted closer to hers until I felt the intoxicating warmth of her breath swirling under my chin.

Her lips parted invitingly. She closed her eyes.

"Elizabeth," I whispered. I kissed her, lightly, once, unwilling to assume too much. Her fingers wove through the hair at the nape of my neck, pulling me closer in response. Again, I kissed her, longer, my tongue parting the moist flesh of her lips, then exploring the depths of her mouth. My heart hammered against my ribs. Waves of blood pounded through every fiery vein in my body. I pulled back momentarily, even as her lips sought mine and a little moan of protest escaped her throat. There was something I yearned to tell her. "Elizabeth, I—"

"Father!" Marjorie's cry shattered the spell Elizabeth had cast over me. Dazed, I looked up to see her running at us, flapping something in her hand. Coll galloped along at the edge of the icy water, his oversized paws sinking deep into the wet sand with each springy stride. "Fatherrr! A letter for Lady Elizabeth!"

Scowling at my daughter, I set Elizabeth down, holding her until she stood firmly on the shore. Although Oonagh was by then already at the edge of town, Elizabeth nervously tucked unruly strands of hair behind her ears and tugged at her clothes to straighten them.

Marjorie ground to a halt and gasped for air. Mud flecked the lower half of her skirt and the hem was sodden. She thrashed the sand from her clothes with her free hand and then snatched her skirt up to her ankles. "My toes are cold!"

"Ohhh, I told you to stay out of the water, Marjorie," Elizabeth chided as she pried the crumpled letter from Marjorie's hand. "Must I watch you even more closely? If you catch cold, you've no one to blame but yourself."

Marjorie's lower lip quavered. "But, but Coll didn't see where I threw the stick and I went to get it and the water came, and I . . . I . . ."

"Enough now, Marjorie." I lifted my blubbering daughter into my arms and began back toward Rothesay. "We'll dry you out in no time."

"But I'm going to be ill now and I'll have to stay in my bed." Her shoulders heaved with an exaggerated sob. "And I won't be able to play with Coll . . . or Elizabeth."

"You will, my sweet, don't worry, you—" I glanced beside me, expecting to see Elizabeth there, but she wasn't. I turned around to find her in the same spot, the letter pinched tightly between her fingers, her face growing long. "Elizabeth, what is it?"

She folded the letter neatly and ran her fingers along the crease. As she came toward us, her eyes cast down at the ground, she slipped the letter beneath her kirtle. "It's from my father."

"Not ill news, I pray?"

"Nothing bad, no." Her frown, however, contradicted her words.

I turned to walk alongside her. Seagulls scattered before us, some puffing their breasts up and clicking their beaks at us, as if indignant of our intrusion. Still, Elizabeth would not look at me.

"Then why the morose look? It can't be good."

She drew a sharp breath, and then expelled a long sigh before answering. "He wants me to come home. To Ulster."

"Nooo!" Marjorie's wail pierced the air. A gray cloud of wings shot upward and a rush of cold air swirled around us. "You can't go, Elizabeth. You can't."

Finally, Elizabeth glanced at me. Even in the growing darkness, I could see the glint of dampness in her eyes. "I can delay . . . for a little while, perhaps. For Marjorie's sake."

Lengthening shadows stretched across the crooked streets through which we strolled. A dog barked from a nearby alley. Coll perked his ears and then slunk along close to my leg, head low. We turned a corner and suddenly the smell of fish and cookfires hung thick in the air. Laughter erupted from the open window of a small house as we approached. Before we could steal a glimpse inside, a pair of grease-smeared hands grabbed the edge of the shutters and slammed them shut. Startled, Marjorie nestled her head against my neck, sniffing back tears. Our footfalls were muffled on the frozen mud; our steps grew ever slower.

When we neared the bridge spanning Rothesay's moat, Marjorie wriggled from my hold with a grunt and ran ahead, her anger evident in the stomping of her feet over the planks.

At the foot of the bridge I halted and took Elizabeth's cold hands in mine, my thumb stroking the ridge of her knuckles. "Your father heard I was here, did he?"

Her gaze slipped to the ground again. "Yes."

"Then I shall have to think of a way to convince him I am not a danger to you."

"Knowing my father,"—she shook her head, raising her eyes briefly, and slipped her hands from mine—"I don't think that's possible."

Hands tucked beneath her kirtle, she went across the bridge and beneath the iron bars of the portcullis, never looking back.

FOR A SHORT WHILE Elizabeth kept her distance from me. But she could not avoid me entirely. I was dogged, if not disarming, and two days later we again escorted Marjorie and her pup to the bay for another outing. By week's end, however, the weather had turned wicked and not a soul would dare venture outside, unless out of direst necessity. A freezing rain turned to a driving snow and the wind howled down from the mountains like the keening of a widow. In the town, pigs and cows were brought indoors. The smell of peat smoke and manure choked the air. Boats sat on the shore, thick with a coating of ice. The letter Elizabeth had written to her father, begging to stay on, went unsent. While snow piled deep upon Bute, Elizabeth and I sat on a bench by the hearth, drinking mulled wine and talking until the hall had emptied. My fingers crept over hers. Then, she turned her hand over, so the heat of her palm touched mine. Soon, she laid her head on my shoulder and we sighed in unison—the only words left unsaid were those we dared not speak.

James Stewart wandered into the hall and glared at me in reproach. I ignored him, downing the last of my wine, and gazed into the flames of the dwindling fire. I did not care anymore who might know of us. By the time her father heard anything, we would not be together anymore. Elizabeth was as willing as I was to risk a scathing rebuke in order to be together. In truth, I would have risked much more.

I dallied at Rothesay a month more, but eventually the time came when it was I who had to leave first, not Elizabeth. The truce King Philip had made with England was due to expire and bloody too soon Longshanks would be on his angry way north again. I did not trust Comyn to leave Carrick in peace and Lamberton and Wishart had already left for their respective sees in St. Andrews and Glasgow to handle various matters.

It was the coldest of February days when Stewart, his wife, and Elizabeth gathered in the courtyard as the horses were brought out for Gerald and me. Brittle winter air shattered our frail words of farewell. Reluctantly, I handed my Marjorie back and she clung to Egidia's skirts. Tears glistened on her pink cheeks. Coll padded across the slick cobbles, leaned against her leg and nuzzled her fingers.

I took Elizabeth's face in my hands and kissed her sweet and long upon the lips. My mouth trembled not from cold, but from the wave of pain pulsing with every beat of my heart. For weeks, I had denied this moment would ever arrive. Now that it had, it was as though some emptiness threatened to devour me whole. Fool that I was, I thought I would be able to endure this parting bravely, like some eager young soldier venturing off to war. Instead, I felt . . . desperate. Or determined. I didn't know which.

Once, ambition had consumed me. But for all that I wanted to pursue what my grandfather had begun, it seemed meaningless without Elizabeth. What I thought I had always wanted—it had changed.

"Say you'll be my wife, Elizabeth. Say that you will and I'll fly back the moment I can and take you in my arms and never let go."

She looked down, as if she sought to hide the tears brimming over her long lashes. "Please, Robert, I . . . I can't promise that. You know why."

Gently, I lifted her chin in my fingers and stared into her eyes, as green and glistening as the Lothian hills after a spring rain. "I thought surely we . . . Oh, damn it, Elizabeth. Do not give breath to such murderous words. Give me reason to hope."

She brushed my whiskered cheek with smooth fingertips. "We can but hope. That is all, no more."

I pulled her in close—yet even as I did so, I realized I had brought this upon myself . . . upon us. "We'll find a way, my love. By all that is true and sacred, we *will* find a way."

I meant it, more than I even knew.

I had mourned long enough for Isabella. I wanted to live again—truly *live*. Not for some tomorrow that might never come, but for *now*.

13

<u>Robert the Bruce – Turnberry, 1301</u>

"DO YOU HAVE THE ear of Wallace?"

"Robert, what is this about?" Bishop Lamberton descended from the grassy dune where his horse began to graze beside mine. He had sped from St. Andrews to Turnberry on faith alone. The letter I had sent him contained only a request that he come as soon as possible—not a word more. He strode toward me, the bottom of his robes sweeping over drifts of gray sand and flakes of shingle that glinted beneath a miserly autumn sun. "Why have you summoned me here?"

"Answer—do you have the ear of Wallace?"

Lamberton shrugged. "We talk often. Why?"

I stared out over a sea that was both calm and cold. "France is at peace. There are rumors . . . of Balliol returning with a French force." I walked to the water's edge, watching the long lines of foaming waves break against the shore. A gentle tide washed over my boots. "I cannot let that happen."

"Rumors, Robert. That is all."

"No, I *cannot* let that happen. Not for me. Not for Scotland."

I turned away and walked along the shore slowly, my head forced down by the weight of my troubles. Lamberton followed in respectful silence.

"Why else have you called me here?" he finally asked.

Beside a pile of rocks that jutted out into the water, washed smooth by an eternity of the sea's angry lashing, I stopped, looked at him, and confessed. "I wish to marry Elizabeth de Burgh. Her father rejects me. Says he will not wed his daughter to a landless rebel. I can't accept that either, your grace." I had not seen Elizabeth since our parting at Rothesay and in that time she had sent only a single letter. The harsh formality of her words had pained me as she relayed her father's blunt refusal.

"Ah, I see more clearly now. You want two distinct things and sensibility tells you that you can only have one or the other. What would you have me say to quiet your mind?" He crossed his arms. Far behind him, the steeply roofed towers of Turnberry Castle pierced a pale blue sky.

"Say what is right, proper, what is best for all. Say it in your usual, wise way with such surety I cannot doubt the reasoning behind it."

He laid both hands on my shoulders. His eyes narrowed. "Robert, have you done something rash?"

"No . . . no! But . . ." I began to shake over my distress and he clenched my shoulders more firmly, as if to still me. I dug at the roots of my hair, stretching my scalp back.

"Robert, tell me what it is. Why do you want me to speak with Wallace? What hand could he have in all of this and what does Ulster's daughter have to do with any of it?"

"Come with me . . . and I will show you." I led him back to where I had dropped the reins of my horse. From a bag tied to my saddle, I took out two letters. I handed the first to Lamberton. "This is for William Wallace to carry."

"Carry to whom?" He regarded the letter warily as I laid it across his open palm.

"King Philip of France."

"Robert," he began, sighing heavily, "I cannot dispatch this without knowing what it says. Do you understand that?"

"What it says is very simple—that I ask him to beseech the pope to uphold the papal bull against Longshanks for his incursions on Scotland and—should that find success, as I think it will—I ask him to demand that King Edward agree to a truce with Scotland."

"A truce between England and Scotland? You do realize that Edward has arranged for his son to marry Philip's only daughter?"

"I have not been living in a cave, your grace. Longshanks took a French bride himself and even that has not kept troubles from reaching across the sea to him." After the death of his first wife, Eleanor of Castile, Longshanks had bargained his French possessions for the hand of Philip's sister Marguerite, but even that diplomatic move did not remove the prickly burr of French pride. Philip was shrewd enough not to trust his new brother-in-law unconditionally. While Longshanks was trying to arrange a marriage between his heir and Philip's only daughter, Isabella, he was also negotiating with the Flemings for a princess's hand for his son. Philip learned of his duplicity and promptly quashed the scheme by taking the little Flemish princess and her father captive.

"And the other?" Lamberton said.

"Is to go directly to King Edward at Linlithgow."

Lamberton stared at me with what appeared to be mounting doubt—or perhaps it was shock. He kept his other hand back, as if the second letter dripped poisonous ink. "Robert, unless you confide in me, I am loath to do this. You are mad with love for this Elizabeth and desperate to hang onto hopes for a crown. It is deathly dangerous to court two kings at once."

"Your grace, I am neither mad nor desperate. I am determined.

And I do not court kings—I court peace and progress . . . as well as my hereditary rights. Scotland will not return to the shameful days of a Balliol as king, not as long as I live. And I will have Elizabeth, however I can get her, but on honorable terms."

"There is only one way to achieve that . . . and I pray that I am wrong in my guess. The letter to King Edward—what does it say?"

"You have figured me out, have you?" I crouched down, picked up a handful of coarse sand and watched it sift through my fingers. "It says that if I submit to his will, he will begrudge me my lands and let me live freely, that he will not disinherit me from anything rightfully mine . . . and in more subtle language, it is to be understood that he will allow me to pursue any rights to which I hold claim."

The wind lifted and beat hard and cold against my back. So much of the future swung on the stroke of a pen.

"Take caution, Robert. Edward is masterful at twisting words to meet his own purpose."

"He did not invent that game, nor is he master of it. It is a ploy meant to buy time." I rose to my feet. "Just as Douglas did at Irvine. Edward has not been a well man, has he?"

"No, he hasn't. He could have expired before we even began this conversation. Or . . . he could live for another two decades merely to aggravate us all."

"Aye, well, be that as it may. By then Elizabeth and I will have a houseful of children and if the crown does not rest on my head, by God, I'll be certain it is not on Balliol's, either. Longshanks' son, Edward of Caernarvon, is profoundly lacking in military prowess. Being weak-stomached, he'll never have it. This summer I kept Turnberry from him and long before supplies would have run dry on us, he gave it up and crawled back sniveling to his father."

Still unconvinced, Lamberton held back. I prodded him further.

"Faith in God, Bishop—where does it come from?"

He lifted his strong, clean jaw and looked at me with deep conviction. "It comes from many places, Robert. The Holy Gospel, the miracles He has performed, life around us."

"But ultimately"—I tapped the gold embroidered cross on the middle of his chest—"where does faith originate from?"

"From men's belief."

"Then I ask, your grace, that you have faith in me. Not as a deity, but as a man who pursues a purpose which serves not himself, but a country filled with people. People who serve God and have faith in Him—faith that one day He will deliver them from injustice and tyranny and set them free. But to do that, He needs an instrument and I . . . am that."

The wind flung Lamberton's cloak back from his shoulders. He gazed at the horizon, where sky met sea a hundred miles out. "Robert, you should have been born to the Church. That sermon would have won you souls by the thousands."

"Much as I would love to lay claim to those words, I think I heard them in a sermon somewhere. One of yours, perhaps?"

"Wisdom, my son, is better than rubies." He put out his other hand and took the letter.

I gave him the bag to put the letters in and held his stirrup while he mounted. "God go with you, your grace."

"More important, Robert, may He stay with you. Something tells me you are going to need His guidance in days to come."

"Fateful words, but I think I'll need more than Almighty God looking over my shoulder and words of wisdom to see me through on this."

Linlithgow, 1302

I WALKED A WALL both narrow and high. One misstep and the fall would be far and long.

It was not for land or title that I knelt to compromise, although I knew everyone believed so. Like a spark to dry tinder, Elizabeth consumed me far more than my call to destiny. How might it all have fallen out if Elizabeth had not captured my fragile heart with her faint smiles that hinted fondness, her glances that begged me closer, her whispers that filled my head with mad longing? When Isabella died while giving me my sweet, bright-eyed Marjorie, I had closed the door to my heart and locked it to the world. Elizabeth alone held the key. It had all led me to where I now was: Longshanks had summoned me to Linlithgow to discuss my proposal.

Gerald and I sat upon our ponies on a road that wound down a hillside through the town. Curls of smoke from peat fires lifted from frosty roofs. Pale shafts of winter sunlight came and went while a stiff wind chased high, scattered clouds through a sapphire sky. At the edge of the market square, a mother and her small child, their hands and feet wrapped in strips of rags to defend against the cold, regarded me warily, unsure of what to make of a Scottish nobleman passing through their midst clad in chainmail and surcoat: friend or foe? I smiled at the mother, but it gave her no obvious comfort.

Ahead was the castle of Linlithgow, where Longshanks had taken up residence. Beyond it lay a placid, silver loch and on the distant reedy shore swans and herons gathered. Longshanks had commissioned none other than James of St. George to transform the manor house, erected during the reign of King David a hundred and fifty years earlier, into a fortified peel. The new gatehouse was made of stone and two stout towers flanked the east and west ends of the castle. Grumbling English soldiers scratched at the frozen earth with shovels and axes, toiling to dig a ditch around the castle in the bitter throes of winter.

"I do not like this, my lord," Gerald fretted. His breath hung suspended in a fog of ice. Despite the harsh cold and a deep piling of snow, he mopped the perspiration from his brow with the edge of his cloak. "Dangerous play, this is. We could as soon end up drowning in our own piss in some forgotten dungeon."

Not like him to be so bold with words. Clearly his nerves were frayed. "A cheerful vision, Gerald. Now come along. I've a meeting to attend."

I kicked my pony in the flanks to urge it forward, gave a last beckoning glance to Gerald and rode toward the gatehouse. A hundred feet from it, in the narrow gap between the town's edge and the makeshift bridge that spanned the widening ditch, I dismounted and handed the reins to Gerald. He stared at me close-mouthed from the back of his pony.

"What?" I said, keeping an eye on the English soldiers mustering in our direction. "No fond words of farewell? No fountain of wisdom sprung from the mouth of experience? Come now. I'm going to meet the bloody King of all England—share a glass of wine, break bread and all that ritualistic nonsense."

"Good luck," he muttered with a roll of his eyes.

"Accepted." I turned and walked toward the soldiers, dropping axe and sword on the road as I went. Then I spread my arms wide in a show of peace and spoke to their captain. "I am Robert the Bruce, Earl of Carrick, here as arranged to meet with my lord, King Edward."

The glint of metal caught my eye. At once, ten swords and five spears were aimed at my bare throat and chest. I was afforded but a moment to look back at Gerald. Swiftly, they closed in on him, too, and dragged him from his saddle.

Feet stomped behind me. I heard a grunt. The whisper of a blade parting air.

Then the sharp pain to the back of my head . . . and the blackness of Hades swallowed me whole.

14

Edward, Prince of Wales – Linlithgow, 1302

THE WIND CUT COLD and sharp across my face. I sat on the ledge of an unfinished window in the west tower of Linlithgow, balancing sideways as I peered down at the scene emerging before the gatehouse. The Bruce had arrived exactly as called for— on mid-afternoon of the appointed date and with only one man. Trusting soul. It would have been easy enough for one of the king's men to cut cleanly through his neck with a single flick of the blade.

Head bared, weapons abandoned, the Bruce walked over the ditch bridge, his arms drifting wide to show he bore no weapons. A dozen guards swarmed like angry hornets around him, swords and poleaxes aimed and ready to sting at his naked throat. Bruce's squire was detained without protest and to my delight one of our soldiers smacked Bruce squarely in the back of his head. The blow sent him reeling to the snowy ground.

I leapt from my vantage point, raced down the winding stairs and burst into the room, where the king was bent over rolls of parchment. The fire roaring in the hearth struggled against the draft and then licked the mantle in protest. Sketches of a dozen castles lay scattered over a huge table while their genius, Master James of St. George, perused their designs for the slightest weaknesses.

"He has come," I announced, almost breathless. "The Bruce has come."

My sire glanced at me briefly, and then back down at the plans.

"Can you manage as well at Kildrummy?" the king said to his master mason.

Master James squinted. His eyes darted from one scribbled page to another. Finally, he twitched his mousy nose and nodded.

"Good then. Finish here first. I want this done with before next summer. You will be provided whatever resources needed. Payment shall be as we discussed before. A hundred and fifty pounds."

"Generous as ever, sire." At that, Master James smiled faintly, if one could call that slanted line of his mouth a smile. He then collected his architect's tools into a box, which he tucked under his arm, and went from the room wringing his hands.

My sire quickly became reabsorbed in the drawings, shuffling them about on the table with ink-stained fingertips. Mottes, peels, palaces, towers, walls—all his life's work. Ever the dilemma to him of how to enslave an entire race with the least effort over the long run. He reached out to pull an oil lamp closer, but before he closed his fingers around it, he jerked his hand back and touched his temple. He gritted his teeth, waiting for the pain to ebb.

"What do you want?"

I shrugged. "When they bring that vile traitor up here, should I stay or go? I rather relish seeing him humiliated."

He began to roll up the parchments. "Stay, so you may learn a twig or two of how to rule those who care not to be ruled over."

"As you wish, sire."

A painfully long time passed while we waited. My father and I shared not a word. When we were forced into conversation, his words became weapons, mine shields. Better the awkward truce of silence than a battle of words.

Two urgent knocks and the doors flew open. The soldiers dragged a limp Bruce into the room by the arms. With a flip of my sire's royal hand, they discarded him roughly on the floor. Bruce squirmed, rolled over into a ball and rubbed at the back of his head. His squire, composed but obviously concerned, was tightly surrounded by four guards.

Finally, Bruce looked up at us and made as if to stand. The tip of a sword was shoved against the throbbing vein in his neck. His brown eyes glinted in a silent plea to my father. His tongue flicked over quivering lips. Hoarsely, he began, "My liege . . ." Bruce closed his eyes in abandonment and went on, "I lay my life at your feet, to command . . . or to extinguish."

Tempting invitation. What scheming could cause this man, who had fought against my father after serving him, to so thoughtlessly and so presumptuously stroll onto these grounds believing for one moment my father would spare him? Pure arrogance.

I invaded the space between Bruce and my sire. The insult of Turnberry still fresh on my conscience, I glowered at Bruce. "I should cut out your false tongue and feed it to the crows. You will regret your lies, Bruce. I will make certain of it."

"Shut up, you idiot," my sire growled at me. "You have precious much to learn before your day comes to wear a crown."

I backed away, reeling from the sting.

"Bishop Lamberton delivered a letter from you." The king rolled up parchments one by one and set them in neat piles. "You mulled it over long before changing your song. Have things gone amiss for you with your Scottish brothers? Or have you finally collected your senses? Perhaps we can come to understand each other more clearly now that we are face to face."

Bruce spat out, "I have but one—"

"You were not given leave to speak." My sire folded his arms beneath the edges of his ermine-lined velvet mantle and studied, long and hard, the man who knelt before him. He had not claimed his portable throne that dominated the far end of the room, as if he desired to be on his feet to tower as far above the lowly Scottish liar as he could. "And you will address us as 'my lord king' in the future."

He circled Bruce, then stopped behind him, staring down at the glorious crown of autumn brown hair that fell in gentle waves around a sun-touched face—a face that glistened faintly with the sweat of cold fear.

"You have cost me dearly," the king said. "Men, money, sleep . . . days and nights tramping through a barren wasteland of thistle to ferret out you and that vulgar Wallace. And yet you would dare plead for clemency? May prayers be said for your damnable soul if you have come for any cause other than to tender an oath of fealty unto me."

With deliberate slowness the Bruce raised his deer-brown eyes. "Plainly I have, sire . . . my lord king, but not without purpose. May I beg one, simple grace of you?"

"Beg all you want. It becomes you."

"Grant me the hand of Elizabeth de Burgh, daughter of the Earl of Ulster."

Turned traitor to his own for a woman, of all things? He was too easily witched by the whisperings of honeyed lips. There lay his soft underbelly. His weakness commanded him like a dog drooling over a bitch in season that had but to flag her tail. Nose to the dirt to pick up her scent, panting to have her.

The king scoffed. "What profit for England in this? You violate royal edict, fly in the face of summonses, ravage my lands, incite mutiny and yet when it behooves you to bed an earl's daughter, who is unwilling to have you unless by honorable contract, only *then* do you prostrate yourself before me?"

He seized a handful of Bruce's hair and jerked his head backward. "In Wales, Llywelyn, Rhys, Madog . . . all thought they could outstrip me. And what has become of them all? Look at my face, you canting beggar. Study every crease the years have carved. Is it written there anywhere that I am ignorant or easily gulled?"

Bruce sagaciously kept his tongue, but my father would finish with his berating before he let the whimpering Scot utter one more word.

The king let go of his hair. "If she indeed drives you mad with lust—"

"Holds my rampant heart in her gentle hands," Bruce interjected in a voice that was soft and longing. He raised his face—a face so beautiful in its symmetry the gods of ancient Greece would have welcomed him to Mt. Olympus just to gaze upon it—and slyly hinted, "And by that, this may benefit us both, might it not? I desire to have her as my wife. You would profit from my fealty."

"Pray tell, arrant knight, how that might pass? As I see, the favor you beg goes but one way. I have you in a rather compromising position."

Bruce tilted his head thoughtfully, then lowered his eyes again to soften the blow. "Scotland has yet to be tamed. The king who was chosen to be its ruler in name was as ineffectual as he was fickle."

"Get to the root. You bore me with the obvious."

"Choose another to be your man in the north. One who would trouble you far less."

"That being?"

"Me."

"You?" The king threw back his head and laughed. "Trouble me less? I think there are scarce few who could trouble me more than you, Bruce." He walked away and proceeded to pour himself a goblet of wine, mulling over the proposition. Then suddenly he lifted his chin and chuckled to himself. "There *is* the blood of kings in your veins, however thinly it courses."

I claimed the throne my father had so far ignored and propped my jaw on my fist. It was the only seat in that barren room and tedium had overcome me. I was sickened by the route of the conversation, distrustful of every radiant syllable that trickled over Bruce's well-formed lips, and highly disinclined to gainsay my father. But no sooner had I resigned myself to its meager, thinly cushioned comfort than I was catapulted from it by my father and cuffed sharply between the shoulder blades.

"As I said—precious much to learn," he chastised. "The first of which is not to presume yourself worthy enough to sit there. Now, any sage words, my son?"

I hesitated. I knew my mind, but if it differed from his did it matter that I reasoned at all?

"Come now, boy of mine." He pinched my left shoulder from behind.

"The chicken does not lie down with the fox," I uttered, writhing beneath his hurtful grasp.

"And which are we? Fox . . . or fowl?" He let go of me and came around to stand before me.

"I suspect . . . the chicken."

"Hmm." He nodded, glancing at Bruce. "You *would* see yourself thus. No gain in this for England, then? None at all? Desperation for one man—opportunity for another, think you not?"

He flashed a sardonic smirk at me. *Ever a trick in his questions. Oh, bloody hell, I should learn to stay silent.* I slumped in bitter defeat.

The king returned his empty goblet to the table and said to Bruce, "We will discuss this further, Lord Robert. However, the grace I begrudge you will not come without price. Your lands will be returned, but on stringent conditions that you side with England against Balliol."

"Done, my lord," Bruce said—too easily in my opinion. "But if I request the assuredness of my due inheritance and my freedom, as I have put forth, what then is the price? You have not yet said."

"I shall hold you to it in writing, so that every Scotsman may know unto whom you grovel in fealty. You will attend my court when I call for you, you will provide men and arms whenever your Scottish brethren disturb the peace . . . and you will remain my vassal. Understood?"

"And so long as I maintain you are my overlord, what of my claim to Scotland's crown? For that I . . . *might* agree."

"I would not be so hasty as to answer that today . . . or tomorrow even. Prove your loyalty, Scot. Swallow the arrogant pride you so easily cast out as cause and argument. Yours was the weaker case. As you recall, courts of law beyond England decided against your grandfather. Your father does not so greedily reach for that which was never his. Perhaps you should spend less of your efforts in dissension and more of it in diplomacy. However, as I said, prove you will cede to the might of England. Do that . . . and the sun may yet shine on your ambition."

Proper rot, as Piers would say. Promises so easily spewed out. Words are but words, my trothless lords. Sounds evoked to conjure up images, however false or imaginary. Politics are spun by fools in search of self-glorification. On the morrow I shall hawk with friends. Lighthearted souls not half as false as the pair of you.

One day, though, one day I will make the Bruce pay for vexing me at Turnberry. And I will prove to my sire that not only has he been duped by the Scottish bastard, but he has underestimated me, as well.

15

<u>Edward, Prince of Wales – Warwick, 1303</u>

I WOULD RATHER HAVE been born on the dirt floor of a peasant's cottage, than swaddled in the silken sheets of royalty. I would rather rise with the sun every morn and feel its gilded rays caress my neck like a starved lover, than waste the night away with nobles who would woo and cajole in one breath and then spit when your back was turned.

Nineteen . . . a man by the standards of most and yet treated as though I had no better judgment than my yowling, infant half-brothers.

My father leaned uncomfortably close and jabbed a long finger behind us at a young auburn-haired lady. "If there were not valuable alliances to be woven abroad . . . that one . . . there in the green, she would give you children fair to look upon."

It was Elizabeth de Burgh, daughter of the Earl of Ulster and now wife to the reinstated Earl of Carrick, Robert the Bruce. Muted rays of a springtime sun in evening fell around her face and shoulders like a false veil of purity. She was seated several rows up and to our right. The stands had been erected specifically for this tournament between the shaded banks of the Avon and the high walls of Warwick Castle. The entire foppish affair had been contrived to celebrate the christening of my newest half-brother Edmund, born only a year after Thomas.

"Her father enjoins Ulster," the king said. "Genteel enough to warm the sheets of England, yes, my son? But for you, the daughter of a king. Nothing less."

I felt his blood-hot eyes upon me and I wondered what snare lay in the twisting rope of his words. He patted the hand of Queen Marguerite, sister to that dough-brained King of France. She smiled in servile adoration at my father before she commenced gossiping with one of her handmaidens behind her. If not for her jewels and silks, Marguerite would have looked no more a queen than some country wench driving geese to market. Her skin was sallow, her nose oddly hooked and her chin too small beneath large, vacant eyes. More harlot than matron, she had not a sliver of the regality my mother, Queen Eleanor, had possessed.

When my mother died, my sire had escorted her body from Lincolnshire all the way back to Westminster Abbey. At every halt, he ordered a cross erected in her memory. He mourned her so terribly it plunged him into an abysmal mood—a chasm so deep and dark I thought he would never crawl from it to join the living again. When he was finally able to return to matters of state, it was then that he called the Scots to him at Norham and forced them down on their soiled knees to cower at his every utterance. And so he sought to do the same with me: to mold me into his slave, demanding I do as he said and when he said nothing, damn me for not knowing what he wanted of me. Damn me twice for being such a fool I might have to ask. A tacit, cruel game of power and I must play the pawn to be flicked about by regal fingers.

I stretched my arms before me and admired the plush purple velvet of my sleeves—a bolt of velvet had been one of my many recent acquisitions shipped from Florence at my express order. If my time was not my own to ride my horses and do whatever else I pleased, then I would make good of the funds afforded me and outshine all others in my presence. Only Piers could outdo me.

Raising my hand to my shoulder, I fluttered my fingers in salutation at Piers as he made his way from the end of the stands to his seat. He must not have noticed my gesture, for he did not return it. My sire had conveniently sent him off to Chester a few weeks earlier on business and so he had arrived too late to enter the ranks. Just as well. Piers would have flattened them all and where would have been the amusement in that? I came to these damnable tournaments not because I gave a whit as to who won, but because I reveled in the pageantry and the flourish of colorful garments. I came to see and be seen. I certainly did not come to have spousal prospects paraded before me like sows before the butcher. That awful business was currently under negotiation, to my displeasure.

"Rush into a union, kind father," I observed, "and you make enemies as well as allies."

A sharp masterstroke . . . or so I thought.

The king's lips twitched above his meticulously combed beard. "If it's your own blood you care to see come after you on this throne, you will value the breeding of the mate I have chosen for you and make use of her maidenhead. Let her be the row and you the plow, with every fertile season. Sons too often die. You have a brother now. Two, in fact. Do not believe yourself indispensable. And I rush nothing. Your union has been carefully searched out since before you were bred."

I turned my face away to hide a sneer. Would he forever use my infant brothers as weapons against me? Little French bastards. Their grasp on life was a single, fine thread I could snap between two fingers. Three infant brothers of mine had died before I held on and survived. The Fates, evidently, had not seen them fit to rule.

Neither would little puking Thomas or drooling Edmund. Oh, they may well live, but only to endure as my underlings. Kingship may not have been my utmost desire, but I could swiftly become accustomed to primacy before my sire was cold in his grave. May an arrow take him if his horse does not throw him first.

"My queen." My sire squeezed Marguerite's pale hand. Her eyebrows flittered in response. "They begin: d'Argentan and Bruce. In all my years I have not seen two knights more finely matched."

Marguerite tilted her head, piled high with plaits of pale yellow, but her eyes roved over the crowd like a butterfly floats over meadow flowers. Pliant enough, but I would prefer a wife—again, if I was to ever have one—who would be less generous with her paint and powder. She had in her wardrobe half the cloth of Flanders. How Father spoiled her. He only showered her with gifts because having a queen half his age and getting her with child bolstered his pride.

The herald's horn sounded. As the two knights bore down on each other across the barrier, I shoved back a stubborn yawn. D'Argentan's horse was smartly caparisoned in black cloth woven with scrolls of gold thread. Well muscled and of the purest blood, the animal was steady in the clamor of tournament and sure-footed. Bruce's horse was lighter in body and it had skittered before every pass that week. As the two beasts came nearer to one another, the knights lowered their lances in aim. The crowd fell deathly silent. Even I leaned forward. Hoof beats thundered on the dusty, packed earth like the rumble of ancient, angry gods. D'Argentan's lance skipped off the shoulder of Bruce with barely a click. But Bruce's landed squarely in the middle of his opponent's breastplate with a terrible clang and snapped in half. D'Argentan reeled backward. The crowd gasped. It was only d'Argentan's iron grip on the reins that held him in the saddle. He struggled to upright himself as his horse galloped on. Then he reined his mount hard around, eager to retaliate.

Bruce tossed his splintered lance to the ground and plucked up a new one from his bushy-haired squire. He bowed stiffly in the saddle to indicate he was ready. His horse pranced. When the signal was given Bruce kicked his horse hard in the flanks and flew forward. He kept his lance up, long after d'Argentan had dropped his and made aim. The long-reaching legs of the horses closed the gap. When they were four lances apart my stomach went taut. Bruce had not lowered his lance. D'Argentan eyed his target and leaned heavily toward the barrier, putting the full force of his weight behind the point of his weapon. But as his lance closed in on Bruce, Bruce pulled hard to the right and dodged it. The more nimble horse and rider had claimed an advantage.

This time, applause . . . not for the favored d'Argentan, the un-equalled champion of countless tournaments, but for the slippery Scot. The crowd had turned. How fickle they all were. D'Argentan was better mounted and better armed by a supreme measure. Only a dolt would be blind to that.

Then, d'Argentan allowed his anger to surface. He spewed French curses at his opponent through the slit of his visor and called for a different lance, even though the one he had just wielded was in pristine condition.

My father watched the whole confrontation through narrowed eyelids. Mindlessly, he plucked a grape from a plate balanced on the left arm of his throne and plopped it into his mouth. Then he curled a finger at Sir Marmaduke Tweng, who shuffled obediently before the chairs, one shoulder sloping noticeably from the batter-ing he had received at Stirling several years before. The old, crooked knight bent his ear close to the king's mouth.

"Double the prize to the winner," the king said.

Sir Marmaduke raised both hands toward the combatants. Their squires rushed forward, received the king's new offer and raced back to their knights.

The signal. They charged. Again, Bruce hesitated to lower his lance. Then, he snapped it downward quickly. The pronged coronel of his lance slammed into the wrapper covering the neck of d'Argentan's headpiece. D'Argentan was vaulted skyward. He slammed into the ground. A cloud of dust exploded above his motionless armored body. His horse veered away at a gallop, startled by the sudden loss of its load. It was Bruce's squire who caught the reins of the lathered, riderless horse as d'Argentan's man rushed to his master's aid. The crowd leapt to its feet, murmuring as one, all eyes locked on the inert body of what, up until a few moments before, had been the most feared knight in all the land. Bruce was neither charlatan nor simpleton. Saint George save me that I should ever face him on the field, man to man.

Then I witnessed something I had never seen. Such an abrupt, inarguable victory was cause for celebration. Myself, had I been inclined to poke at others with long sticks, I would have ridden up and down the length of the stands ten time over, head bared to receive my laurels, my ears uncovered to soak up the lauds. Instead, Bruce lowered himself from his saddle, walked stiffly in his armor encasement toward d'Argentan and pulled the stunned—some I'm sure thought dead—knight to his wobbly feet. Hands on knees, d'Argentan leaned over. Bruce cupped him once lightly on the back and approached the king's stands.

Bruce motioned for his squire to help remove his helmet. The straps undone, Bruce put a hand on either side and lifted it. A crown of thick, dark hair stuck to his sweat-soaked forehead.

"In lieu of your generous prize, my lord king," Bruce said, "may I claim a kiss from my bride?"

My sire squeezed his wife's hand and a flush of color fanned across her cheeks. "You Scots should always be so easily pleased."

It was no modest kiss Bruce placed upon his wife's waiting lips.

Many were the ladies who must have simmered with jealousy upon witness of his brazen passion for his countess. But when the stands erupted into applause I read the intention beneath the act. Chivalry was a game to Bruce. Love in lieu of money? He played for the world's adoration and my sire was part of the audience.

Since Linlithgow, the king had kept the Bruce at his breast like a suckling infant. Bruce had not only been given blessing to wed the de Burgh maiden, but he had also been granted the wardship of the young Earl of Mar, heaping the Scottish traitor with ever more power to serve his own purpose. Thus far, his hollow oaths had preserved him. And I could but stand by mute and enraged whenever he fell short of showing any genuine loyalty.

KING AND QUEEN WERE first to retire as the sun slipped behind the treetops, but I lingered and caught up with Piers at the foot of the old motte tower. I parted him from friends and led him by the sleeve toward the shade of the sprawling oak halfway up the hillside. He climbed the steep slope beside me with his chin forward, the lips of his fine mouth unbending. As ever, he was resplendent in his white-plumed hat with an upturned brim, an ermine trimmed gown split down the sides that swept the ground and his bicolored hose of red and gold.

"The tournament was bland as bean pottage without you in it, Brother Perrot," I said, trying to curry favor with him. "You would have won against Bruce ten times over."

He stopped abruptly and turned to me. "I heard the news."

"News?"

"That you are to be plighted to Isabella of Valois. They say she is beyond beautiful."

I laid a comforting hand upon his shoulder. "She is to be my consort. To bear me sons. A union devised purely for political convenience and posterity. Nothing more."

Piers turned his face aside and fell silent as a small group of twittering ladies passed by.

"Besides," I added, desperate to salve his wounds, "she is several years too young yet to . . . She is a little girl still."

He shook his head and I saw the glint of a tear in the corner of his eye. "You will forget me."

"How could I ever? You will become dearer and more important to me with every year."

"You say now."

"And I will prove it. You'll see. Lands, office, titles—I will hold nothing from you that, in your devotion, you have not shown yourself worthy of."

He looked down. His mouth twisted with worry. "But you? Will I have you?"

"Do you doubt? You have me now, don't you?"

"And Ponthieu? Nothing would mean more to me than the fief of Ponthieu."

"I would give you the sun if it would not burn my hand to reach for it."

His fingers crept up and closed around mine. He stroked my hand and smiled, satisfied. "You're right. I would have won. Bashed the Scotsman's bloody skull in."

In that moment he was all to me: shining and tender. I would have stood against an entire army to keep him at my side. He tugged my hand, then let it drop as he went toward the great oak that clung with fierce stubbornness to the hillside.

"Shall we hunt tomorrow, Edward? Just . . . you and I. Leave Gilbert and the others behind."

"Impossible, I'm afraid." I hung my head and scraped at the earth with the pointed toe of my shoe. "The king and I are to leave within a fortnight for the north. Parliament has approved the funds, although they quibbled terribly over it. Nasty lot of cantankerous old men, more concerned with their wine cellars and rabbit warrens than anything. Neville recently routed Comyn from Selkirk Forest, but not without losses, and so my father is bent on revenge."

"I see . . ." Piers sank down and leaned back upon his elbows in the grass. "If not a wife's bed beckoning you to duty, then war is to be your mistress."

"I will be king one day." I drew my shoulders up, listening to my own statement and pondering on the strangeness of it.

"You will. And as king"—Piers lay on his back and gazed at me as the rays of a lingering sunset fell copper upon his face—"can you make the world disappear? Will the king command the king-dom—or the other way around? I think, Edward dear, it will only close in on you more."

Try though I did, I could not rid myself of the sickening por-tent of Piers' words.

Two months later, on the same day my sire, King Edward of England, affixed his seal to a treaty with France, I was joined by proxy to Princess Isabella, daughter of King Philip.

As with all things, Piers was right.

16

<u>Robert the Bruce – Lochmaben, 1304</u>

After my humbling, public submission to King Edward, the reprieve, oddly enough, was a pleasant one. In the mornings, when I was not away on the king's business as sheriff of Lanarkshire, Elizabeth woke me with sweet kisses and soft words. When I came home, she greeted me with her slender arms flung fiercely about my neck. At night, she gave me endless comfort and delight.

There was some reward in swallowing my pride . . . ecstasy even. But still, deep inside, I could not stomach the cost of it.

Meanwhile, my father had remained firmly ensconced on his English estates in Essex and Huntingdon, weaseling his way back into favor in any fashion he could: sending Longshanks gifts, issuing public proclamations of his agreement with every policy the king spewed out, supporting him with whatever troops his restricted funds could bear. Aside from a handful of carping letters that had found their way to my headquarters in Ayr, my father and I had not spoken in nearly seven years. But when I received word from my brother Edward that my father had returned to Lochmaben in Annandale and was mortally ill, I bowed to a son's duty, however difficult or unwelcome, and went.

It was late when I arrived at Lochmaben. The residence, lately refortified by Master James, had been recently returned to my family's possessions—a token of the faith I had gained from Longshanks himself. Mary, the sister who always put a smile on my lips, however weary or heavy of heart I was, greeted me in the dimly lit hall.

"Mary?" I put my hands on her shoulders and gazed at her long before I embraced her. "What happened to that frail wisp of a girl I knew?"

"I'm nineteen, Robbie. Hardly a girl anymore. I've a husband now, mind you," she said, referring to Neil Campbell, whom she had wed this past year while I was about on Longshanks' never-ending business. She kissed me sweetly on the cheek and pulled her wrap snug around her upper body. "And not at all frail."

"Aye, hardly a girl. I shall have to post a guard outside your door to keep the men away when your husband's not about."

As I embraced her, I heard the rushes on the floor rustle and peered through the half-darkness to see my sister Christina. Her jet-black hair swung loose at her back. Her high-belted gown was modestly cut, but of a deep red that drew attention to her dark hair, eyes and long lashes. I drew her into my arms and saw a few steps behind her a young man of about her age, who was obviously captivated by her every movement.

I whispered into her ear, "Would this be the proper time to express my condolences on the loss of your husband last year?" Christina had been married to the Earl of Mar, who had died young, but like so many marriages, it had been a contract meant to weave alliances, little more.

"A hunting accident. Quite unexpected." She pulled away and took the hand of her admirer. "Robert, this is Sir Christopher Seton, my betrothed."

"My lord," Christopher said, bowing slightly. He was as lean as a willow sapling.

I cuffed him sharply on the upper arm, sending him sideways a step. "Look after her well. I'll not have my sister unhappy. Understood?"

He nodded and they smiled at each other in that secret way lovers do.

"Where are the others?" I asked.

"Asleep," Mary said. "It's nearly midnight. I'm surprised you would travel at such an hour, dear brother. You're lucky the robbers did not get you." She bunched up her chestnut brows at me in disapproval.

"You still worry enough for all of us, Mary. But I thought it urgent." I pulled off my riding gloves and laid them on the main table, then unfastened the clasp of my cloak. "Father, is he . . ."

"He is very, very ill, Robert. He hasn't long, I'm afraid." She extended her hand. "Come, I'll take you to him."

I took her hand. Mary lifted a rushlight from the wall and guided me through the narrow corridors. Gently, she nudged open the door to father's apartment. A sickening stench wafted from within.

"Who's there?" came a voice so frail and cracked that I wondered if I had heard it at all.

I took the rushlight from Mary, kissed her on the forehead and nodded. Then I stepped into the room. The awful smell suddenly grew stronger. I held my breath a moment and swallowed, until the impulse to vomit passed.

"Father, it is me—Robert." I rested the light in an empty sconce on the wall and moved closer to his bed. "Edward asked me to come."

"Come to sniff out your inheritance, have you? Who says I'll give you any? He was always my favorite, you know. Edward, I mean." His voice came from behind the heavy curtains hanging from his canopied bed.

I moved closer, but a shadow from the curtain fell across his chest and face. Ever contrary, he played us against one another so that we would compete for his attention. "You used to say Alexander was your favorite."

"That changed when he left me."

"He hardly left to spite you. He's been at Cambridge. I hear they offered to make him Dean of Glasgow." Brilliant beyond his years, Alexander had a passion for learning as large as my brother Edward's love of women.

"Why have you come, Robert?"

My eyes, by now, had begun to adjust to the darkness in the room. I could discern the lumps and blotches on his face that betrayed his illness. A shudder went through me and I looked away. "I told you. Edward sent for me."

"Ah, I remember now. I told him to do that."

"Why?"

He attempted to sit up, but the effort strained him so much that he only sank down further. "Merely wanted to congratulate you."

"For what?"

"Coming to your senses."

"Ironic. Longshanks said the same thing. I was never aware I had lost them."

"Clever of you to strike a deal and wed the daughter of one of the king's faithful. Very, very clever. There is spiced wine on the table there. Have some. You look bedraggled. You could use it." He grappled at his blankets with hands wrapped in loose strips of cloth. "I had not thought you capable of such duplicity. Tell me—was this your ploy all along? You have played it exceedingly well."

I swept the half full jug of wine and cups to the floor. Gritting my teeth, I gripped the edge of the table and leaned as close to his shadowed, putrid face as I could stomach. "Do *not* pretend to know my mind—even less my heart."

He eyed me from the cavern of his pillow and shook his head. "So, Robert, this was not some clever plot, after all? You fell in love with her—followed your heart. That is never wise."

"Coming from one who seeks naught but self-preservation and comfort? My heart tells me one thing. My head, two or three or four. And you yet another."

"Such anguish and confusion, son. Let it be. The match is wisely done—profitable and politic. You have returned to the fold. Even after all the grief you have caused me, I shall die with joy in my shriveled heart."

Your heart has ever been that way.

I watched the yellow light on the folds of the canopy over his bed dance and sway, interplaying with shadows. His words were always like that—light and shadow mixing. Telling me to go in one breath, asking me to stay in another. Any wonder I questioned my heart, even as wildly strong as it beat inside my chest? I turned my back on him and walked away.

EARLY THE NEXT MORNING, Mary woke me to tell me father had worsened. I did not go to him. What else could I have said? That I loved him? I did not. That I hated him? That neither. Simply put, I did not care, cruel as that may sound. Instead, I dressed and asked her which room was Edward's. I could tell by the way Mary stammered and blushed that he had a woman with him.

The door was not barred. I pushed it open so slowly it made no sound. The sight of Edward's bare back greeted me as he mounted an eager wench beneath him on the bed. All I could see of her was a pair of curving ivory thighs beyond bent knees. The room was small and the scent of sex powerful.

"Mmm, Edward, have you any idea how you delight me?" she purred.

"Aithne?" I exclaimed. "Why, I think you used to say that to me."

Edward rolled from her, snatched up a pillow and launched it at my head. "Have you abandoned manners, brother?"

"And you morals?" I retorted with a grin. "Well met, Edward. How is your husband, Aithne?"

She pulled up the sheet, but only far enough that her breasts were still half exposed. Her coppery hair fell like a rope of silk over her shoulder. "If I ever saw him I would be able to tell you. How are you, my dear, sweet Robert? You have wed, too, I hear. Or is that a wild rumor meant to crush the hearts of hopeful women?"

Aithne of Carrick had been my first lover. And the first of many a young man as I later discovered. Mostly lads just sprouting their whiskers, like myself, tumbling with her in the stable hay, but she had a skill and hunger for pleasing men that brought them crawling back over and over again—including me. Edward, as well. In our youth, it had driven a deep wedge between us. I had thought I loved Aithne and might have married her, had my father agreed. But that was not to be. Rather than have us squabble over her, father had found a willing suitor for her and sent her away. Obviously, her allure had not waned with the years, nor had a marriage contract tamed her. I pulled up a stool.

"Elizabeth de Burgh," I said. "My second wife, actually. The first, Isabella . . . she died in childbirth."

"I'm so sorry, Robert." She turned on her side so that the sheet fell away. "So this Elizabeth—she is well bred? And beautiful?"

"Exceedingly." I could not help but glance at her plump, white bosom.

Edward yanked the sheet up to her shoulders. Then he slid an arm possessively around Aithne's waist, pulled her buttocks close against that part of him seeking to know her and drowned her neck in wet kisses. "Perhaps we could continue this conversation *later*?" he said with a swift glare at me. "If you don't mind, Robert, I believe Aithne and I were in the middle of something. Or rather, *I* was in the middle of *her*."

"Of course." I rose and made toward the door. "Meet me at the stable at noon, Edward. We shall ride along the River Annan. The rain will lift soon and I have a proposition to make."

But when I stole a last glance, I doubted that Edward had heard me at all. He was already indulging himself in Aithne's gifts with selfish, ravenous fervor. If he had meant to rouse a shred of jealousy in me, it only made me long for Elizabeth more.

EIGHT ROE DEER STUDIED us from the far bank of the River Annan. A late fog that followed a soaking rain overnight had kept them about well past their usual hour. They stood with their backs to the pines, lifting their heads from lush, new spring grass to reflect our own fascination.

"Thomas brought down two stags a week before last," Nigel informed us. At the sound of his lilting voice, they bounded back into the mists.

That morning, I had roused Edward, which took great effort, and my youngest brothers, Nigel and Thomas, and told them to come along. Nigel would rather have been whispering prayers from Prime until Lauds. He yearned to join the Church, so he had told me that very morning, even though we had all known that since before he was five. Shorter than myself by a head, he was constantly bested by the rest of us in every pursuit and so he had taken early to a life of devotion, although I suspected he had secret aspirations higher than an abbacy. Thomas, however, yearned toward nothing that was not directly in front of him. Take him on the hunt and he was the first to spy and take aim at the boar, but getting him out the door and on the horse to begin with was a near to impossible task. Upon first impression, he might have followed Edward's traits, but Edward had ambition, however thwarted by a quick temper and impatient mood. Handsomest of us all, naturally gifted in physical talents, Thomas was indolent and indifferent. He never complained, never took sides and, in general, made a joke of life.

Even though we had only paused to view the deer, Thomas had already slipped from his saddle, led his horse to the river's edge for a drink and then climbed upon a rounded boulder clinging to the bank. There he laid belly down, dangling his fingers in the white swirls of water rushing by. Before I could say anything, Nigel and Edward followed.

I surrendered and went to join them. As I neared the lip of the bank and knelt to take a drink, a rock the size of my fist plopped into the river. A shower of ice cold water doused me.

Thomas slapped Nigel on the back and laughed raucously.

"Always were an easy target, Robert," Thomas remarked, his face luminous. For Thomas, amusement was easy to come by.

"Do I need to remind you, *weeee* Thomas, of the last time we wrestled?" I pushed my hair back from my face as streams of water ran onto my shoulders. "You ended up with your head in a bucket. Had difficulty breathing, didn't you?"

Thomas rolled his chestnut brown eyes at me and stuck out his tongue.

"How was she, Edward?" asked Thomas, as he flipped over and sprawled on his back to look up at a cloud-wrung sky that threatened more rain. A flirting sun had been chased into hiding and the day was yet no warmer than when the first silver hint of dawn broke above the distant hills. "Sweet as honey?"

"Little boys brag," said Edward. He bounded up on the rock and stood there, hands on hips, watching the young salmon slip along the water's rippling surface. A full minute later, he traced a finger from his chin, down his neck, to his collarbone and said, "More like wine, really, she was. Intoxicating. Numbing. Every taste left me wanting more." He moved his hands in the empty air as if caressing her outline.

I picked up a flat stone and tried to skip it across to the other side, but the rapids were too deep and strong from the winter run-off and my little stone sank after the first skip.

"When Longshanks dies," I declared, "I am going to take the crown."

"Of England?" Thomas exclaimed, bolting upright.

"No, France, you dolt." Edward smacked him in the forehead. "Bother, Robert. I was in a mood for boasting. Must you always outdo me?"

"I mean it. I need to know you're all in with me."

"In?" Nigel looked from face to face in bewilderment. He pulled at his tight brown curls as his neck shrank down to meet his shoulders. "But I am to go to the Sorbonne to study theology."

"Then go. I'll not hold you back. But when the time comes, Nigel, know that I will need you in whatever way you can aid me."

"There is more to the world than women and fighting," Nigel grumbled, arms clutched around his knees and pouting as if he were a lad of five and not a man full into his twentieth year.

"Aye, he's right." Thomas chuckled. "There's food, ale, and a good soft bed to greet you afterwards. War I could do without, but women . . ."

"I would hardly call those pock-faced milkmaids you've been groping '*women*'." Edward leapt from his perch jauntily and came toward me. "So you get a crown and what do the rest of us get, Robert? A pat on the back, a wreath of laurels, a herd of cattle? Maybe a fine house in the country?"

"*You* get to be second in line to the throne, my brother."

"But you have a wife . . . and you'll have sons."

"But until and unless I do—you are after me."

"You have a daughter. And she could have sons."

Argumentative as ever . . . and never pleased with second help-ings. "Are you saying you want none of this?"

Edward hesitated. His hands swept wide. "I'm trying to make things *clear*, Robert. Not muddy. Scotland does not need another throne left vacant. It only invites contention and opportunists. And I have no intention of taking part in your brawl and getting nothing but scraps."

"Scraps are what we have had thus far, brother. This will be a fight in the name of all Bruces—the rightful heirs. You, me, Alex-ander, Nigel, Thomas. I would not treat you thus, Edward."

"Good, because I don't take kindly to being maltreated."

He meant it even more than his words conveyed. Edward resented being born second. The problem with Edward was not in garnering his support for the quest. It was in gratifying him afterwards.

Rain began to fall, not in a fine mist, but heavy and hard as it does in April, as if the clouds had suddenly wearied of their burden and surrendered to it. Nigel and Thomas scrambled for their horses, but Edward and I just stood there face to face, the rain slashing at our faces like cold steel. He looked away for a long moment as our younger brothers sped off, back toward the castle.

Finally, he nodded. "Better the brother of a king," he mused, "than a mere earl. I only pray I do not die in the attempt. It would be a pity to waste such talents as mine."

"I daresay you will never be mistaken for being humble."

He smiled broadly, raindrops running in little rivulets between the bristles of his unshaven face. "*Humble* is merely knowing how to hide the truth. Lying to oneself, in effect. I am what I am and in that I am honest . . . as I trust you are being. Now, tell me—if you have no sons yourself, who will come after you?"

"You drive a hard bargain, Edward."

"Make up your mind. I'd like to get out of this rain."

"*You* will." I braced my hands firmly upon both of his shoulders. "I swear to it. Not because I want to appease you. Because I know you would never let anyone wrest anything from you. You would surrender the clothes on your back and your last crumb of bannock before you'd allow the slightest scratch in your armor of pride. In that, I trust Scotland is secure."

No sooner had he clasped my hand than he was upon his horse and flying over ground back to a roof and fire. I watched the hooves of his horse slapping showers of water behind them as they drove through the gray rain.

IT WAS NOT UNTIL I rode through the gates of grim Lochmaben that I felt the chill invade my flesh. Unhurried, I returned my horse to the stables and entered into the hall where my brothers and little sister Mary waited. Edward wore a sardonic smile, but the rest were entirely somber.

Mary came to me and took my hands. Her fingers were cold. Her eyes, red.

"He's dying," she whispered.

"All hail," Edward said with a bow, "our soon-to-be new Lord of Annandale: Fair Robert."

When I entered my father's chamber for the second time upon my return, the odor of rotting flesh stung inside my nose. His stone-still form beneath his coverings looked like a corpse upon its funeral bier. If not for the occasional flickering of his eyelashes, he might well have been mistaken for dead.

As I reached his bedside and made the sign of the cross, he turned his face to me.

"A priest?" he croaked.

"Nigel has already sent for one."

He labored to breathe. His malady had devoured his insides. Like many who had journeyed to the Holy Land, he had harbored the leprosy until its later manifestation. While on Crusade with Longshanks, then prince, my father's friend Adam de Kilconquahar died, leaving behind a wife heavy with child. Her name was Marjorie of Carrick and she first met my father when he returned home and brought her the sorrowful news of her husband's death. Within the year they had wed and she bore him ten children in all before a fever took her swiftly away one harsh winter. Death was not coming so mercifully to my father. It had haunted him for years like an unseen shadow and finally he gazed at its hideous face in the full light of day.

That was how he looked as he stared wordlessly at me, mortality meeting death and realizing the strength of its power—his mouth parted to show his loose teeth and pale gums, the flesh on his face lumpy and splotched, one eye long since swollen shut. *God spare me that I should ever suffer such infirmity for such a length as he, or such gruesomeness that I must hide from the world.*

With fingers like gnarled twigs attached to his swollen stump of a hand, he reached for a cup on the table next to his bed. His numb fingertips grazed it as it skidded out of reach and tottered on the table's edge.

"The drink, son. Give me the drink. It will ease the pain."

I raised my arm to reach for it and then stopped. I took a step backward and watched him writhe as the agony gripped him. His mottled hand, dangling over the edge of the bed, trembled violently.

"Give it to me," he commanded in a raspy, failing voice.

I shook my head. "Give me your blessing first."

"I told you—the marriage is well done. Now, give it to me . . . or curse you."

"I want your blessing to claim what is rightfully mine."

"Fool to think you can so easily take or keep it."

I went to the door and silently slid the bar across to persuade him. "Your blessing. You can die in peace . . . or in agony."

Even on the precipice of death, he nurtured no remorse, sought no penitence, desired no salvation. Naught but his own comfort mattered to him.

He shook from head to toe, his breath catching with each spasm. Finally, he curled two of his fingers at me and said over his drooping lip, "Then come be blessed."

I knelt at his side. He laid the club of his hand on top of my head. "For all you endeavor to gain—I bless you, son. Let it be not in vain . . . as my life has been."

His hand slipped away. Quickly, I lifted his head and let him drink. Most of the liquid spilled from the side of his mouth. He coughed and swallowed, then mumbled something, which I took to be a request for more. Slowly, the tremors subsided.

When the cup was empty, I stood and clenched it in my hands. I fought the tear that sprang to my eye.

"I would have given it to you anyway," I uttered, staring into the cup. "Good God, I would have run through a rain of arrows to save your fading bones . . . and all for only your blessing."

I heard him breathe once more—deeply, peacefully.

It was seven days before we laid my father, Robert Bruce, fifth of that name before me, to rest, without his last rites. The local priest that Nigel had gone to fetch had refused to come to Father's bedside or preside over the funeral of a leper, but another was finally found who, although even less ardent about performing such a task, was more easily reminded of who filled his collection box.

The body of Robert, Lord of Annandale, lay wrapped in a plain white shroud in a coffin of lead. Upon the coffin was draped a pall of black and centered there in tight threads of gold embroidery was the lion of Bruce: claws outstretched, its mouth wide open in a roar of dominion.

17

Robert the Bruce – Selkirk Forest, 1304

I AWOKE TO THE scent of pines and hay. Next to where I had slept, sweet woodruff bloomed in abundance. Beads of morning dew clung to its whorls of leaves beneath airy white petals. I reached out and tipped a leaf so the dew dripped onto the ground. The generous rains of April had lately been followed by warmth and sunshine more like July than spring. I could have lain there all day, staring up at the blue-green boughs above me where a golden-eyed, horned owl roosted . . . except for Gerald stooping over me, his stale morning breath suffocating my daydreams. He inclined his head toward the edge of camp, where my brother Edward was washing his hands in a stream.

I pulled on my boots while Sir John Segrave, Longshanks' man, watched me. I sauntered toward a tree nearby, undid the cord on my hose and relieved myself. My brother, Edward, approached me. His mare, sipping from the cool brook, trailed her reins along the stony shore.

"Did you find him?" I knelt at water's edge to rinse yesterday's dirt from my face.

"Wallace? Ah, well, no . . ." he revealed with a sly grin. "But he did find me. Drove a spear into the trunk of an oak tree not half a foot from my head. Sweet Jesus, but I thought my next heartbeat would be my last."

"And you told him?"

"Aye—follow the Ettrick Water. Keep to the hills. Then west to the Nith and on to Ayr, where a ship will carry him to France." Edward rubbed at his beard pensively. "If Segrave suspects anything, Robert . . . you know?"

"Aye, treason. My head on the block. Yours as well." I stood up and with the corner of my cloak wiped the water from my chin. "But how else am I to play the part of the faithful dog than to 'follow' orders? I will just be the hound that never quite catches the hare. As for Segrave—in with Neville since the start. A tangle of snakes. Cover your tracks well, when he is about. Better yet, leave none."

Edward unslung the short bow from his back and removed the bowstring, then coiled it around his fingers. "I thought it was particularly clever of you to omit the windlass when that devil, Longshanks, ordered you to forward the siege engine to Stirling."

"Omit? Misplaced by careless sailors at the port, that is all. None of it my doing." I winked at him, then plucked a twig from the ground, frayed the end of it and picked at my teeth.

We stood there in the dampness of the lifting mist, going about our morning business as if it were any other uneventful day. I itched to ask my brother about his morning—what words he might have said to Wallace and Wallace to him—but I knew it would have to wait. Before the day was over there would be more than enough cause for Segrave to watch us more closely in the future. Silently, we watched as a scout rode into camp, dismounted and immediately made way, not to me, but to Segrave.

The scout poured out a river of information as Segrave

received the news stoically. Segrave glanced at us, then uttered a few words to his men. They kicked dirt on their cooking fires as they shoveled down handfuls of cold porridge and scooped up their weapons in haste.

Edward gathered up his mare's reins and scratched at her pink nose. "The executioner comes."

Segrave strolled toward us, hands clasped behind his back. Always, he wore the expression of a fox—the small, scrutinizing eyes, the long, pinched nose.

"Wallace was seen fleeing to the southwest less than an hour past," he said.

I feigned surprise. "Are you certain it was Wallace?"

"Completely," Segrave acknowledged. "He is unmistakable: they say he is a giant among men who goes about bare-legged and bare-armed and wears his hair loose and wild like a lion's mane. Who else fits that description?"

"Many a Scot would," I mused, then added, "but, if you say without a doubt it is him—"

"How far is he now from us?" Edward's forehead wrinkled with the appearance of genuine interest. My brother was a fine actor—no doubt he used the skill to flatter his women and woo his way into their beds. So many times as a lad he had turned the blame on Nigel or Thomas when he played mischief and our mother had never been the wiser to him.

"Miles. Sir Edward . . . the sentry says you were off long before dawn this morning. Where did you go?"

"I was near to starving, Sir John," Edward answered. "What do you think I was doing? Plotting your murder with rebels?"

A moment hung suspended as Segrave's smooth, hollowed cheeks sucked in further. Then Edward reached for the back of his mare's saddle and untied the game he had collected. He swung two hares and a plump, wild goose by their feet.

"All I had time for, really. These parts have been picked over."

Segrave suppressed a sneer. "Save them for later. We've a rebel to hunt now."

Edward smiled and tipped his head of chestnut waves in something of a nod.

"Gerald, at once!" I called. "Saddle my horse. We're riding out."

As Segrave went to gather up his arms and don his mail, Edward draped an arm about me.

"Thank Wallace for filling your belly when you sit down to eat tonight," he said, pleased with his own resourcefulness. "I never let go a single arrow."

WE RODE ALL THAT day and most of the next before Segrave relented. The trees in Selkirk Forest were as thick as hairs on a dog's back. Segrave was either too obsessed or too stricken with the fear of going back to Longshanks as a failure to realize he may as well have been searching for a single pearl in the whole of the ocean. We picked up Wallace's trail from where the scout had led us to, but it grew quickly cold. Wallace knew the hills and the forests, knew how to live off the land and become a part of it. If he was ever taken, it would be either by trickery or sheer luck. I prayed that would never come to pass.

Wallace's flight should have resurrected hope. But the year was a failing one for Scotland. A year in which self-reliance gave way to self-preservation. When Soulis departed for France to plea for Philip's allegiance along with a contingent of others, among them Stewart and Umfraville, the guardianship was then turned over to Comyn. A fatal move, because Comyn connived however he could. If bowing to Longshanks would buy him time and keep his lands from being plagued, then that is precisely what he would, and did, do. He bartered for fines over punishment, so that the Scottish no-bles could keep their possessions, never mind their pride. But who am I to condemn for such?

Again, in legions they capitulated. Would nothing ever change? Only Sir William Oliphant at Stirling stood firm. Before Soulis left, he had commanded Oliphant to defend Stirling at all costs and that is exactly what Oliphant tried to do.

Longshanks had other plans. If Stirling would not surrender of its own free-will, he would raze it to rubble. Preservation, as I had learned, meant setting aside dignity, if only for a while.

18

James Douglas – Paris, 1304

THE SUMMER FATHER LEFT for Irvine, Hugh and I would sit high on a hill, day after day, watching the kestrels glide and swoop. One morning, our patience was rewarded with the sighting of a vixen. Ears twitching, she loped cat-like through the rustling grass. The short tail of a plump vole dangled from between her teeth. Vigilant, she made her way back to her lair beneath the roots of the yew tree where her kits awaited. Another time, we saw a pine marten stealthily hunt down a red squirrel among the treetops. It stared and crept, closer, closer. Then with a burst of speed, it pounced, clamping its jaws on the squirrel's neck. With every squeal and squirm of its victim, its teeth pinched deeper and deeper, until finally the furred russet body hung limp from its jaws.

The road over which we kept vigil stretched across the land, disappearing around a hill to the south where a spur of black rock forced a twist in its path. Every time a traveler appeared in the distance, we raced down the hillside, slapping our hands against the pine trunks to keep from sliding, and waited anxiously to see who it was. We saw many strangers: merchants and soldiers, nobles and beggars, farmers and robbers.

But we never saw our father again.

I cannot remember the last words that I shared with him. I do remember him standing on the wall walk of Berwick, his eyes fixed on the horizon, his voice strained yet sharp with commands. I remember him patiently teaching me how to pull a bowstring when I had not half the strength needed. I remember him that final winter stooped over on his bench before a dying hearthfire, head in hands, as Eleanor kneaded his bunched shoulders. Images as strong as if only a moment past.

Before autumn arrived, I was sent off to the College of Cardinal Lemoine in Paris. No one told me how long I was to stay there or even why I was sent in the first place. For awhile, Lady Eleanor wrote to me. Although her letters were glossed with words of hope, after a time even that trickle gradually ran dry.

Then, before I had turned thirteen, I received one more letter from my stepmother, delivered by an associate of Bishop Lamberton's. It stated, simply, that my father was dead in the Tower of London. I have no doubt his tongue had cost him his life, for he had no love of England or its wicked king whatsoever. I heard no more from Eleanor after that.

I had no father now. My stepmother was lost to me. And my brothers and I had been flailed apart and cast like wheat chaff to the wind.

OF SCOTLAND, I CHERISHED both the sprawling days of summer, when dusk and dawn were one, and the witching darkness of winter, when I would warm my hands by the hearth while song and company wrapped themselves around me like a cloak against the cold. I loved the height and breadth of the mountains and the mysterious depth of the lochs. I marveled at the matrimony of blue-green pines embracing a meadow of yellow-faced daisies; glittering ribbons of shoreline and forests thick with deer; snowy hills and starry skies.

Among all those things that filled my heart and gave me breath, Paris had none. Seven years had lapsed since I left home. Seven years of wretched solitude, during which I had invented my own means of survival.

The stars winked faintly from the tiny window at the end of the room I shared with some twenty other students at the College of Cardinal Lemoine. Beneath my threadbare blanket, I curled my fingers around the purse and squeezed. The hard edge of three silver deniers indented my palm through the softened leather. I dug within and pulled one out to run my fingertips over the cross imprinted on it, then tucked it back inside, clutching the pouch to my chest.

As I rolled over, pain seared through the stripes of broken skin on my back. Ten lashes—the usual punishment. Between each bite of the willow switch, Master Marten had quoted scripture to me: *'Because of these things cometh the wrath of God upon the children of disobedience'.*

I had been late to Master Datini's Latin lecture. A quarter of an hour, no more. For a reason.

Earlier that afternoon, I had been at the fair in the streets leading to Notre Dame Cathedral. A Genoese cloth merchant sidled up to a market stall to inspect a pot of weld, a yellow dye. I edged up to him, my knuckles brushing the leather purse that swung at his hip. Then, he began to haggle, loudly, with the dyer. I drew my hand back into my sleeve, the blade of my short knife cold against my wrist. Only when the crowd erupted in near hysteria did I have my chance again. People jostled forward from alleys to see the annual Procession of the Relic, led by the Bishop of Paris. Sweating bodies pressed in around the stall. A zealous pilgrim dressed in rags bumped the merchant's elbow. As he bellowed curses at the pilgrim, I looped the strings of his purse in one hand, then slipped my knife across them. Shoving my way through the throng, I had put twenty paces between myself and the Genoese before I heard him accuse the dyer of stealing his money.

My lawlessness had bought me a hearty serving of Lent fritters and salted herring smeared with mustard, which I greedily washed down with a jug of mulberry wine. Enough food to quell the rumbling of my empty stomach. Worth every lash.

As a *boursier*, or student on scholarship, I was allotted only two loaves of white bread daily and one meal in the refectory, usually pottage or thin stew—hardly enough to sustain an infant, let alone a ravenous, sprouting lad. In my seven years in Paris, I had learned as much of theology and philosophy as I did of begging and stealing. The begging, actually, I had long ago given up on. It suited little boys, but no one took much pity on a young man of eighteen. Besides, thievery was much more profitable.

At the time, I did not ponder too long on God's disapproval. Survive or starve—those were my choices.

I probed for the hole on the underside of my straw mattress and tucked the purse deep within. I would still get several more meals out of my cache—whenever I could slip away from my lessons and chores long enough to indulge myself. That might be days yet.

A cough broke from the far side of the room. Someone else sniffed with tears. The boy next to me muttered in his dreams. Our beds were stacked like cords of wood with barely enough room to squeeze between them. I felt the tickle of a louse and scratched at my scalp. Unable to sleep, I turned to face the window. My back stung with the feeble effort.

There, through the window, the stars still glimmered. For hours, I gazed at them, until I drifted off to welcome sleep.

I dreamt of home. Of mountains, burns and lochs. Sea and sky. Kestrels, foxes, squirrels. Meadows, moors and forests . . .

THE NEXT MORNING, I sat in the school refectory—not on a bench at one of the tables like the other students, but alone on a stool by the hearth. It was my job to tend the fire, a task usually given to much younger boys. I wore the perpetual soot marks to show for my menial labors. I was the last to begin eating, but a few others still lingered in conversation over their bland meals. The flames were fading and so I set aside my bowl of dark bread and cabbage to feed the fire. Kneeling, I arranged the charred wood and reached for another log. At the table behind me, the German boys jeered, but I did not look. It was better, I had learned, to ignore their taunts.

A troop of feet padded over the floor. I poked at the logs, hopeful my tormentors would pass me by. Then, directly behind me, I heard the scrape of a stool across the floor and the loud crack as the seat struck my skull.

A flash of white across my vision. And daylight vanished.

The stink of filth and moldy rushes slowly filled my nose. Broken voices came to me through a gray fog. I struggled to understand them, then slipped away again.

My next recollection was of looking up at the ceiling. My back burned from scabs torn open. Scowling older boys swarmed above me. Ten, more maybe. Their shapes blended and swayed dizzily around me. One at a time in turn, they kicked at my head, groin and ribs. I squirmed. Pain thundered through my every limb. Blood oozed from my lip. Every part of my body ached with bone-deep bruises.

"Shove hot coals down his throat, Frederick," the fat one said. "If he doesn't vomit fire that will keep him quiet . . . for good."

Frederick's belly rippled with laughter. His uncle was a bishop: a fact which had collected a small army of worshippers to him. Without ever lifting a single, ivory finger, he always had a full purse of coin, supplied by his father, a count of some importance, while I had to scrub floors and muck out stalls to earn my fare. While I memorized the Latin verses of Thomas Aquinas by moonlight, for I often had no candle, Frederick played at dice. When it came time for exams, Frederick would lazily nudge his quill across his parchment and then fall asleep, while I wrote copious pages.

I hated Paris. I hated that school. I hated my teachers. And I hated Frederick most of all.

I grabbed a pot hanger from above the ash-cold hearth and slashed him in the thigh. Frederick shrieked, like a little girl whose hair had been pulled, and fell to the floor. He pulled his leg to his chest. Blood sprayed like a fountain from his gaping wound and seeped into the rushes.

I rose to my feet. The circle of boys, who moments before had thought me so weak of will and limb, now retreated from my furious reach. I strode from them with a limp, clenching my jaw against the pain in my ribs that screamed with every breath. As I reached the end of the long room, I turned around to face them. I opened my fingers and let the pot hanger fall to the floor with a thunderous clatter. Only Frederick's whimper cut across the silence.

A hand pinched the curve between my neck and shoulders.

"Young Douglas," Master Martin, one of my schoolmasters and a Dane who dissected the tedious subtleties of rhetoric more days than I cared to endure, spoke in his edgy, crackling voice, "come with me. It is time we decide what to do with you, given your intractable nature."

Send me back to Scotland, I prayed.

HIS WIRY FINGERS DIGGING into my upper arm, Master Martin escorted me to office of the Headmaster, Julien Andreae. The door groaned on its hinges as he led me into the musty, book-cluttered confines. Motes of dust danced on shafts of sunlight through half-open shutters. Behind the desk, however, it was not Headmaster Andreae who greeted me to dole out my penalty, or more hopefully my expulsion. There, in gold-lined ecclesiastical vestments, sat a man who had been pointed out to me once during one of his previous visits to Paris: Bishop William Lamberton of St. Andrews. For a moment, I wondered if God had sent him to make me atone for my wrongdoings. I would much have preferred a public flogging. Less disgrace in that.

"Your grace." Master Martin prodded me forward as he knelt before the bishop. Clumsily, he pulled at my shoulder, dragging me to my knees.

Bishop Lamberton offered his hand. Stiffly, Master Martin pressed his thin lips to the ring above Lamberton's creased knuckles.

"You may leave." The bishop withdrew his hand and brushed his fingers toward the door.

"Shall I bring his things?" Martin inquired. "It will not take long to gather them."

"Yes, yes, do. I had thought to leave him here a day or two until after I am received by King Philip, but by the sight of him perhaps it is better to remove him now."

"None too soon, your grace. Had I not intervened on his behalf he would not be in one piece now."

I turned my head to sneer at the lying Dane and spied, hidden in the shadows, the outline of a form I could never forget. Master Martin nearly skipped from the room with obvious joy.

Behind him, William Wallace stretched an arm out and closed the door. I shuddered, though whether out of awe or fear I knew not. He had grown more ragged and fierce-looking in those few years since Irvine. Falkirk, I assumed, had stolen the passion from him. Those wild blue eyes that once reflected the broad sky of Scotland were now as dull as puddles of rainwater on a muddy road.

"James. James?"

I turned my eyes back to the bishop. His clean jaw propped upon his knuckles, he sighed and reached a finger toward my bleeding lip, but I turned my face away.

"Sir William, have someone bring a clean cloth and water."

"Don't need it," I protested vainly. "Doesn't hurt."

Wallace shook his head. "Your father once said you were independent and willful. He forgot stubborn."

"I said it *doesn't* hurt," I told him, even though moving my lips without grimacing was near to impossible. A warm line of blood traced its way from the corner of my mouth down my jaw and neck toward my collarbone. My lip, I could tell, had already swollen to obvious proportions.

Wallace grabbed me by the ear and tilted my head toward a stream of dusty light to get a better look. "You should clean that up . . . unless you prefer to have it fester. I can sit on your head and douse you if I have to. You're still half my size."

I wriggled from his grasp and scrambled on my hands and knees away from him. Brute strength was not everything. He, of all folk, should know that.

"Sir William," Bishop Lamberton interrupted, "let be, for now. He will not die from that gash in his lip. At least not likely. Besides, we have . . . sensitive matters to discuss." He straightened in the chair, folding his hands in his lap. "I am sorry about your father, James."

I had not thought often of him, tried not to, or of Hugh or Archibald. Slumping back against a shelf burdened by the weight of its books, I looked down at the floor to hide my welling tears.

"Why was I not sent home before now? I have lands to look after." Surely Lady Eleanor was overwhelmed. Hugh could be of no help and Archibald was far too young to be anything but a burden. "What of Hugh and Archibald?"

"Safe," Lamberton assured me. "Your absence is something I will venture to remedy in due time. Because of your father's involvement at Irvine, however, the family estates were duly confiscated and granted to Sir Robert Clifford of Westmorland. Surely you understood why you were subjected to such hardship here. Did they not tell you? Ah, no, I can see they did not. Nor, obviously did they treat you as the son of a proper noble."

Confiscated? How could someone else take away what was rightly mine? Still, not even the loss of my family's lands would keep me from going home. "You said you were going to take me from here. When do we leave for Scotland?"

"*We?*" The bishop sighed and rolled his eyes heavenward. "Not yet, James. It is too soon. You will be transferred to the Sorbonne, given a small pension . . . our Good Lord allowing I remain in the munificent graces of King Edward."

I could scarce believe what I had just heard. I shot to my feet. Too soon? *Too soon?* "I want to go back. Now! Do you hear me? I won't stay in Paris. It reeks!"

"And what would you go back to, James Douglas?" Wallace posed. "You have no lands. No home. Nothing."

"I don't have '*nothing*'. I can fight . . . against Longshanks. And I will take back what is mine."

"What do you think the rest of us have been trying to do all along?" Wallace moved so his frame blocked the shaft of light between us and he was naught but a silhouette—a mountain blotting out the sun.

"James," Lamberton intervened, "the realm is in confusion. Today you might have your lands back; tomorrow they could again be taken from you. I simply came to look in on you and arrange better schooling for you. Your father and Sir William here were good friends. I owe it to both of them to see that you make it to a proper age, when you can be of more value to your homeland."

"I'm eighteen now!"

"I will send for you, when the timing is more propitious. Master Andreae says that, although not exceedingly gifted, you are a diligent pupil. Your determination is wasted on these teachers. But understand—any improprieties will propel you into the streets. I will not rescue a rebel. If you wish to return to Scotland in due time, then you will display a measure of self-control. King Edward is not likely to be impressed by a tally of misdeeds."

I clenched my fists at my sides. "I don't care what Longshanks thinks of me."

"Do you want your lands back?"

"Aye."

"Then you *should* care. For now—you will leave this . . . this place of squalor and attend the Sorbonne, as a young noble should."

"Then if you put me there, tomorrow I shall be gone. I will work, beg or steal my way back to Scotland; but however, I *will* get there."

Wallace gripped my shoulder. I expected him to spin me around or volley admonishments at me, tell me I was too young, too weak, too inexperienced to make a difference yet.

"Your grace," he addressed the bishop, "take the lad home with you. Let him petition for the return of his lands. He'll only cause trouble if you keep him here."

Lamberton rose from the chair. He went to the open window and for a long while stared expressionless out over the crowded streets of Paris, tapping his ringed finger on the stone ledge. In the undersized courtyard of the school, spring's first buds dotted the tree limbs and birds flitted from branch to branch in courtship. The sights may have been promising, but the warmer breeze also brought with it the pungent smell of rotting food and waste dumped in the streets. He inhaled and without expelling the air, looked my way and said, "Perhaps I never took the time to notice before, but it *does* reek."

THE FOLLOWING DAY, I was fitted with better attire and properly scrubbed. Then, I accompanied Bishop Lamberton and Sir William Wallace to King Philip's palace. Although relegated to the kitchen for my meal, I was never so enthralled in my entire life. Elaborate dishes were labored over and sent out to the main hall: boar's head served on silver platters, fishes in white wine jelly, pears peeled and cored and filled with honey, and steaming bowls of rabbit stew cooked with cloves and ginger in almond milk. In time, servants returned with the remains and I gorged myself gluttonously. The silver deniers, still hidden in my mattress back at the college, could not have bought me a meal half as fine as this.

I was not privy to what went on between Bishop Lamberton, Wallace and King Philip. I only knew that Wallace carried letters of delicate importance and that the King of France had his nose quite out of place for some time afterwards.

On the road beyond Paris, the bishop and I parted ways with William Wallace. He was on his way to Rome to meet with the pope and beg for Scotland's cause. The treaty carved out between France and England had dealt a horrible blow to Scotland and Lamberton told me Longshanks had already begun on his way again to march through Scotland.

It was late May by the time we made port in Berwick and there my joy ebbed and gave way to a tide of grief. Nearly eight years had crept by since I had left my easy boyhood far behind and hardened to the world. I knelt and touched the earth and wept. Wind whipped at my hair. Clouds of dark blue-gray brought the sky down low and thunder shook the earth.

We set out for Stirling as showers of warm rain poured over us. There, we would meet with King Edward and petition for my inheritance.

19

<u>Robert the Bruce – Stirling, 1304</u>

I WENT FROM SELKIRK direct to Stirling, myself to play the king's
henchman, while in secret I prayed for some miracle that would
spare Sir William Oliphant within those high, towering walls. There,
I witnessed the antics of an aging king, keen to impress a blushing
bride less than half his age. Longshanks raced to and fro on his
majestic steed beneath the castle walls. His head bare, he dismounted to hurl threats, even as arrows grazed his ears. Once, a stone
launched from the battlements startled his horse and he was tossed
to the ground. One man lost his life trying to drag the
injured king to safety.

While King Edward mended, I received a message. Oliphant
offered surrender. Inwardly, I sighed with relief, hoping few, if any,
of those within had succumbed to starvation or sickness, as was the
usual course.

In a merchant's house above a jeweler's shop, the king kept
quarters in relative comfort. From there, he had a clear view of the
castle walls. Nearby, sentries were on constant vigil with barrels of
water and buckets at hand, for more than once a flaming arrow had

sizzled through the night sky to land on a nearby roof. The bed-chamber was small and cramped, but crowded with the objects of opulence so familiar to a king's existence. I knelt before him until the blood left my legs.

Longshanks raised his arms, elbows bent, as his physician wrapped his bruised ribs in a cocoon of linen bandages. The morning sun poured brazenly through the open window, outlining his form. Air hissed between his teeth as the physician poked and prodded at his chest. He possessed a remarkable physique for a man who had thus far survived six-and-a-half decades—much of it spent in the dust and brutality of the Holy Land and numerous battles on the continent. His skin had sallowed with the years, but he remained lean and lithe. The backs of his hands were spotted from the sun and his hair, once a shining dark gold by all accounts, was now a streaked blend of yellow and silver-white. When the physician was done, he bowed and left. The king's page began to dress him. Longshanks eased his battered body down onto a stool while the page pulled the king's chausses over his long legs and tied them to the laces that dangled from a belt at his waist.

"Rise, earl," he said. "Had Wallace . . . and lost him. How unfortunate for you."

I rose, my feet numb, and kept my head down in humility. "My lord king, we were never so near, I'm afraid, to even come close to him. He slipped away after the first sighting."

Longshanks stood and raised an arched eyebrow at me. "I see. Elusive as a pine marten, isn't he? You know he's there, some-where, you can even at times smell him, find the hole to his den, but . . . you never see him. Now, what is it you want? I have very little time today for unimportant matters."

"Indeed important, my lord. Oliphant extends an offer of sur-render."

The king absorbed himself in straightening the sleeves of his padded jacket. Then he strutted stiffly to the window and jabbed a finger at the object of his delight. "Come here, Lord Robert. See there, that brilliant example of machinery? A monstrosity. A marvel. The War Wolf, I call it. It took them awhile to refashion that windlass you mindlessly misplaced, but there it is at last. What utter geniuses my engineers are. Constantly outdoing themselves. Tomorrow, if not today, it will be in position and loaded and they will unleash its power on the castle walls. I regret that I will have to mend them later, but 'twould be a terrible pity not to put the thing to use."

The trebuchet towered over every house in Stirling. To think I had some part in it. But as I had told myself on so many occasions, I had merely followed orders. Its verge, or main arm, was hewn from a single, gigantic tree trunk. The frame itself, which supported the pivot point atop a staunch set of trestle legs, was a massive work. His engineers had already loaded the counterweight and hooked the end of the verge and were laboring at the windlass to winch it back. Most of the time, the damned contraptions missed their mark, but when they hit, they could leave a hole the width of a tithe barn door. I thought of the people inside, women and children among them.

"But . . . I said Oliphant is prepared to surrender," I repeated, desperate to get through to him. "On your terms, sire. Unconditional. There is no need to put it to use."

God be kind, how does one stand back and watch your own people battered and butchered for amusement? How could I persuade him to mercy . . . if he had any at all within him?

"Oh, but there is, earl. I do not believe in leniency. If a subordinate wishes to display obedience, he should do so long before the whip is brought back for the first lash. I intend to leave a mark or two—as a reminder."

As I gazed into his transparent eyes, I realized I was looking into an empty soul. Fed by half a century of bloodshed and carnage. How easy to rule by fear. How much harder to forgive and embrace.

"Is there something else?" Like a cat that has cornered its prey, he still wore that cruel grin of pleasure. He returned to his page, who was now securing him within his armor shell.

"What?" Deep in my own thoughts, I had not moved my eyes from his face.

"Something else, I asked. You may escort me while they load the first stone. They are further along than I expected and we may yet have a show of it today. I can hardly wait to hear the first crash and see how much damage one machine can do."

"Uh, I beg your pardon, sire . . . but, I have other things to . . ." I broke off and shook my head. "There is something I must know, sire."

"Ask if you must."

For weeks I had stood by and watched the stones and arrows fly, knowing that within the castle walls my own folk suffered and trembled in fear as they watched the great war machine assembled and loaded for its virgin volley. I was tired of keeping my peace. Tired of following orders. Tired of complacency and groveling. Longshanks had tested my loyalty to its fullest by demanding my presence at Stirling. But I would not be content to try to prove it interminably. He, too, had made promises.

"The crown of Scotland," I broached. "We entered into an agreement—that you would support me when I laid claim to it. Stewart and several others are abroad. Comyn has capitulated. I see no better time."

His laughter shattered the air like a rock hurled through a pane of glass. "Do you think I have nothing better to do than win kingdoms for you?"

Not so long ago my impetuousness would have won the better

of me, but I had learned since then—learned to hold my tongue and to wait. I had assumed the role of the beggar, and beggars learn patience or die of blighted hope. For now, if I wished to return home to Elizabeth, if I wished to one day be of such a might and mind to take on this cruel, soulless bastard or overcome his milksop of a son, then patience must be my preservation.

Bowing as I backed away, I left.

For three bloody days, Longshanks battered the walls of Stirling Castle with his treasured toy like a small boy taking aim at birds with his slingshot. It was not enough for him to gain the surrender of his enemies. He meant to grind them into the ground so they would never rise again.

Glasgow, 1305

I MET WITH BISHOP Lamberton at Cambuskenneth Abbey. We put our names upon a document with only God as our witness. He would support me, he swore, in whatever fight for freedom I might take up, because that would remove the chains that linked Scotland's church to England's, a burdensome cross he could no longer bear in silence.

King Edward was ill again. They said he could barely rise from his bed. For months it went on like that. My time was drawing closer.

Early the following winter, I met with Red Comyn at Bishop Wishart's home in Glasgow, supposedly on the king's business. There, I made him an offer: support my claim to the crown and have my lands or take the crown himself and give me his lands.

Comyn did not need long to ponder on it. "Are you some kind of blathering fool, Bruce? What good is a crown without possessions? A title, little more." He leaned back in his chair and studied me, then snorted loudly. "Call yourself 'king', if you like. Annandale and Carrick are proper compensation for that."

I was skeptical not because he accepted my offer, but because he did it so easily. If he hated me, though, he hated Longshanks and the threat he posed to his welfare even more. "You're in agreement, then?"

"Put your oath to paper," Comyn demanded in a voice that rumbled even when he kept it low, "so that I might remind you of it when the time comes to exact payment."

I glanced at the amber flames wavering in the hearth of the stark meeting room that the bishop had set aside for us. A cross of driftwood on the wall opposite the fire was the only object of significance in the room. Four plain chairs, unadorned by intricate carvings or velvet cushions, sat about a small table, its surface worn smooth by decades of use. Everything so in contrast to the lavish homes of English bishops, with their crosses of gold studded with pearls and tapestries of the Garden of Eden, where I had on many occasions been housed while at Edward's beck and call. If I claimed Scotland's crown, it was not to gain wealth.

"Come now," Comyn chided with a quake of laughter. "You should want the same of me. What are we but men, whose memories fade and blur with time? Let us put it to ink, Lord Robert, so we forget nothing."

His smile shot a chill up my spine. But he was right. Neither of us fully trusted the other. I pushed back my chair, opened the door and called for a servant to bring us parchment and ink. I smoothed out the parchment on the table and dipped the goose quill in the inkhorn. When I was done, I passed it to him for approval. "Your support for my lands."

Comyn nodded, signed his name and pushed the contract back to me.

I drew the quill across the parchment to mark my name. Its tip skipped and caught, the ink blotting messily. My stomach lurched.

"Done," I breathed.

I hated Comyn. Hated the ground he walked on. But I would rather have him as an ally than as an enemy.

FOR YEARS AFTER THE Battle of Falkirk, William Wallace had lain low, often as far away as Paris or Rome, before finally returning home where he kept quietly to himself. Then one day, he was lured to the house of a fellow Scotsman in Glasgow. There, agents of the King of England took him prisoner. They tied him beneath the belly of a horse and transported him all the way to London. The English gave him what they called a 'trial' at Westminster Hall, but he had no lawyers and was never allowed to speak in his own defense until the very end. When they asked him if he admitted to the acts of which he was accused, it was then that he finally spoke.

"I have never been a traitor to King Edward of England," he said, a crown of laurel leaves placed crookedly on his head and his hands and feet oozing pus and blood beneath the ring of rusty shackles, "because I never swore allegiance to him."

A simple truth. A condemning one. But no matter what his words, there could only have been one fate for him.

Bound about his wrists, they tied him to the tail of a horse. Then the horse was whipped smartly, so that it took off at a canter, dragging him behind. The skin was scraped raw from his legs so that he bled from hip to heel. His relief came when the horse halted before a tall gallows. There, they dangled him by his neck until he lost consciousness . . . and then they cut him loose. If he was not dead by then, they made certain of it by taking off his head and quartering his body.

William Wallace had never stood for anything but Scotland. Never loved anything more than the land where he was born—and for that, he gave his life.

If Longshanks had wanted to crush the memory of Wallace from Scottish hearts, he only served to make it larger and greater.

20

James Douglas – Stirling, 1304

FROM BERWICK TO STIRLING, we journeyed on swaybacked hill ponies over winding roads, first taking the coastal road north, then cutting across the green Lammermuir Hills before we skirted the Firth of Forth.

A noisy escort of seabirds glided above us. I inhaled the salt air, drank in the view, and closed my eyes as I twisted my fingers in my pony's shaggy mane, wondering where Hugh was now or when I might see him again. So many years had passed since I had seen Archibald, I doubted if I would even know him were he to appear before me.

A handful of the bishop's immediate household accompanied us. They elbowed each other and laughed at me when I spoke, so I soon learned to keep my thoughts to myself. Although I had forgotten neither my Gaelic nor my English, seven years in Paris, surrounded by students from a dozen or more kingdoms, had burdened me with a strange accent of which I fought to rid myself constantly.

Even though our journey seemed all too long and tedious, I

think it was more the dread in my heart than the distance that made it so. We drifted past Edinburgh and Linlithgow, pausing only long enough to rest and take a hearty meal or two, then pressed on our way again. When I could, I wrote to Lady Eleanor and my brothers. Hopeful, I then sent the letters off tentatively in the hands of name-less messengers with a few pieces of silver and the promise of more if they returned a letter from one of my family to me. My joy at coming home, however, dissipated with each day. I was grateful to the bishop for his generosity toward me, but I was as alone as ever. Bishop Lamberton kept his eyes on the road and his conversation sparse. I sensed that he had business to tend to far weightier than the dispossession of my family lands.

Finally, we neared Stirling. For hours, I watched the castle on its high, stony hill grow larger and larger. We rode along the Roman road, past the low-lying Bannock Burn. I swatted away the midges diving relentlessly for my ears and squinted against the dazzling light of a summer sun as it bowed from its zenith. We climbed the steep road from the burn to the town, our ponies snorting with the effort.

Stirling buzzed with industry. Wagons loaded with rough-hewn stones rumbled by, throwing clouds of dust into the air. Scaffolding ran the length of the southern wall of the castle, where masons labored. Hammers and chisels pinged discordantly. Workers dug at shattered and chipped stones with their picks. At the end of a groaning rope supported by a huge winch machine, a cut stone swung dangerously.

As we waited at the castle gate, my stomach knotted. I could not take my eyes from the shambled wall, nor cease to wonder at the purpose of pummeling it to pieces only to reconstruct it later at great expense. An hour or more passed. The masons and laborers toiled on, even as dusk settled. Everywhere, women carried buckets of water and loaves of bread to the workers. Our ponies were led away to be fed and looked after. I leaned against the wall of the gatehouse to keep myself from falling over from hunger.

"Is it an English custom to keep a bishop waiting?" I mumbled loud enough to be overheard.

Bishop Lamberton surveyed the progress studiously. "We have requested an audience with Edward Plantagenet, King of England. He will see us at his convenience, not ours."

I rolled my eyes and tucked my hands under my armpits. Loose mortar littered the ground and I kicked at it. A flake of stone skidded across the gate opening in front of an English soldier who scowled at me. Despite the fancy clothes the bishop had forced upon me as his squire, I was aware of my rough looks and insolent smirks. Bishop Lamberton did his best to correct me, but in the company of Englishmen it was ever a struggle.

"Your grace," the English captain addressed with a jerking bow, "the king will see you now."

As the captain turned on his heel to lead the way, the bishop grabbed my arm and uttered in a low voice, "James, leave this to me. Say not a word. Be mindful that there is more than your inheritance at stake here."

My life, perhaps? What would King Edward have cared about striking the breath from me? Who was I to him?

I was a Scotsman. Filth. Trouble. All the worth of pig shit scraped from English boots. Once before, I had struck out against Longshanks. He would hear my name and he would remember. My tongue went to the place in my mouth where the tooth had been knocked loose—a hollow reminder of that day. I remembered the bench smacking against my jaw, the tang of blood, the tooth wet in my palm.

WE ENTERED THE GREAT hall of Stirling Castle. Great beams of oak glowed golden in the fading light of sunset. A row of tall, narrow windows lined one wall and on the opposite were intricate paintings of the earth's bounty: plump clusters of grapes and golden bundles of wheat. A handful of English lords and barons parted before us as Bishop Lamberton made his way down the center of the hall; I stayed ten paces back. King Edward of England sat rigidly upon his throne on the dais. He, too, looked as if he were painted there. Or perhaps carved from stone, for surely that is what his heart was made of.

Bishop Lamberton had given me clear orders earlier: do not speak, keep my head down, do not look at the king and if spoken to defer all responses to the bishop.

The first thing I did was raise my head and gaze into Longshanks' icy eyes. The look he returned was one of annoyance mixed with indifference. He had no idea, as yet, who I was.

I now hated him more than I did that day in the hall of Berwick, when my father had knelt before him and spoken false promises. Father had died in the dungeons of the Tower, put there by Longshanks' orders. He had been beaten and tortured to extract information. My stepmother had nearly been raped by one of the king's men. My brothers sent into hiding. My lands taken from me. The pride and dignity stripped from my kinsmen. King or no, I *hated* the man. I felt a drop of blood on my tongue as I bit back my anger.

"What business brings you to Stirling, your grace?" Longshanks questioned. "Word from the council at Berwick?"

"No, sire. Another matter." Lamberton dropped his chin. "I come to request a courtesy."

"In what matter?"

"On behalf of my squire, my lord." Bishop Lamberton turned and lifted a hand toward me.

"The wheels of our kingdom do not grind to a halt to indulge mere squires. Put your request in the form of a letter and the matter will be addressed . . . as time permits."

"I beg you, indulge me but a minute sire. It will take no longer. The resolution of this issue is long overdue. Five years ago, Sir William Douglas died while under your arrest. His son, my squire James Douglas, was a minor at that time, pursuing his studies in Paris. His family lands were later granted to Sir Robert Clifford. I ask for the return of those lands, following the laws of inheritance. He is of age now."

Longshanks rested his jaw on the ridge of his knuckles. He looked down the length of the row of lords until his sight came to rest on one particular man there.

"What do you think, Clifford?" Longshanks asked in a sardonic tone.

Sir Robert Clifford came forward. His gaze swept over me, walking in a circle about me as I kept my head still. I watched his every movement from the corner of my eye.

"I think not, sire," Clifford proclaimed. "It would be dangerous to deliver such wealth and holdings into the hands of a traitor's son. Fruit seldom falls far from the tree. This one, I say,"—he sniffed the air—"is already rotten."

Clifford was close enough to me that had they not taken my knife at the gate, I could have slipped my blade between his ribs before he ever saw my hand move. Another time. I smiled coolly at him. He took a quick step backward.

"There is your answer." Longshanks leaned more heavily on his fist, tucked his angular chin to his chest and swallowed back a yawn.

Bishop Lamberton bowed, taking a few steps backward. "I thank you, sire, for your wise judgment."

He turned and as he passed me, put a hand upon my shoulder

to guide me from there.

I pulled away. Lamberton reached for me again, but I darted from him, toward the king. The guards that flanked the ends of the dais gripped their sword hilts.

I halted and said with a shrug, "How then?"

"What? Speak up." Longshanks' lips curved into a snarl.

I raised open hands. "How then . . . do I get my lands back? I am home and yet I have no home to go to."

He straightened his back and gripped the arms of his throne with fingers that flashed with jewels. "I am old, Douglas. But my memory has not slipped away yet. I remember your father's treachery. Once—forgiven. Twice—dead. And I remember you. You have not changed, either. You are still the same surly, misbegotten spawn of that Judas Iscariot I tossed into the rotting darkness. Be happy you have your life, boy. If you want to keep it, stay out of my sight."

He brushed one of his ringed hands toward the door. "Take him away."

But before the guards could get to me, I had already turned and was on my way out with Bishop Lamberton stomping on my heels.

In the courtyard, where the pink of dusk surrounded us, the bishop dug his fingers into my arm and shook his head fiercely.

"I told you not to say anything."

"Then why did you bring me here?" I said.

If he had an answer, he did not share it. "In the morning, I will be going to Cambuskenneth Abbey to meet with the Earl of Carrick. You will go back to Berwick, James. Wait for me there."

I could but stand there, wordless, as he turned his back on me and went to find his quarters for the night. I did not join him until much later. Instead, I climbed the tower stairs to stand upon the wall walk and look out over the darkening land. All the masons and laborers were done with their duties by then. I watched them stagger drunkenly through the streets of Stirling. Some were gathering around their flickering campfires in the city of tents scattered along the Roman road to the south, perhaps to share stories. To the east, the River Forth wove like a black ribbon through the land, yearning toward the open sea.

21

Robert the Bruce – Lochmaben, 1305

TURNBERRY, WHERE I HAD wiled away much of my youth, was always closest to my heart; but it was Lochmaben, a more stately place for a rising earl and his lovely countess with its herb gardens, mews and wine cellar, that became home to Elizabeth and me. From there it was a swift ride to Carlisle, where I was often summoned—sometimes whimsically it seemed, as if to test my obedience.

Ever since the tidings of Wallace's heinous death, I had felt a dark, vaporous cloud hovering over my soul. It is a burden to grieve and be unable to reveal it. Elizabeth was my consolation. Into her open ears I poured every dream and doubt, every hope and fear. She received it all and gave back to me nothing but love and comfort. There were nights when I awoke from nightmares, sweating with fury, when I might have clutched up my sword and ridden alone to London to murder the heartless Longshanks on his throne before a hall full of councilors, but Elizabeth would say my name over and over, pull me back to bed and return me to the moment. There were days when I stood on the turrets and gazed out over the brown and dying countryside. Brisk autumn wind tore at my cloak and rain soaked into my bones as I lamented on the hopelessness of it all. Elizabeth would retrieve me to our chamber. She peeled away my wet clothes and set a peat brazier next to my chair to return the warmth to my flesh. She stroked my whiskers, and then settled into my lap. As I looked at her, nothing existed but the bewitching green of her eyes and the shining red-gold of her hair. A touch from those soft fingers and all was forgotten.

And then came a few, brief, cherished days when we believed Elizabeth was with child. She hummed and smiled like a young lass in love for the first time. I took her to bed often—morning, evening and afternoon. Afterwards, we smiled and stared long at one another. We talked of the child: whom it would look like and all that it meant to us and how many more we would have. Then I would kiss her belly and lay my head there and imagine a heartbeat, strong and full of the force and wonder of life.

One morning, I arose and, upon seeing her soundly asleep, slipped from our bed, dressed and crept to the door. I went to the stables to look in on Elizabeth's favorite mare, which was close to foaling. She paused in her feeding only long enough to investigate whose hand was running along her protruding flank. Two more weeks, I surmised. As I left the stable groom in charge of the horses, a gray mare for Elizabeth and a black for me, a messenger galloped into the courtyard, dropped from his steaming mount and placed a letter into my hands.

A summons from mighty King Edward to shatter the sunlight of my bliss into a thousand shards.

I found Elizabeth alone in her solar, curled up in a corner in her crumpled nightclothes, knees tight to her chest and tears flooding over her cheeks. Perplexed, I pulled the door shut and went to crouch beside her.

"I truly thought . . . I'm sorry, Robert. So sorry. There is no child." She buried her face in her hands.

I wrapped my arms around her and kissed the top of her head, her hair still messed and knotted from sleep. "Another time, love. You are young and strong. There is no hurry."

She wept long and hard while I stroked her hair. Outside, the rising sun poured strongly through the single glazed window, as if to say the world had not ceased to go on because of our tiny sorrow for a child that never even was.

"Shhh, shhh." The cloth on the shoulder of my tunic was soaked through with her grief. All I could do was hold her. "Elizabeth, do not think I love you less. Come with me to Christmas court at Windsor. We shall bury our sorrow along the road and feast on puddings and wine and dance till our knees give out. Come with me, love."

She pressed her tear-wet palms against my cheeks and shook her head. "Robert, no, no. You cannot go. Stay, oh, please stay. I need you. And I fear for your safety."

"Fear? What cause have you to fear? Besides, I have been commanded. To refuse to attend Christmas court, well, I would need a very good reason and I believe I have run dry of excuses, used up every last one over these past few years to frolic with you. Well worth the insult I may have caused him, but just the same . . . this time, I . . ."

Those lips that had urged such waves of passion within me trembled faintly.

"Then tell him I am ill . . . and you cannot leave me," she pled. "You have too much to lose if . . . if Comyn—"

I pressed a finger to her lips. She may as well have plucked at my heart with her very fingers. "I promised him more than Longshanks will ever even hint at. The man has no loyalty but to his purse. So I must go this once, my love. The time for me to make myself known is not yet upon us. Soon, though. Very soon. I wish to see for myself how the king fares. This court that he has conjured up is a façade, meant merely to reassure his subjects that he yet breathes."

"Stay."

"Elizabeth, you know I cannot. I *must* go."

"Then you shall go without me. I have no wish to sit among those hooded crows and feign joy. Oh, I will be sick at heart until you're safe at home again."

She turned her face toward the winter sunlight that marched boldly in through the window. The dry tears that now streaked her face with salt left marks like the beginnings of tiny cracks in shining enamel. She had taken Marjorie in and loved her like her own, wanting her own flock of bairns with a fierceness that until then I had not been aware of—mayhap in the same tenacious, foolishly impatient way that I wanted to give life to my grandfather's dream and hold it as my own. And she, who had been a pillar of stone for me, was now a fragile lamb, quivering in my arms.

I smoothed down the errant wisps of her hair, and then traced a finger down her neck, shoulder and arm until I clasped one of her hands. I brought it to my mouth and kissed her fingertips, one by one. With woeful tenderness, I turned her hand over and laid a kiss within her palm. "Ah, Elizabeth, sweet . . . My heart aches as well for want of a child, not only for us . . . but for an heir to a kingdom yet without a king."

Still gazing into the light, she said, "For you, I suppose, a man, it is about heirs and kingdoms. For me, it is all I have to give in this life. All I am."

I cupped her chin and turned her face to me. "Say that and you say a lie. You will always be the reason I will fight to live another day, Elizabeth, children or no."

I crushed her delicate frame to me, as if the ardor of my embrace might impress upon her the depth of my love for her.

22

<u>Robert the Bruce – Windsor, 1306</u>

DUE WEST OF LONDON, Windsor had all the splendor and convenience a king could fancy, without the stench and stir of the city. Fertile pastures patched with woodland surrounded the royal residence in rustic tranquility. Within the mortared walls, however, the scandal of court life teemed. I endured Christmas court in the company of the two Edwards and sundry barons of blessed England, although I would much rather have been enjoying the intimacy of my gentle Elizabeth at humble Turnberry. I was miserable without her. Even Gerald, for all his stale attempts, could not humor me. But somehow, I managed to wear my mask well and discoursed with a gaggle of English bishops with their upturned noses and glittering ringed fingers of gold. They sniffed at King Philip for quarreling with the pope, while in the next breath they intimated the pope's own iniquities in dabbling in Edward's affairs. Christmas came and went, anything but merry, and all the judgmental prelates drifted off to their parishes.

Although I yearned to return quickly home with Gerald at my side prattling away the hours, I took the road northeast to Essex, the area my father had favored, to look over the vast stretches of family farmland: rich, loamy soil deep and frozen beneath stubbled stalks of grain. All was serene and every penny accounted for. If nothing else, my father had kept a tight fist on his coffers, hiring only the shrewdest and most parsimonious of constables and stewards. There was nothing more to do, but go home to my Elizabeth. On the way, I would stop for a day, two at most, at Huntingdon and take a quick tally of affairs there.

We had not gotten as far as Cambridge, when a messenger caught up with us. Another damnable summons from Longshanks. And so, instead of a swift journey home, hearts alight with anticipation, we pressed back toward Windsor. Dread sucked at my insides. We skirted Epping Forest, hardly aware of the tall, smooth-trunked beeches around us, which stood in silent array like ladies in gowns of pale, green silk.

The business might have gone quickly, but for the king's frequent absences. Each day that I arose, I thought, hoped, prayed perhaps that would be the day Gerald would come to me with the news that Longshanks had received his final rites. Yet, it never came to pass. The king would drag himself to the council chamber, a countenance as gray as ash and eyes drooping to his jowls for lack of sleep, his cheeks hollow, a cough rattling every breath, his limbs obviously compromised for strength as he leaned upon his page to rise from his chair at the premature end of every day's session. All the while, his unavailing heir scrutinized me as if I was an orphaned lamb abandoned in an open field and he was a lion in need of a meal.

In mid-January, the king's health took a turn, sadly, for the better.

He was in such lofty spirits he called a feast. In my chamber, I laid out three of my best shirts on the bed, studied them for awhile and finally picked up the red one with the dagged edge bottom and pleated shoulders and pulled it over my head.

Gerald's mouth twisted in disapproval. "Not that one."

"Why not?"

"It's not fit for such a grand occasion. You have better." He readjusted his growing paunch beneath his embroidered tunic, fastened at the neck with two ivory buttons. When at court, Gerald was fastidious about his dress, if nothing else. It was a trait that had given him fits when we were hiding in the forests only a couple of years ago, with rarely a change of clothing, let alone any lye and tallow soap to wash with or a chamber pot to shit in. I chuckled to think of those days: Gerald mumbling every time he caught wind of his own bodily odors or distressed over a rip in his cloak.

"Better?" I remarked. "This is the shirt I married Elizabeth in."

"And how many times have you worn it since?" His forehead shrank between those expressive eyebrows and peaked hairline.

I snapped the shirt off and tossed it onto the bed. "Who needs a wife when I have you? Now, your advice?"

He tugged at his shaggy beard with a thumb and forefinger. "Hmmm, I'd wager on the green. Fine cut. Rich cloth. Aye, that's the one."

As I reached for the green silk tunic and began to pull it on, there was a knock at the door. Gerald went to open it.

"Robert!" Ralph de Monthermer held his arms wide. A warm, pleasant smile graced his lips beneath a dark moustache streaked with gray. Ralph and his kin had been close friends of my grandfather's. The bond, strained as it might have been by Anglo-Scottish relations, had never dissolved.

We embraced in the doorway. "Ralph, you look well, thin perhaps, but—"

"Been down with a fever. Nothing serious. I am well enough now."

"And things in Gloucester?"

"Ever the same."

"I have seen your stepson about—Gilbert de Clare, a handsome lad, indeed. And a fine soldier in the making, I hear. When Edward needs to call on him one day, he'll be a worthy opponent on the battlefield." And as close to the Prince of Wales as a mole on his backside.

Suddenly, Ralph's brow clouded. He leaned out into the corridor, glanced both ways, then dove back into my chamber and pulled the door shut behind him.

"A moment to speak with you." His fingers ran back and forth over the fur trim at the neck of his shirt. "Your grandfather, rest his soul, was a fine man. I was a stripling at Lewes when he saved me from one of Montfort's men. I shall never forget that."

I nodded. "That was a long time ago, Ralph."

"And I am still alive, thanks be to him and Our Father." He paced over the loose planks. Every time he turned they groaned with a secret, begging him to let it out. At last, he stopped, looked at me in a probing manner and took a deep breath. "You are not safe here."

"What do you mean, Ralph? What have you heard?"

"Rumors, whispers . . . that when they took Wallace, letters were found on his person, letters that, that—"

"Out, man! What letters?" My veins clogged with ice. There should not have been any letters yet in Wallace's possession that carried my name when the traitors took him. He had delivered them to Philip and Boniface . . . and come back by then. Might he have had one from them addressed to me that never found its way to me? But how? My heart fluttered. Ralph de Monthermer was indebted to my grandfather, but in these ever-shifting times how could I know enough of the man's character to trust that he, too, would not betray me? I gripped his arms tightly, as if to force the truth from him. "In honor of my grandfather, your friend, if there is danger to me here, say it. If you never had the chance to repay him—at least save me."

His countenance went soft, as if a tide of memories had washed over him in that moment. Ralph preferred music and philosophy to politics and war, that much I knew of him from the times he had thrown open his doors in hospitality to me. His stepson Gilbert was of a different vein. Shoulders sagging, his jaw slack, Ralph pressed his hands together, as if in a prayer for guidance.

"It bodes ill, Robert. Letters from various nobles of Scotland, suggesting your name over and over as king."

Shrugging, I relaxed my grip. "But how does that put me in danger? Because others say that? It is what Longshanks himself swore to me."

"Far from the worst of it, Robert. When I arrived here, Gilbert received me. He had a secret and could not keep it to himself. Recently, Prince Edward received a correspondence from John Comyn of Badenoch, promising to deliver proof of your treachery. The prince then told the king of it and it is that proof the king awaits now . . . and why he called you back from Huntingdon."

I spun on my heel, threw open the chest at the foot of the bed and began to cram my belongings into it. Then, consumed with urgency, I dropped my things and rummaged for my purse of coin, figuring I could make it home with that alone and the clothes on my back. "Gerald, our horses, we've no time."

"No, not yet," Ralph begged. His hands fluttered in the air as he continued to pace in tight circles. "It is yet daylight. I could have been seen coming here. And if anyone sees you leave in haste . . . they will talk. They will know. Every tongue from here to London will be wagging. The king does not yet have the letters in his possession. There is still time. I beg you—attend the feast. Excuse yourself early. Say your head aches or your stomach disagrees with something. I will linger. If there is any hint of danger, I shall send a signal of some sort through the keeper of my wardrobe, Waldhar. He is an old and feeble soul and none will think anything of him ambling about the corridors."

My heart hammered so loudly I could barely hear Ralph. What if his appearance here was a trap, meant to coax me to self-incrimination? And yet, it was all too close to the truth to be a lie.

I stopped his motion with a steel hand on his frail shoulder. "Spurs for haste."

Ralph nodded and returned, "And a shilling then, if the honor of your name has been bought and sold."

Oh, it had indeed. And I had Edward of Caernarvon and Red Comyn to thank for it. How could I have been so terribly naïve? So trusting of a selfish pig? How now to preserve myself and fly home? But first, to endure a hall thronged with lords and ladies, some of whom undoubtedly had caught wind of this all and who would gaze upon me haughtily, whispering of the false Scot who had nuzzled up to the king and been treated as his own favored son, heaped with offices and holdings and housed under the king's own roof.

Lord, Holy Spirit . . . Blessed Virgin and Savior Above . . . bring me safely through the night. See me home. Spare me. For the sake of beloved Scotland, spare me. Let me see my Elizabeth again.

IN ALL MY LIFE, I had never seen such gluttony and excess. The king himself drank from a gilded chalice studded with pearls, while those at the head table were given hippocras, a sweetened, spiced wine, in rose-colored goblets of glass. Servants ceremoniously brought forth the Great Salt in a silver saltcellar fashioned in the shape of a sleeping unicorn. Then they brought out spit-roasted lamb; herbed capon stuffed with suet, bread crumbs and saffron; fried almonds over a pudding of white rice; and a purée of apples in almond milk laced with ginger. Afterward, there were congealed sweetmeats heady to the tongue, spiced and garnished with coriander, orange peel, anise and cloves. The aromas alone overwhelmed the senses. I nibbled here and there at the offerings before me, but the impulse to flee continued to charge through my veins, distracting me at every moment.

Seated close at my right, for the hall was stuffed to the vaulted rafters with guests, was Aymer de Valence, the Earl of Pembroke and Longshanks' favored general in the field. He poked a knife at the barely touched food on my overflowing trencher. "Indulge yourself, Lord Robert. One never knows how long a time will pass before such luxuries come our way again."

His words raised an alarm for me. How much did Pembroke know of Comyn's divulgence? If the prince had told Gilbert de Clare, and de Clare in turn told Ralph de Monthermer, then how many more knew of my impending doom? Prince Edward had left his place in between courses and was dangling above the shoulder of his favorite, Piers de Gaveston, an opportunist loathed by the king from all accounts and adored and lavished upon by the prince. The prince, a perpetual sneer on those thin, pale lips of his, whispered into Gaveston's receptive ear. I thought I noticed a glance from both of them and my whole chest tightened with panic.

"You should at the least try the custard," Pembroke urged. "It is the king's favorite dish. Mine as well."

Sir Robert Clifford of Westmorland, seated next to Pembroke, leaned forward. I could smell his drunken breath as he slurred, "Too sweet, if I may say."

"And you, Clifford," Pembroke remarked dryly, as he dipped his fingers in a bowl of scented water and dried them on his napkin, "are too full of drink to hold anything down until the morning. A perfect waste of fine food."

I smiled wanly and brought a morsel of food to my mouth. I swallowed it, tasting nothing. "The cook is to be commended. I regret that . . . I was stricken with some ailment of the stomach while in Essex. It lingers yet, much to my discomfort. Everything runs clean through."

"Pity." Pembroke tilted his head of silver-black hair at me. His eyes, dark as a Saracen's, flashed at me above a curious grin. "I hope you improve soon."

Short, with little hands and small features, Pembroke compensated for his stature with both cunning and resolve. He was a shrewd man, one I would have felt security in had he fought at my side, yet one I would have faltered in courage before, had I to face him as an enemy. Longshanks had greater faith in no man than him. And he returned it with a depth of loyalty the king reveled wholly in. For that, I feared him, feared for my life even as I sat there as an honored guest in the king's hall.

Pembroke knew. He must. Perhaps they all knew and this was some contrived spectacle in which to reveal my betrayal. Would they lash me to a horse's behind and drag me through the streets of London, as they had done to Wallace, jeers and rotten fruit flung at me while the cobbles scraped the flesh from my bones? What twisted torture would the king concoct to draw out my death? Or would I languish in a lightless dungeon, rats nibbling at my flesh until I was nothing but bones and sinew? I preferred a swift death on the battlefield to either.

Between the two long side tables, the juggler flailed knives in circles through the air and balanced a long sword in the center of his palm by its point. Little dogs sailed through fiery hoops and jesters tumbled and mocked the King of France to tides of laughter. A tightening circle formed around the prince and Gaveston, as eyes darted boldly to me. I watched as if in a dream, or rather a nightmare, and weighed when to make my exit—afraid to do so too soon, more afraid to wait. As I glanced around, I noticed Clifford had disappeared.

To the left of King Edward sat his queen, Marguerite, her hair piled high and woven with jewels, her youthful body enveloped in a gown of pale cream and gold. With her blank eyes, her plain mouth and her small chin bobbing at every word that passed over the king's teeth, she looked more ornament than regal consort. The king flipped his fingers at me in salutation. I returned a nod and as I lifted my hand to reach blindly for my goblet, it toppled and a river of blood-red wine poured over a field of snowy linen.

"Earl?" Pembroke laid a hand on my upper arm. "You look pale. Perhaps you should take to your bed after all?"

An opening, at last. I pinched the bridge of my nose between clammy fingers. "Aye," I breathed. "Advice I will take." I dabbed at the stained tablecloth with a grease-smeared kerchief and pushed my chair away.

As I made toward the door, a voice cut above the clamor.

"What, Lord Robert?" The prince brought his drink to his lips and took a long draught. "Leaving so early?"

I bowed. "To bed, my lord, with a disagreeable stomach, unfortunately."

He sauntered toward me, his goblet stem pinched between his fingertips. "Well, if you think the festivities will cease without you, you are gravely mistaken." He waved a delicate hand in the air. "Play on, minstrels! Something less melancholy. We grow weary of ballads. My stepmother requests a dance."

For a moment, Marguerite's face shone like the sun, but as the music struck anew her husband merely sank deeper in his chair. He was too brimming with wine to keep step in a dance and too feeble yet in the bones to even rise from his chair. The corners of her little mouth plunged in disappointment. She shot a pitiful glance at her stepson. Scowling, the prince set his goblet down and bowed shallowly before Marguerite. Her smile watery beneath painted eyes, she rose and joined him.

As I backed away in retreat, I caught eyes fleetingly with Ralph de Monthermer. I prayed he would prove true and deliver me warning in time to be gone from Windsor and out of England for good. Next to Ralph, Gilbert de Clare—so beautiful he would have rivaled the fairest lady in the court—hugged a deep tankard and gazed dreamily into the midst of the dance. My heart faltered as Gilbert's face turned my way. *He knows, he knows. They all know.* But his eyes lacked focus; his lips were tilted in a drunken smile.

I wove my way through a snake pit of bodies, as dancers clasped hands and twined in and out across the floor. Drumbeats followed me into the corridor, pounding in my head, growing louder as they echoed through the emptiness. I shuffled through the dimly lit passageway. Two yellow, writhing shadows reared up before me. I pulled back behind the dark refuge of a column, listening for voices, watching for the glint of weapons. But all I heard nearby was the heavy panting of two lovers, stealing a moment of sin. I hid there for too long a time as they groped, their clothes rustling against one another, the wet smack of kisses eliciting groans of pleasure from the woman. Her whispers carried through the dank air, a heavy French accent—one of the queen's maids perhaps, followed by the hushed, drawling murmur of her lover.

Cursed devil, would I be trapped here forever? How long before the damning evidence arrives? Did the king have it already? Or was Comyn merely bluffing, pitting the king and I against one another?

I shivered as cold beads of sweat dampened my forehead. Further into the shadows, I shrank. The stones of the wall pressed hard against my rigid back. *Perhaps I should just scurry past them? They might not even notice.* Then I heard the lady's breath catch, the man grunting as he probed clumsily beneath her raised skirts. *Good God, could they have chosen a less discreet place?*

"Ah . . . ahhh, sooo sweet, love."

The voice had a familiar hiss to it. Creeping forward, I hugged the column and there in the dead end of the corridor adjacent to the main stair was Clifford, his buttocks bared, taking the willing French handmaiden while standing. A marvel, considering how drunk he was. Her pale hands kneaded at his sweaty flesh while her mouth hung open, stifling the cries she must have longed to release. That was not his wife and the maid herself was recently wed to a lesser knight from Cornwall. I realized I was in no danger of being revealed by either of them.

"Your pardon, my lord." I stepped forward into the wavering rushlight. "I do not wish to interrupt. Carry on."

The lady gasped when he tore away from her. I brushed past them with a shaming glance and plunged up the stairs. Behind me, I heard her begging and moments later they were going at it again— this time more arduous and less abashed, eager to peak in the ecstasy of each other's flesh, mindless of the vows they had spoken on some other forgotten day with some now forgotten mate.

When I reached the door to my chamber, I looked down the length of the dark corridor and keened my ears. The animal sounds of Clifford and his vixen had ceased. Far, far away, I could still hear the strumming of strings and the rhythm of the tabor. I nudged the door open. Then it was flung wide by Gerald and he yanked me in. A single tallow candle resting on the window sill lit the room.

"I was beginning to wonder about you," Gerald admonished with a grimace as he drew the bar across the door.

"Ralph's man?" I queried.

"Come and gone." He held out his hands and dropped into my palms the spurs and a handful of coins. "You had no sooner left than the king, in drunken state, poured out his intention to arrest you as soon as the evidence was brought forth."

Betrayed by Comyn, one of my own.

"Your cloak, m'lord." Gerald held out my hooded, fur-lined cloak as I stepped beneath it. With deft fingers, he fastened it in a single motion.

"To horse, Gerald. It will be a hard ride to Lochmaben . . . if we get there at all."

"They are ready and waiting."

"Whatever would I do without you?"

"Don't think it, my lord. I will be with you until we are too old and decrepit to remember any of this."

I pounded him hard on the shoulder. Together, we stole through the passageways, avoiding all who had drifted from the drunken revelry of the great hall, across the gaping courtyard beneath a brittle winter sky, studded with starlight, and to the stables, where our horses waited with steaming breath.

23

<u>Robert the Bruce – Lochmaben, 1306</u>

FIVE DAYS FROM LONDON to Lochmaben, day and night on a lathered horse, February wind biting at my bones. Riding so long and so hard I thought I would never see the end of the road. Two more days while I sent Nigel and Thomas to Dalswinton with an urgent message, asking Comyn to meet me at Greyfriar's Kirk near Dumfries, where the council was holding sessions.

I drifted between wakeful sleep and restless pacing. Long, vacant nights wrought with muddied thoughts; short, dreary days through which I floated in a numbed haze. I kept from the hall, confining myself to my chambers, robbing Elizabeth of sleep as I wore at the planks. Back and forth, back and forth. I moved across the floor in angry, chopping strides. Turned, pulled at my hair, muttered curses.

When she could stand it no more, Elizabeth bolted from the bed and threw herself at my feet. Raising a face reddened by weeping, she clamped her arms about my legs. "Robert! I beg you—for all that is sacred, do not go."

"Do you know what he has done? Do you know?" White with

fury, I could not meet her pleading eyes. Little more than a week ago, I had wished for nothing more than to be at home holding her in my arms, renewing our love with every heartbeat, every gentle touch. But now, even my devotion to my wife had been thrust aside, my thoughts consumed with devices and schemes for revenge. My anger was so excessive wee Marjorie had run from me in tears that morning when she asked me to watch a trick she had taught her dog and I had exploded at her.

"No, Comyn will never change," I said. "Why did I think that he would?"

Elizabeth clawed at my arms and said my name over and over. Finally, she buried her face against my thigh, her breath blowing damp and hot with each anguished sob.

"I did not think at all, apparently." I tore myself from her and sank down into a thinly cushioned chair. The peat brazier next to it was stone cold. "Or maybe I thought . . . greed would overrule his hatred. Now I see differently. I am done with thinking. Done with Comyn. Enough of the bloody, life-sucking bastard. May his deceit consume him. And may the flames of hell melt his flesh from his bones for all eternity."

She struggled to her feet. Her blanket hung loosely from her shoulders, then dropped to the floor as she approached me. She knelt before me on the cold floor and pressed her hands upon my knees. "And what will you do, Robert, when you see him? Avenge yourself? To what end? How will that serve this country or your dreams of a throne?"

I looked away. "No, Elizabeth, I have turned a blind eye long enough. He laid his hand in mine and swore . . . *swore* alliance. Brother to brother. Scot to Scot. And it was all false. All of it. Every word, every breath, every drop of ink. All a trap. A lie. A damnable lie."

She pulled back, her hands clasped as though in prayer. "But what will you do? Robert, this is not who you are. You are too angry now to—"

"Will I ever be less? How many times can I allow him to attack me and do nothing? No, this must be dealt with now. Let him admit to his brazen pack of lies. With God as his witness, all will be out between us."

I had been betrayed—my life offered up for the gallows. I brushed her away and went from her—the one person who should have been able to stop me.

But my mind was made up. I would confront and condemn him and vow, then and there, that we would be mortal enemies.

And on my honor, I would let him walk away, with his life. Then, the battle would begin.

Greyfriar's Kirk, 1306

I WAITED IN THE sanctuary of God's house for the brutal traitor, Comyn. Endless, agonizing hours I waited. Every muscle taut. My temples throbbing incessantly. I paced in monotonous rhythm outside the church, up and down the icy steps, searching within and then down the road for any sign of him. Above, a crescent moon pierced a black dome, where stars glittered like diamonds in the echoing depths of a lightless cave.

"He will not come." Nigel wrapped his cloak tight around him. His breath hung in a white cloud before his pale mouth. "The day is gone. The hour long past."

Thomas leaned against the shoulder of his sorrel horse and scratched at the flecks of mud on its hide. "There's an inn next road over. Warm fire. Drink. Women." He grinned boyishly to himself.

"I'm going inside," I told them.

Nigel lurched forward, but I shook my head to stay him. His

piety and my ire would mix as well as water and hot oil. I motioned to my brother-in-law, Christopher, to follow me. Long of arm and keen of eye, he knew how to use his fists as well as his weapons. I had seen him split an Englishman in two with one swipe of his blade at a full gallop. More prudent to have him watching my back where Comyn was concerned than my future priest-brother.

"But what if the coward comes with a host of twenty or thirty or more?" piped Roger Kirkpatrick, a friend of Thomas's.

"That's why you're waiting out here," I told him.

James Lindsay, who stood next to Roger, thumbed the hilt of his dagger and nodded his willingness. They had all been innocent visitors to Lochmaben when I had stormed in there in a monstrous wrath. No friends of Comyn's, they had accompanied me to the church, eager to see what would unfold, and I hoped to protect my back. Nigel and Thomas stood mute in judgment, probably realizing no good would come of this.

The cold hush of a winter evening cloaked the world. "Send him within, when he arrives," I said bitterly. "The words I would have with him are meant for his and God's ears alone."

I lit a dozen candles upon the altar, said prayers for the souls of Isabella, my father and mother . . . and Wallace. Then I sank down next to a stone column and fixed my eyes on the Holy Crucifix.

Sleep had crept upon me—although I do not remember my eyelids drifting shut—when at last the hinges of the door creaked. The candles were burnt to stubs. Slow, heavy footfalls like dying heartbeats pounded closer. I knew without looking that he had finally come. And with a purpose no less than mine.

Christopher, who stood guard vigilantly to the side of the altar, narrowed his eyes. He shifted his arm beneath his cloak.

"I never thought the day would come," I said aloud, without turning to look, a smirk of irony tainting my words, "when John Comyn, Lord of Badenoch, former Guardian of Scotland, would sell his soul to the King of England."

His steps ceased. Another pair, more halting and heavier, followed. Slowly, I rose from the floor, still facing the altar. The cold of the column seeped into my palm as I braced against it. My ire, which had been smoldering with each drawn breath, now erupted into flames as I turned around. Behind Comyn stood his uncle, Sir Robert Comyn—a man well into his years, but one who had seen more brawls and battles than I.

"What? Bruce, I confess there is madness in your eyes and words," Red Comyn drawled. "What do you want with me and why here? I have business to attend to at Dumfries and no time for your babbling."

The light within was dim, wavering streaks of orange cast by short wicked candles. Comyn's countenance gradually drained of color. He stood tensely, arms stiff at his sides, not daring another step.

Everything poured out of me—every drop of hatred, every shred of injustice—everything crying out for revenge. Reason was as remote from my conscience as the stars from the earth. I moved into the aisle to face him squarely. The floorboards groaned ominously beneath my shifting weight. From the corner of my eye, I saw Christopher inch forward.

"Letters were found when they captured Wallace. You linked me to them. Told Longshanks of our pact. Sold my name to the very devil himself and all . . . all for what? Spite? Greed? Certainly not glory! Even less for love of your country." I reached wide, lost for understanding. "Is it even remotely possible you could put aside your hatred of me and my kin for the well being of this land and its people? Does any of that matter to you? Or do you despise me so completely you would court your own ruin to see me dead?"

He tugged at his riding gloves finger by finger as calmly as if he had heard not a word of my unleashed fury. Then he tossed them to the ground and swaggered toward me, thrusting his big, overfed belly before him. "Maybe I did it for sheer humor? Do you think I cherished every day I was forced to sit beside you in council meetings while you spewed out your lofty lineage? You call yourself in the right whether you stand across the battlefield from Longshanks or beside him. Who is the traitor, I ask? Bloody whoreson Bruces— no better than any of the rest of us, though you think yourself gods. Gladly would I burn in hell alongside you for all eternity . . . if I could keep you from the throne."

With a macabre smile on his twisted mouth, he charged at me. I saw the glint of a dagger and instinctively drew out my sword. I held it straight out, but only to warn him off. I thought surely that at any moment he would step aside, pull back, stop, something. But he kept coming and then . . . my sword plunged deep into his big, round belly. The slurp of a blade parting soft flesh mingled with Comyn's grunt. His knife clattered to the floor. The shock of his weight slammed up my arm. I let go of the hilt. Comyn tottered, jaw agape, and then crumpled. He clutched at the double-edged blade with bloodied fingers, too consumed in agony to cry out for help.

I reached out, wrenched the blade loose and dropped to my knees beside him.

In that same moment, Christopher lunged forward as Sir Robert leapt toward me. In the swift scuffle that followed, a scream was cut short. Comyn's uncle dropped dead before me. Christopher snatched back his knife, then nudged at the lifeless Sir Robert with his boot.

"Merciful Father, no, no. Please, nooo," I moaned.

This was not supposed to be. Not like this. Not here. Not now. I had called Comyn here trusting he would never do something so rash, but how could I not have protected myself? *He made me do this—to raise my hand against him in a holy place.*

Red Comyn glared at me as if through a heavy fog. A crooked

line of blood trickled from the corner of his mouth and into his beard. His lips parted to a gurgle. He swallowed back the blood and coughed weakly.

He drew breath and I leaned in closer, pressing my hand across the wound to try to stop the river of blood.

He clamped both hands around my forearm. "In hell, Bruce."

His hands fell away. He closed his eyes and just when I thought he had stopped breathing altogether his chest rose and fell again. Christopher's light touch brushed my back. My knees shook as I stood. I picked up my weapon with slick, blood-soaked fingers and looked around. A host of angels, carved wooden figures perched up high along the length of the nave with wings outspread, gazed down at me in judgment.

"Robert, Robert," Christopher pled, "come. We must be gone from here."

And leave them? One dead; one dying?

"My lord? Christopher?" Roger Kirkpatrick called from the doorway. "What happened? I thought I heard—"

I staggered past Christopher, spurred by the terror of my crime. Left and right I wove, blinded by tears of madness, down the central aisle. Christopher trailed after me and shoved Kirkpatrick outside, slamming the door shut behind us.

Nigel seized the sword from my hand and gazed at my crimson palm in shock.

"Robert? What . . ." His face blanched, Nigel pressed my fingers into a fist, as if to hide the evidence of my sin. "Is he—"

"I . . . I confronted him with . . . with his lies." I was shaking violently, a man who had seen battle, bodies half-hewn and piled in bloody heaps upon the muddy ground. But this, dare I think it, murder in God's house? True or not, they would say it. Condemn me. And all my dreams would be but ashes blown away by stormy winds. *Oh, Lord. What have I done?* I leaned upon Nigel and pinched his shoulders with my blood-wet fingers. "He came at me then. I only meant to stop him, Nigel. I did not mean to harm him. Believe me, *please*."

Nigel touched my face. His fine mouth twisted with words that would not come out. There was comfort in his dark eyes and even a trace of forgiveness. *Ah Nigel, you will make a fine bishop one day. Do not judge me too harshly. I am not a man of God, like you. I am flawed and from this day forward the proof is upon me for it. The blood is on my hands.*

He stroked my cheek and suddenly I became aware of the iron smell of blood. It came from me.

"Is he dead?" Nigel asked.

The others pressed in close. Silence resounded. God himself must have leaned down from the heavens to see if I would speak the truth.

"His uncle is dead." I glanced at Christopher, who wore his shame plainly. Eyes downward, he crossed his arms over his chest. There was blood on the top of the scabbard of his sword, blood on his shirt and drops of it above his knees. I swallowed. My words were like boulders of guilt that I could hardly nudge over my tongue. "But Comyn, I think, heaven have mercy . . . I have wounded him. I do not know if he yet lives."

I searched their faces, but there I saw nothing of reproach or repulsion. Nigel's lips whispered prayers of forgiveness.

"If he yet lives," came Roger Kirkpatrick's voice from the top of the stairs, "I will finish him for you."

"Roger, no!" Nigel screamed.

But it was too late. Roger was well ahead of us all. My brothers scrambled after him as they flew into the church. Their rapid footsteps clattered through the cold, brittle air. I could not move. I did not want to know or witness what I could not prevent. Comyn, if he had not already claimed his last breath, would die by my hand. *Merciful God, what had I done? Why couldn't I stop it from happening?*

Why hadn't I heeded Elizabeth, bowed to sensibility, waited? Christopher stepped up to my shoulder, his mouth agape like mine.

I turned to him and laid a hand on his shoulder. "You saved my life."

He grasped my arm. "And you had to save your own, as well. This is none of your doing."

"But . . ." I bunched his cloak in my fingers, pulling him closer, "how will anyone know?"

Before he could say anything, if there was anything he could say, Roger emerged, knife flashing in his hand, and dashed to his horse.

"Done," he growled, gritting his teeth. He shoved the knife back into his belt. "He will never stand in your way again."

How could I tell him this was not the way I had meant it to be? This was not loyalty, it was stupidity, madness.

As Nigel and Thomas descended the church steps, I could see the panic plain on their countenances. Nigel came to me.

"What now? Where to?" Nigel questioned.

Thomas grabbed the reins of his horse from where it was tethered. "Act swiftly, brothers, or they will have an army after us and I am not about to stand here waiting for them to arrive."

James Lindsay and Christopher were soon up on their mounts, their reins clenched impatiently, their spurs catching the glimmer of snowlight. The horses tapped at the packed snow with their hooves and tossed their heads in anticipation.

Christopher leaned over his horse's neck. "Robert? We need to act first. Where to?"

For a moment, my mind was blank, my heart still gripped with terror and disbelief. It was as though I had dove into a frozen lake and when I came up there was nothing but ice above me. I heard my name over and over. I saw their faces, silver-pale like specters from the otherworld, beckoning me to yield to nothingness. But slowly, I returned. Their voices grew clearer. Then, I heard other, unfamiliar voices from further down the street—townspeople arriving to take inventory of what had happened—and that shock brought me from the edge of delusion back to the living. Aye, we had to go from there, had to act. But where, how?

"Dumfries," I muttered. "Then . . . Glasgow."

Nigel and Thomas glanced at each other and then Thomas was the first to put spurs to his horse. As I rode after him, I looked back. A small crowd was running down the road toward the door of the church.

Before morning, word would spread across the countryside like the flood of Noah's day.

24

<u>Robert the Bruce – Glasgow, 1306</u>

BISHOP WISHART RECEIVED ME in the same barren room where Comyn and I had sworn to our pact. Its starkness echoed my fate. The garrison at Dumfries had surrendered almost immediately and its English inhabitants were chased back across the border. But this was not as I had planned it.

The pale, pink light of dawn surrounded the simple Crucifix on the wall. God and all the saints in heaven gazed at me in judgment, surely. If ever I thought myself a man of faith, I questioned it now. How could I ask forgiveness for what I had done? I was so full of shame and regret at that moment, I would have committed myself to a monastery if I thought Longshanks himself would not drag me from it and hang me by my own entrails.

On bruised knees, I knelt before the bishop and kissed the hem of his robes while cold tears betrayed my tormented soul. He laid his hands upon my head.

"Your grace, forgive . . . me." I buried my face in trembling hands. Visions flooded through me—blood upon the altar, the fuller of my sword blade streaked in crimson, the last words of Red

Comyn: *In hell, Bruce. In hell, hell, hell* . . . "I have committed a mortal sin for which there is no forgiveness. I took the life of another, John Comyn of Badenoch, in a place of worship . . . upon the very altar of Greyfriar's Kirk."

"Robert, my son." He lifted my chin with a single, stout finger and gazed into my eyes with endless sympathy. His head tilted sideways as he shook it. "I can scarcely believe it was ever your intention to do harm. Tell me."

"I cannot, in my heart, say that is true, your grace. Comyn betrayed me to Longshanks. Rage consumed me. I called for him to meet me at Greyfriar's Kirk. He came and . . ." I turned my face aside.

"Go on."

"And when I asked him why he had sold my name to Longshanks, he came at me. I only thought—" I gasped for air. Why was this so difficult? I had not slept more than two hours at a stretch since leaving the church that fateful, bitterly cold night. My dreams and waking moments were haunted by Comyn. He would follow me to my grave, whether dead or alive. "I thought he would stop. He didn't."

"So, you defended yourself?"

I nodded.

"And if you had not, what then, Robert?"

Exhaustion swept over me. I sank to the floor. "I would be dead."

"And the future of Scotland?"

I looked up at him. His eyes, small and bright, spoke of larger things. His hands slipped to my arms and somehow lifted me up.

"God has plans men will seldom understand. For many years now, Robert, I have watched you struggle with that which you hold deep inside you. You want freedom for Scotland . . . and you want peace. But you cannot have both just yet. One must give way in order to achieve the other."

"It is all nothing now. Nothing. I have sinned and I must do penance, for all my life."

"Oh, doubtless you will, in ways you do not yet know. But for now, you live and you must go forward. You should be king, Robert. It was meant to be. At Irvine, you asked how long was long enough to wait. I had no answer for you then. You are no longer King Edward's man, but your own. There is no turning back from here. Waste not another day."

My head swam in confusion. "But what I have done . . . it will keep me from the throne. Who would want a murderer for king? No, I should go from here. I can take a ship to Norway. Hide there. My sister is Queen Dowager and if—"

"Hide? Fie. Shame the thought. Have you heard nothing?" He gripped me with a strength I was unaware he possessed. "If you had not raised your own hand in defense, you would be the dead one and we would not be speaking now. That would have left Scotland in the clutches of Red Comyn. Do you think that was God's plan? Hah, I doubt He is that merciless. Or that His humor is that twisted. You have done us all a favor. If you find relief in it, I absolve you of all transgressions, my son, and may God Himself punish me by skinning me alive if I am in the wrong, but I do not think He deems you a sinner for living to see another day. It is obvious to me he wanted you to. Besides, justice is not restricted to courts of law, Robert. At times it is brutal and raw."

For a short while, I leaned a hand against the wall. Bits of plaster crumbled at my fingertips. Muffled voices drifted up from the courtyard below. I went to the only window and looked out. There, my brothers Edward, Thomas, Nigel and a growing collection of faithful gathered, fully armed and ready. They numbered over fifty now, not including those we had left along the way. We had taken the castle at Dumfries with such surprise that there had been no bloodshed at all.

"Those men down there," Wishart said, shuffling to my side, "do they think you a murderer? No, they look at you and they see their king. They would follow you into the bowels of hell to prove it. Years ago that's what you hungered for, but didn't have. Now you do. Will you cast away their faith because of your own self-doubt?"

I wiped a cold, cracked hand across my mouth. My beard had grown ragged. My hair hung down into my eyes. In two weeks' time, I had pulled my belt several inches tighter. "You say . . . that I should shed my guilt because it serves no end? In the name of all that is holy, how? I took a life in God's house. Committed sacrilege. I have no hope of heaven."

Wishart pounded a fist on the wall and I startled. His fat cheeks flamed scarlet. "Go to Norway then. Live there in a puddle of guilt, safe and far away across the North Sea, and forever wonder what could have been, what might have been, while you hear of England's rape of Scotland. Let all you have striven for crumble into dust while King Edward croons and bleeds us dry."

Ah, Wishart, my cherubic ecclesiast, you deal me a greater guilt than God's by calling to question my loyalty to Scotland.

I scratched at the frost on the window to see the men in the courtyard more clearly. "Your words are like wine on an open wound. They burn and cleanse all in one."

"I do not grovel, Robert. It is demeaning and in contrast to my nature." He shooed me away from the chest beside me, lifted its lid on rusted hinges and dug within. Velvet and silk spilled over the edge. From beneath them he produced a circlet of gold and held it in his old, shaking hands.

"When King Edward stole the Stone of Destiny and the coronation crown, I hid these things. Not near as grand, but they belonged to King Alexander and he used them in matters of state.

This circlet was upon his brow when he was found, sadly, dead at the foot of the sea cliffs. It is yours, if you will have it."

Extending a finger, I traced the gold filigree and heard the sound of my own sigh, floating on the frigid air. "Will the Church, the Scottish Church, will they follow suit—uphold your absolution of me? Is it possible?"

He bent and lifted the folds of velvet, laying the circlet protectively inside the chest. "Lamberton will and between the two of us, we carry a good weight, if I may so boast. If you swear an oath to defend the Scottish Church against the interference of England and rid us of their pilfering prelates, I dare predict you will find yourself with a host of holy followers."

The corners of my mouth curved into a slight smile. "An army of monks? Perhaps we should battle Longshanks by cudgeling him with the Holy Gospel?" The morning sun through the window warmed me and the world took on brighter hues as fingers of sunlight parted the clouds and touched the land.

"There's the spirit, Robert." Wishart hobbled over to the table, where he had leaned his walking stick of polished walnut. "You will find a way, *Deo volente*."

In the few years since he was released from his imprisonment, I had witnessed his gradual decay. His sight had faded so that he could not recognize me until I was two arm lengths from him. His joints troubled him, apparent in the stooped manner in which he walked, the way he struggled to rise from his chair, and the ease with which he tired. He pressed his full weight upon the burled knob handle of his stick. "Hungry?"

For the first time in many days I felt the rumble of my stomach. "Aye," I admitted, "but for more than bread."

He cuffed me lightly on the arm and winked. "Come then. We'll see what we can do."

25

James Douglas – Berwick, 1306

WHEN BISHOP LAMBERTON WAS called to preside over a council at Berwick, I had no choice but to go with him, despite that it was the last place I wished to be. We rode the miles at an unhurried pace, all seeming peaceful. Snow ran in ragged lines of melting drifts over the rolling farmland of the borders. A bold sun parted cumbersome clouds, lighting the land with shafts of amber light. Shaggy cattle lifted their heads to watch us pass, while sheep scattered from our path. Along the way we heard rumors, many of them, about the Earl of Carrick. Lamberton, however, never discussed it openly, never forced his pace; in fact, he never decided anything without long contemplation. His pragmatism nettled me.

At Berwick, Longshanks' envoys surrounded him. They pried and probed for information about Bruce, but he showed no reaction or divulged anything.

Tedious weeks later, the bishop called me to him.

He was reclined in his high-backed chair at the long table of his library. The smell of old parchment, leather and soot choked the air. A pile of documents sat untouched in front of the bishop. A snuffed candle of beeswax, meant for sealing documents, cooled nearby on the table. The ink in his inkwell was full to the top, the quill lying clean beside it. I began to bend my knee to kneel before him, but he waved me off and then pointed to the bench nearest to me.

Tentatively, I sat down. The length of the table yawned between us. Only a smoking oil lamp shed any hint of light in the dusty confines of the windowless room. I glanced momentarily at the bishop, who was rubbing his temple with a forefinger, and then stared into the yellow flame of the lamp. His voice startled me.

"You have heard," he began slowly, gathering breath, "of Lord Robert's actions at Greyfriar's Kirk? Of his seizing of castles in the southwest: Ayr, Rothesay, even Comyn's own Dalswinton? His open defiance of King Edward?"

I laced my fingers together and nodded. "They say Angus Og of the Isles promised him galleys. I hear others have joined him, as well."

"And what would you think if such a man were to become King of Scotland?" he asked.

The flame, which moments before had seemed so small as to be on the verge of extinction, flickered and grew, consuming its fuel now ravenously and throwing brightness into every corner.

Bishop Lamberton's chair groaned as he shifted in it, awaiting an answer.

I raised my chin and looked at him squarely. I remembered the earl there in my father's hall many years ago, denouncing his fealty to England. And even when I later learned he had returned to Longshanks' embrace, I knew it would not last. At times, men say and do things against their conviction, if only to preserve themselves to fight another day. My father had done so.

"I would serve him with all my heart," I declared.

"And if King Edward had not refused you your inheritance,

what then?" He leaned forward. A stack of maps and parchment between us fluttered at his movement. "If you had Douglas back, by Edward's grace, would you feel the same still?"

"I can take my lands back myself, if need be," I said, the muscles across my stomach tightening, "but I can never bring back my father. I was here, in Berwick, ten years ago. I heard the screams, smelled the blood, saw little bairns limp and lifeless in their mothers' arms . . . Need you ask?"

He pushed back his chair, came to me and laid a hand on my shoulder. "Lord Robert will soon leave for Scone where he will receive the crown at the Abbey there later this month. It is impossible for me to abandon council business here of a sudden. Too many eyes upon me. I shall send you to Lord Robert with a message that I will depart when I may safely do so and join him for the coronation. Ride swiftly, James. Let no army deter you. And give my message to no man but Robert the Bruce."

I rose from my bench, knelt and kissed his hand.

"On my life and my honor," I swore.

Lochmaben, 1306

THE VERY NEXT DAY, in the silver hours that precede dawn, I rode out from Berwick on the road to Lochmaben on the bishop's best horse, a snowy gray with a flaxen mane. The message I carried was written nowhere but in my heart. Days were yet short this time of year and so I rode on into the night, guided only by moonlight reflected in puddles on the muddy roads.

Twice the next day I encountered detachments of English soldiers, no doubt scouring the countryside in search of the very man I was going to meet, but it proved easy enough for me to swing far from their path, plunge into the woods and emerge later without ever being noticed. It was an English custom to be as bloody obvious as possible. It was not a Scottish one.

By mid morning of the second day, a persistent mist began to fall from the sky, melting away the last traces of snow and soaking me to the bone. Mud spattered every inch of my mount. His glorious tail was a matted clump. His muscles trembled with exhaustion and yet he forged on through the rain and the dark at my bidding. I reached Lochmaben just short of midnight, my nose dripping and a cough rattling my chest. I nearly exhausted myself trying to convince the garrison captain of who I was and that I carried a message meant only for the ears of Robert the Bruce. Finally, I was told the earl had left the previous day, but in consolation I was given hospitality. I slept, or tried to, on a pallet of musty straw by the great hearth. The links of my new chain mail hauberk, a gift from the bishop for my endeavor, were already beginning to rust.

By the time the bells of the nearby church rang lauds, I was dressed in my still damp clothing and given cold pork dumplings and a pint of cider to invigorate me. Servants and visitors, still deep in slumber and wrapped in blankets or cloaks, lined the floor of the great hall of Lochmaben. At my rising, one old man lifted his head to spit in my direction, mumbled and went back to sleep. A servant shuffled quietly in and stoked the hearthfire before adding new logs. Even though I was reluctant to leave my dry blanket and a warm fire, the drumming of my heart beckoned me on with my mission.

The hinges of the door nearest the dais creaked and a lady entered. From her shoulders hung a plain, gray cloak, although beneath it she still wore her nightclothes. At her knee, a large, wiry-coated hound whimpered. It curled around to gaze up at her and she scratched one of its long, sandy-colored ears. A thick plait of dark reddish-brown hair wound down the lady's back. Her round eyes glistened like light playing off the waves of a stormy sea as she looked toward me.

I felt the blood rush hot to my face and cast my eyes down. I had spent far too much time in the repressed air of a bishop's household not to be affected by the nearness of any woman, let alone one so beautiful, even in such a plain state of dress. I was nearly twenty now and more chaste than some monks I had known—many Scotsmen my age had already married and sired a small brood of children.

She approached the end of the trestle table by where I stood.

"They told me you are James Douglas, Bishop Lamberton's squire. I am Lady Elizabeth." She glanced over her shoulder and called softly into the shifting darkness, "Marjorie?"

At first there was only silence. Then Elizabeth called the name again. Somewhere, between a pair of tables where a column rose to the ceiling, a faint sound arose like the stirring of a mouse. The dog whined, then swished his long, thin tail back and forth. A little girl, of ten years or so, peered at me from behind the column, twisting her fingers in her long yellow curls. She flashed a smile and scampered forth, dragging a piece of clothing behind her.

The countess took the garment from the girl. "Tsk, Marjorie. You know better. This was clean when I told you to fetch it, wasn't it?" She shook the dust from it and then held out the finely woven cloak to me. "Not entirely clean, perhaps, but dry and warm. Someone will bring you food shortly to carry you on your way. Tell Lord Robert . . . my husband, that I wish him well and ask forgiveness for my cross words. I-I-I . . . I meant them not."

Her voice cracked. The countess could not have been much older than me. Her eyes shimmered with woeful tears that reflected the firelight. She sniffed and tried to smile, but the effort produced only a frown.

As I reached out to take the cloak from her outstretched hands, I heard a low rumble from the dog's throat. His lip twitched.

I drew my hands back slowly.

"Coll, fie," little Marjorie uttered. The dog dropped its head and slunk behind her.

"You have a loyal friend," I said, recalling how Fingal used to follow me everywhere and bravely watch over me as I courted mischief. Fingal would be long dead by now. He was empty in the eyes and deaf as a tree stump when I left home.

"Egidia Stewart gave him to Marjorie as a pup," Elizabeth said. "Shamelessly, he has become more of Robert's dog than he ever was hers. 'Noble Coll' he calls him, although the dog seems more stubborn than noble to me. I have to lock him in the kennel when Robert leaves. The one time I didn't he followed the road Robert had taken, trailed him all night and caught up with him the next day. Robert had to send a man back with the silly dog on a rope. Fortunately though, when Robert's not about, the dog's content enough with us. Here, please, take this. You'll need it."

"You are too generous, my lady." I lifted the cloak over my shoulders. Its hem was hand-embroidered with gold thread and black cord was stitched in intricate patterns over its deep red cloth. It was a lord's cloak and I was completely unworthy of it. I fumbled with the clasp of silver fashioned in the shape of two knotted snakes.

Rescuing me from futility, the countess fastened it with slender but deft fingers. "You must be exhausted to have arrived so late and be leaving so early."

I stiffened when her fingers brushed my chest and she quickly pulled her hands back. Coll peeked at me from behind Marjorie with his big, black eyes, taking measure of me. His tan eyebrows jumped up and down as he studied me from head to toe.

"Not half as much as my horse . . . the bishop's horse, I mean. I fear that he may be too spent to carry me with any speed, or much further."

"I already asked the stable hands to ready one of mine for you. Morel."

I took a step back, uncomfortable with such generosity when I had done nothing to earn it. "I cannot. It is too much."

"And should I have you standing over a dead horse on a deserted road? Take it. Carry my message to my husband and the bishop's, as well. You're not far behind, but if you leave now and follow the road to Lanark, you may well find him. Godspeed."

I bowed to her, but before I turned to go, I asked her one thing. "Have you heard anything of my brothers? Their names are Hugh and Archibald Douglas."

She tilted her head, as if sifting through thoughts. Then her long lashed eyes narrowed and she nodded. "Aye, I think . . . aye, they have oft been at Rothesay in the company of my cousin, Walter Stewart. He would be close to them in age."

I wanted to snatch up her hand and kiss it, but I could only manage a fleeting smile. I turned, plucked up my sack and pulled from it a letter, tattered from my rushed and hard journey. "Will you see they get this?"

I entrusted it into her care, confident that at last I would hear from Hugh, or more likely by now Archibald, and soon I would see them again. After so many years, finally.

Lanark, 1306

ON A FRESH HORSE, I rode hard on the north road along the River Annan and then on toward the Clyde. My will was tested as I flew past the road that led off to Douglas Castle. If I went there now, I would find only Englishmen, eating from my table, sleeping in my room, stabling their horses where I had passed my youth with Hugh beside me and Fingal at my heels. The rain had relented, but a gray, windless sky kept everything wet. I was somewhere near Lanark when I finally caught sight of what I assumed was the earl and his company. With reckless enthusiasm I sped along the road, the hooves of my horse slapping mud onto the rich cloak flaring from my shoulders.

A swarm of weapons greeted me. I jerked back on the reins barely soon enough to keep a spearhead from plunging into the breast of my mount. A dozen or more mounted men in chainmail surrounded me, backed by a small army of roughly equipped footsoldiers. My horse danced nervously. She reared and I gripped my legs tight to stay on.

"Make way!" I commanded. "I have messages for the Earl of Carrick."

One of the men dropped from his saddle and pushed the others back with a punch of his gloved fist. A long mustache covered his mouth and matching bright red locks of hair strayed from beneath a battered conical helmet. "Drop your weapon." He smiled to show missing teeth and drew his sword. "Unless you want to swallow mine."

I tossed my sword to the muddy ground and as I reached for my knife—the one my father had given me on the battlements of Berwick during the siege—a spear tip pricked the vein in my throat.

"I'll take that one," the red haired man said.

"And you'll give it back when you hear who I am," I told him.

"Perhaps." Taking hold of his bent noseguard, he readjusted his helmet and grinned. He reached up, slid the knife from my belt and tossed it to a tall, dark-eyed knight standing behind him. Then he snagged the hem of my cloak and yanked me from my saddle. I landed with a 'thump' on the soggy ground.

"Gerald?" The tall knight holding my father's knife elbowed a portly squire beside him. "Do you recognize that cloak?"

Gerald twisted his bushy brows into a knot, shuffled to me and laid a thick finger on the clasp. "Indeed I do."

I pushed myself to my knees and gazed at the tall knight. How could I not have known instantly? At once I bowed my head in obeisance. "My lord earl, I am sent from Berwick by the Bishop of St. Andrews."

"Of course. We'll get to that. First, how did you get my cloak?" Then the earl studied the dark roan mount that had carried me from Lochmaben. "And Morel? This bears explaining."

"Your wife, the Countess Elizabeth," I began, my head still lowered, "she gave them to me to use not two days past."

"And how are we to know you did not steal all these things?"

"Would I be here if I had?"

"He has a point there," Gerald said.

"True enough," agreed the earl. "Go on then."

"She says that . . ." I looked up and was overcome with awe of his towering height, "that she did not mean her cross words. That she is sorry for them and wishes you well and good."

He hardened his countenance, as if smote with embarrassment over the private nature of my message. "Ah, well, wives are never joyful to see their menfolk depart. Isn't that so, Boyd?"

"Don't know 'bout that," Boyd, my surly interrogator, admitted. "Mine seems happy to see me go and I'm even happier to leave after being harangued and badgered by the witch for a fortnight. This scar by my right ear is from our last quarrel. These two teeth knocked out by a flying bowl during our first." He drew a line from his ear to his missing teeth. His half-empty mouth gaped open and with a guffaw he snapped it shut.

"And which of the two of you looks the worse?" someone shouted.

"Och, I would never, *ever* strike a woman," Boyd protested. "All part of the dance. I suffer her fury and she bears my children. Eight of them now with Murdo's arrival. We make up splendidly."

Laughter rolled in waves through the men.

Lord Robert stomped his foot once to halt it. "Enough. Now, you," he said to me, trying to divert attention, "name and business?"

"James Douglas, my lord, squire of Bishop—"

"*Wee* James?" He came to me, bent over and studied my face closely.

"Once," I said.

"Aye, no more. How old are you now? Sixteen, seventeen?"

"Twenty."

"Indeed?"

I shrank within my muddied cloak. I knew I did not look my age. Probably I never would. "I am Bishop Lamberton's squire and he—"

"Paris. Did you learn anything there?" he interrupted again.

I sighed inwardly, frustrated at his casual nature. "A great deal of French, some Latin, and how to cut a merchant's purse from his belt and disappear into a crowd before he ever noticed it was missing."

He nodded with interest. "Sly. A bit like your father. A good man. I admired him." He straightened and handed my knife back to me. "You were saying?"

"Thank you, my lord." I tucked the knife back into my belt. "The bishop sends word that he could not leave Berwick immediately. But he will be in Scone on the appointed day . . . to see you crowned."

"Good then, if all falls out as it should, I should like to have him there." He walked a few feet away, lifted my muddy sword and handed it back to me. "On your feet now. Back to Berwick for you then?"

As I stood to sheath my sword, the mire sucked at my boots and I had to pull them free before I could move from my spot. My leggings were thoroughly soaked, not to mention sagging in a rather unflattering fashion, and my cloak, the earl's cloak, was a terrible mess. Lord Robert was already headed back to his horse and I followed him every step through the crush of curious soldiers. "If you would allow, I should like to serve you, my lord. My father's lands, they were given to Sir Robert Clifford and I want to join you, so I might one day get my home back and bring my brothers and step-mother there."

As his squire Gerald held his stirrup, the earl put his foot in and hoisted himself up. His armor was like the chain mail I had on and he was dressed no better than any of his knights.

"Ah, I see," he said, looking down at me. "And if by serving me you get your lands back, what do I get from you in return?"

My hand crept over my heart. "I shall serve you, my king, until my final day, through all fortune—good or ill. And I vow to be your ablest and most faithful knight."

He looked about him and guided his horse so they were again headed northward. His men cleared way and began to fall in behind him. Over his shoulder, he said, "Some here would challenge you for such honors."

Gerald snorted from behind his forearm and then muttered as he took his own saddle, "A right grand oath, coming from a mere squire."

"Come along then, good James," the earl said, lifting up his reins. "If you've half the mettle of your father you might be an asset to this company."

Boyd and Gerald exchanged glances as they pricked the flanks of their horses with their spurs. I stood there wet and growing colder as two by two they passed me by. Above, the sun struggled to break through, but clouds in sheer numbers overcame it. I scraped the mud from my knees and turned to find my horse, which had by then drifted off the road to graze on the first tender shoots of springtime.

<u>Scone, 1306</u>

ON THE 25TH DAY of March in the year 1306, the highest clerics and lords of the land assembled at the Abbey of Scone to witness the crowning of Robert the Bruce as King of Scots. The bishops of St. Andrews, Glasgow and Moray were there, as well as the earls of Lennox, Mar, Menteith and Atholl. For the first time I saw all of Robert's brothers gathered together before me: proud Edward with his roving eye, fair Alexander the noted scholar, staid Nigel and young Thomas who could barely endure the length of the ceremony. Behind the throne hung a silken banner of scarlet lilies and a golden lion. From Robert's broad shoulders, a velvet cloak of blue flowed to the floor. When the crown, a simple circlet of gold, was placed upon his head, Robert cast his eyes heavenward and whispered a prayer and a word of thanks to the Lord.

Some said Robert the Bruce had murdered a man: Red Comyn of Badenoch. Some said it was to save his own life, that when Comyn came, he meant to kill the Bruce. Others said it was not Robert the Bruce who ended Comyn's life, but one of his men. Who thrust the blade into Comyn's chest was not the matter. What mattered was that it had happened in a house of God: Greyfriar's Kirk. Ill portent for one who had clamored so long and so loud for his right to the throne. But hungering for a champion, men had gathered about him who were holy, sage or skilled in arms and because of that he had swept through the southwest and ascended the throne.

Upon hearing of Robert's coronation, Longshanks called on his knights to gather at Westminster in May. From there they would march on Scotland. It was exactly the delay King Robert was counting on.

There are some who say God has no hand in the affairs of men. But those who believe in kingship would declare that not to be so. I, for one, believe the Almighty put Robert the Bruce here for good reason: to teach us the cost of freedom and to humble the bloody English.

26

James Douglas – Kildrummy, 1306

EVEN WHEN I WAS in Paris, if I closed my eyes I could see the Lothian hills of my boyhood: green swells brushed by the gentle wind, a golden eagle soaring above. If I listened, I could hear the murmur of winding rivers that emptied into deep lochs. I thought it beyond beautiful, that nothing could compare. I think now that I was wrong, for to traverse the Highlands was to shrink beneath the vastness of the sky. As we moved in the purple shadow of the heathery mountains, it often seemed heaven and earth would meet somewhere, just beyond the next rise.

From Scone, our ever-growing army went on to Moray. There David, the Bishop of Moray, had rallied an impressive host to our cause. Robert believed he could gather more loyal men in Atholl and Mar, and so we turned south and east again. Alliances were so layered, it was a hazard to bargain for fealty. Where one chieftain or lord might swear a blood oath to stand by the new king, there was no guarantee his kith or kin would do likewise. But Robert, ah, he was a man of reckless faith. You either supposed him a fool or admired him for it.

Whenever Robert fell back in the column to talk with his men, Edward Bruce was quick to take the lead. Edward believed, by all appearances, that to lead all you had to do was burst to the fore. Robert understood otherwise—that you led from within. Nigel and Thomas had been stationed at Kildrummy, which Robert intended to make his base in the northeast. Shortly after the coronation at Scone, Alexander had been dispatched to Lochmaben to secure matters there.

We were well past the Spey and bearing down on the River Don, just upstream of Kildrummy, when lowering clouds pushed their way across a clear sky. Thunder rolled over the land—faint, at first, then strong enough to shake the ground. A blast of cold wind tossed my hair over my eyes. As I reached up to rake it away, lightning stabbed through the clouds and cracked like a whip on the earth a hundred feet away. My flesh tingled. Morel's ears flattened. Her head dipped sharply. The shock of her forelegs locking slammed through my thighs. My torso shifted hard to the right. I grappled for her mane, but my fingers slipped over, grabbing nothing. Patches of pink and gold whirled across my vision and then I struck the ground—my fall broken only by a prickly tuft of heather. Muttering curses, I rolled over, a lichen-covered stone scraping my cheek.

Drops stung at my face. Through the deafening roar, I heard Boyd's coarse laughter as he clambered down from his saddle and stuck his hand out. I flashed a sneer at him and shoved my fingers down into oozing mud, then rose to my feet. My hip ached with a fresh bruise. I called to Morel. Rain pounded against my chest and shoulders, pushing me back a step. Another rumble of thunder moved the earth and she skittered sideways. I called to her softly and crept closer, hands at my sides. For a moment, I thought she would bolt into the bleary grayness, but she remained still. Calmly, I reached out and took her reins. Over and over I said her name until her quivering hide calmed beneath my fingertips.

Once my bearings returned, I guided her toward a shallow gully to the right of our procession to escape the threat of lightning, but then thought better of it. Rainwater was collecting there as quickly as it had begun to pour down. Robert shouted to Boyd and Gerald to shepherd all the men toward sloping, lower ground. There were no caves or groves in which to hide. No village or croft within sight. It was all waterlogged land and rumbling sky. And us like mice quivering in our sodden rags, caught in the open, waiting for the end.

Cold rain slashed at my face. My fingers cramped as I held onto Morel's reins. I hugged her broad neck. When once the lightning struck close again and I flinched, Boyd smiled like a madman at me, raindrops dancing off his jumbled teeth.

He laughed. "That was nothing. Ever seen a boulder tossed from a trebuchet? It can take down a whole wall. Terrible noise— especially when you hear bones cracking under the weight of mortar."

More than you know. I looked elsewhere. Instead of bunching amongst the others or close to his horse, Robert was off from the group fifty paces, leaning against a solitary upright boulder, peering into the west. Water poured from his cloak like a waterfall. I patted Morel and guided her through the huddle of bodies and over the open expanse of soggy ground.

"Almost over, my lord?" I asked of Robert.

"It will pass, James. All storms do." He sank down on his haunches to hide from the lash of wind. "Men are born and die. Kingdoms soar and crumble. Yet still the sun rises and sets. Few things are sure, but that there will always be a tomorrow and everything that has a beginning, also has an end."

He closed the front of his cloak, as if it were any protection from the elements, hugged his knees and chuckled to himself. "I only hope this is not my end. Would not make much of a tale, would it? Robert the Bruce was crowned in March of that year. In June, he drowned in a thunderstorm atop a hill."

The daggers of rain that had assaulted us were now but gentle splatters. The rumbling had begun to fall away. "I think your tale will rival Ulysses'."

"A tragic hero, young James. I would prefer to drown on this spot, than suffer his years of wandering."

Morel nickered in my ear. She perked, looked at the road as she blinked through her long, curling eyelashes, and then nudged at my shoulder with her soft muzzle.

"I should give you back your cloak and horse," I said.

"Consider it payment toward your future services. I think I shall have need of them sooner and more often than I would like to call upon." Robert wiped the rain from his face and beard and rose to his feet. "That was fast done. I expected more after all the show."

Then his forehead creased. "Now who might that be?"

I looked to the east, where the road ahead of us led over a ridgeline. A lone rider sped over the muddy road, across a swale that was now a knee-high river and toward the little cluster of dips and gullies where we were huddled. The men by now were up on their feet.

"Friend, I assume. And someone who was expecting you," I surmised. "No foe would fly into our midst like that."

Suddenly, Robert's face lit up and he broke through the line of men in the front as they raised their spears.

"Alexander!" He threw his arms wide.

"Hail, brother." Alexander plunged from his horse. He plucked up the hem of his cloak and snapped the rain from it. "But I wish I could say we are well met."

"What news? Say naught but good, or I'll return you to your

dusty books and windowless rooms—though knowing your nature you would probably choose that over food, even if you were but one swallow from starvation."

Alexander touched his head briefly to Robert's shoulder as they clasped each other tight. "Not a time for jests, Robert. English. They . . ."

Robert stepped back, his hands firm upon Alexander's shoulders. "What?"

A long moment passed. Alexander raised weary eyes and sighed. "They have already crossed the Forth."

"Who? Who is 'they'?"

"Valence, the Earl of Pembroke. He moves swiftly. He took Dumfries shortly after you left Scone. Elizabeth was judicious enough to abandon Lochmaben and flee north. She awaits you in Kildrummy."

A MANTLE OF FOREST green drawn around her, Elizabeth stood behind a crenel of the western most tower of Kildrummy Castle. By the time we neared the gate, she had descended from her eyrie and come out over the drawbridge. Robert spurred his horse ahead into a gallop. She lifted up the hem of her skirts in both hands to run out over the muddy road. Her damp hair clung to her neck and her cloak was dark-wet with rain. As he reached her, Robert sprang from his horse and wrapped her in the circle of his strong arms like a giant cupping a dove between the palms of his hands—gently and fiercely all in one.

As his knights rode by, Robert kissed her full on the mouth and long. Uncommon conduct for a king and his queen. Having met Longshanks face to face, I could hardly imagine him doing more than giving his French bride a cold kiss on the knuckles. But that was the difference with Robert. You never forgot he was a man as much as anyone, never doubted that he hoped, grieved, toiled with despair or loved with a passion as vast as the ocean.

I stopped behind Gerald, both of us still on our horses, while we waited to receive orders.

Robert helped Elizabeth onto the saddle of his horse. Their hands caught and lingered as they stared into each others' eyes.

"Knights in the hall for the night, sire?" Gerald prodded. He glanced at me and rolled his eyes.

Robert placed his foot in the stirrup and swung himself up behind his wife. Next to him she was like a child. Delicate and small of frame, she had the pink bloom of youth on her cheeks and the bright, innocent eyes of first love. He was heavily muscled, a head taller than most men, including myself, and had the first fine lines of maturity etched at the corners of his eyes. When he held her, there was a trace of melancholy behind his pupils, as one who had loved and lost before. Gerald had told me of Robert's first wife, how she had died in childbed, and the terrible sorrow Robert had suffered.

"Aye, Gerald, the hall and a big fire in the hearth." Robert slid an arm around Elizabeth's waist. "The rest wherever you can hang them out to dry. And plenty of ale to go around . . . but ration Boyd and my brother Thomas on it, else there'll be none left for anyone else."

He pressed his whiskered face against Elizabeth's cheek, her back close against his chest, and they rode slowly on over the bridge and through the gate.

The clouds over Kildrummy laced through the sky. Above, a kestrel glided effortlessly on the summer breeze. Then she tilted her wings and went away southward. My clothes by then were nearly dry, the sun overhead growing warmer, but still I shivered.

WE WERE ALL RAVENOUS by the time supper was brought to the tables in the great hall of Kildrummy. With a swish of his hand and a lusty command, Edward Bruce gave word that we were to begin eating without the king, who was resting in his chambers. I sat at the very end of the high table with the king's rambling squire Gerald to my left. Even though the fare was not near as refined as in the bishop's house, the plates and pitchers were full and in a fleeting few minutes I shoveled away half my weight in meat alone. My lack of manners did nothing to impress the young ladies present. Rather, they were a source of elbows prodding at others' ribs followed by whispers and giggles. I had felt in more welcoming company huddled with gruff and drunken Scottish soldiers around a sputtering campfire.

Most of the men were over-full of ale and some already asleep with their heads on the table. Some snored beneath the tables. A few were still singing slurred and bawdy songs to embarrass the few womenfolk there—Robert's sisters and some serving women, the latter of which unfortunately for them could not escape an occasional playful slap on the rump. Boyd led the rounds with a sloshing tankard held aloft in one hand and a plump kitchen maid on his other arm. Gerald saturated me with stories about Robert, Robert's father and grandfather, his brothers, his queen, daughter, first wife . . . I suppose it was my own fault for asking a few questions of him here and there and then going silent as if in invitation of a monologue.

When at last the king entered the hall, Robert paused before Boyd, gave him a look of reproach, to no avail, and then sauntered past. Slumping down in his chair, he jabbed at the food on his trencher with the point of his knife.

To Robert's left, the Earl of Atholl, John of Strathbogie, who had arrived midway through the meal, raised his drink in tribute, but the king merely nodded and dropped his eyes to his plate again.

Beside Atholl, Gil de la Haye, a seasoned knight of many battles, and Sir Neil Campbell, husband of Mary Bruce, one of Robert's sisters, shrugged at each other and thrust their cups at the rafters.

"Elizabeth doing well?" Edward leaned against the table in front of his brother.

The king watched without comment as Edward sampled from his trencher. Edward had eaten little from his own serving, instead making the rounds from table to table, guest to guest, as if the gathering were on his behalf. Finally, Robert picked up his goblet, looked inside absently and set it back down. "Well as one might expect. She understands the Earl of Pembroke is a shrewd commander—Longshanks' best—and that I cannot ignore his presence so far north. Lives are at stake with each passing day."

Edward's jaws ground at a piece of venison. He licked his fingers clean and wiped them on the sleeve of his shirt. "Fragile and easily worried, poor Elizabeth."

Beside me, Gerald stiffened. He had made it more than clear to me he did not care overmuch for Edward. Further down the table, Nigel and Alexander glanced at each other and then at Robert.

"She cares for others," Robert said. "More than can be said of you."

Seemingly impervious to the barb behind his brother's words, Edward grinned. "Still seething about Aithne, are you? I have no claim on her. Once had, never the same. We shall not speak of your lady then, Robert. That would be near blasphemous. One can only imagine what wiles lie beneath that dainty exterior, what with the way you rush to her and abandon the world for hours at length."

"You should not drink so heavily, Edward," Nigel chastised. "The ale speaks for you."

Edward smiled crookedly. "Indeed not, my reverent monk. I have not had a drop of the stuff. And unlike you, when I awaken in the morning it will not be with my blanket clutched to my chest, but something warmer, sweeter and vastly more pleasing." He flipped a strand of errant hair from his forehead and took two quick, prancing steps over to his youngest brother Thomas's chair. Lowly and with implication plain in his craving smile, he said, "See that lass just come into the hall? Her name is Seònaid . . . I fancy a sampling. She has a friend you might favor. Not so much pretty, really, as . . . wickedly willing."

Draping himself across the table, Edward whispered rapidly into his brother's ear. With a heave then, he pushed himself back and strode across the room. Once on the other side of the hall, he tossed his head toward a flirtatious serving girl with flaming hair and her plainer, but equally bold friend.

Thomas threw his ale back, sprang over the table with amazing agility and joined his brother, arm in arm.

"He shall have at least one disciple in this lifetime," Alexander mused as he dabbed a hunk of his bread in butter.

"And a hundred bastards," Nigel added. "I hear the count is three already. Possibly four."

The king leaned forward and raised his voice just enough to reach me. "James," he began, "what is your impression of our brother, Edward?"

"I believe he thinks himself bigger than he is," I said in brave honesty.

A tide of laughter rippled down the length of the table. At first I could not understand what was so humorous. Then it ocurred to me just how they had all construed my words and I let it be. At the college in Paris and in Bishop Lamberton's household, such bawdy sarcasm had been frowned upon. Here it was not.

Then the king's knife clattered to the table and he shoved his chair back. The laughter tumbled away. Dressed in a gown of green velvet, the Queen of Scotland stood at the far end of the hall. A collar of fine needlework in a Gaelic pattern as old as the tombs of the Pictish kings encircled the broad neckline baring her ivory shoulders. A sash of amber silk cut high across her tiny waist. The simple headdress that hid her hair only accentuated the clear beauty of her countenance. If I thought her well-favored in the wee hours clad only in her nightgown or a plain, rain-soaked kirtle, now she appeared worthy of worship. At first I was so astounded, I barely noticed the willowy, yellow-haired girl, King Robert's daughter Marjorie, at her sleeve.

Robert rushed to them and snatched up the girl's fingers as he kissed her forehead. With his other hand on the small of Elizabeth's back, he led them both to the head of the table. Coll the hound loped alongside, licking at Marjorie's fingers. The three took their seats at the table's head and servants scurried forth with warm food. The dog squeezed beneath the table, his bony back brushing the underside, and then curled up at Robert's feet, tail thumping away. With renewed spirit, Robert greedily stuffed himself.

"How long before you go again, Father?" Marjorie asked.

"Marjorie," Elizabeth intervened, almost too quickly, "your father is a king now. You should not bother him with such small questions. He will go as needed. He'll return when he can."

Robert's hand went still. If everyone else presumed the two had spent their hours in arduous rapture, I could see beneath his clouded brow it had not been entirely so. A man's eyes, at times, say far more than a book's worth of words. Their meeting had likely been bittersweet; their passion dampened by Robert's preoccupation with the news of an English force. If any man ever wished himself king, he had but to look at Robert the Bruce just then to see what enormous burden a crown carried beneath its glittering gold and jewels.

Talk at the head table evaporated for a short while, although Gerald made heroic attempts to revive it by asking Alexander about Cambridge and life there. I looked around at the knights and soldiers who had traveled from Galloway and Annandale to Scone and onto Moray and now back to Mar. Living out of a sack and off the land, appearances and manners were apparently the first things to suffer neglect. They cursed and boasted and tossed about idle threats to each other. Their clothes went unmended and beards untrimmed. They belched and shouted and drank until they fell over. Boyd, encouraged by the gale of laughter, accounted for most of the noise. But perhaps this is what it meant to leave the sheltered confines of school life or the piety of a bishop's household and join the world of men. Absorbed with curiosity, I did not at first see the letter a servant had slid in front of me.

I read it not once, but ten times over. Finally, Gerald shook me hard by the shoulder.

"From a lass?" He winked.

"Ah, no. I have no lass." I ran my finger over the beaten edge of the letter and glanced down the length of the table at Elizabeth. She smiled at me, then returned her attention to her meal.

She had kept her promise—sent word to my family. My debt to her was ever-increasing.

"From my brother—Archibald. The youngest one. He and Hugh are safe at Rothesay, though he says Hugh has not spoken a word since I left for Paris. My stepmother, Lady Eleanor . . . she has taken the veil at an abbey. He will not say where for now." My eyes dropped to the blur of ink. I knew what had sent Eleanor to seek sanctuary from the world and I prayed she would know peace until the end of her days. Someday, I would go to Archibald and find out where she was and go to her. Gerald did not ask me more.

"Thomas Randolph? Is that really you?" Edward boomed. He abandoned his swooning maiden and bounded toward the doorway.

There stood a young man of shockingly pale flaxen hair, several shades lighter than Marjorie's, even. His eyes were such a startling blue that even at so many paces I could make out their color. He bowed his head as he looked toward the king. Robert began to rise, but Elizabeth placed a hand firmly on his forearm.

"You forget who you are now," she said to her husband.

"I forget nothing . . ." he returned, looking at her long and sincerely, "least of all who I am."

Edward extended his hand in greeting. Thomas Randolph hesitated before clasping it coolly. He made his way to the king, where he paused and looked Robert over, then bent his knee ever so slightly. He was the son of Robert's much older half-brother, also by the name of Thomas Randolph, through Robert's mother Marjorie of Carrick.

"Rise, nephew," Robert commanded. "You are welcome here."

Robert's nephew stood rigid and straight of spine. He had the Bruce height, but none of their more informal nature. "Your assumption being that I come inclined to your cause."

"Have you?"

He tilted his flaxen head. "Blood binds me."

Randolph's rigid accent revealed he had spent a fair amount of his years, though that be not a few more than mine own, south of the border.

"Ah, but in Scotland," Edward chimed at his back, "sometimes the water is thicker than blood."

"Infamous kin aside, what brings you, Thomas?" Robert said.

"I have with me men of honest repute who would join you: Alexander Fraser, John Somerville, and David Inchmartin." He indicated a small group of knights at a distance behind him. "I also come to urge haste, Uncle Robert . . . sire."

"We've heard of the Earl of Pembroke's advance," Edward informed him.

Randolph cast a cursory glance at Edward, and then looked again upon Robert. "And have you heard as well that he has crossed the Forth and stands now at Perth, ready and waiting for you?"

"Aye, we have heard as much." Robert leaned hard on the left arm of his chair.

"And that at Kinross, Bishop Lamberton fell into his hands? And at Cupar, Wishart did likewise?"

King Robert crumpled beneath the weight of the words. His wife's small hand crept over the top of his.

"This is true?" Robert whispered. Coll lifted his great head from the floor and laid his muzzle in Robert's lap.

Randolph nodded once.

"The Earl of Fife is a ward in England," Nigel put forth, rising from his chair. "It would follow that England would strike that earldom first. Why does Pembroke not come north now?"

Randolph grinned faintly. "It is easier to wait there behind high walls while the Comyn sympathizers flock to him, than to go around the country collecting them himself."

"And how many do they number now?" Alexander asked.

Every person there was rapt with attention toward the young, outspoken Randolph. Rebellion, a clandestine crowning—soon enough it would all come to open war and this was the hue and cry.

"Nearly six thousand," he said.

Stunned, Robert stared wordless at his nephew. Half a minute crawled by before any response came to his tongue. "Nigel? How many are we?"

Nigel's forehead bunched as he tallied the numbers in his head. "With Atholl's men from Strathbogie and Strathaan just come, hmmm . . . over four thousand, I reckon."

"Then for the avengement of Wishart and Lamberton, for the citizens of Perth—tomorrow we ride to Fife." Robert swept a hand across his eyes and down over his face, then pulled at his beard so hard it looked as though he would strip the hairs from it. "Nigel, you and Boyd will stay here in Kildrummy. Protect my family at all costs. If events do not favor us, you are to escort them to Aberdeen, where a ship will take them to Norway."

I saw him turn his other hand over and give Elizabeth's hand a little squeeze. Her chin fell to her breast. Tears flowed from her eyes like a river into the sea.

27

Robert the Bruce – Methven, 1306

WITH THE JUNE SUN strong at my back and a fit army arrayed behind me, I sat upon my horse before the walls of Perth. I stripped off my mail hood, then signaled to Christopher and my nephew, Thomas Randolph, to stay put.

Christopher lifted his reins and edged his mount forward. "My lord, you can't—"

"Pembroke is a man of honor, Christopher. He'll listen to what I have to say."

The warmth of the sun beading my brow with perspiration, I rode forward, alone, up to the gates of Perth. A competent archer could have skewered me with one clean shot. But this was as much a test of Pembroke's honor as it was to prove my courage and faith to my men.

"Show yourself, Lord Pembroke!" I shouted. At the might of my words, gulls exploded from the rooftops of Perth in a cloud of beating white wings and dithery calls. While the bright pennons of England fluttered above the drab walls, I saw strings go tight and fingers flex as a hundred arrows marked my heart.

A minute later, the swarthy Earl of Pembroke appeared atop the wall nearest the city gates. "Lord Robert? You look more hale than when last I laid eyes on you. The trappings of kingliness have imbued you with an air of confidence."

"You have taken captive my good friends, Bishop Wishart and Bishop Lamberton. Hand them over, along with the city, or come out and fight."

His smile flashed white in the long rays of early evening sun. "Bold as ever, you are, Bruce. But Wishart and Lamberton are no longer mine to decide the destiny of. Already they are in chains, somewhere to the south, and their fate is at the whim of my king, Edward. I venture to say their frocks shall spare them . . . for a time. A shame my brother-in-law John Comyn was not afforded the same grace by you." He tilted back, gloating, then pitched forward and leaned out from the wall. "As for a fight—the day is too far gone, don't you agree? Although I welcome the invitation, if it should extend to the morrow."

"It does."

"Good." He pulled back and although he disappeared from view, his voice still smacked with authority. "Rest well. I promise a good fight."

As I turned my mount around to rejoin my men, a single arrow whistled through the air. It twanged as it pierced the ground between Christopher and me. He blinked, but did not flinch. Ignoring the taunt, I put spurs to my horse and we rode back to my army. My men had seen enough of the aftermath of Pembroke's destruction on their way here—entire crofts reduced to rubble and charred timbers, graves so fresh the stench of rotting corpses still permeated the air. There was no dearth of inspiration to take English heads for trophies.

"We'll pull back to Methven," I told Edward, "and make camp. A good meal, a good night's rest and tomorrow . . . Pembroke will get what he came for."

Last night we had been encamped near Methven along the River Tay, just north of Scone. Several days earlier, my brothers Thomas and Alexander had left us to continue gathering arms and men elsewhere. I cannot say I sent them off without reluctance, but I had to gather what help I could and there was no time to waste now that the English were north of the Forth. I had left Nigel in Kildrummy, for I knew he would take no unneeded risks where my family was concerned. Edward, as always, I kept near me, for his sake as well as my own.

The men were not happy being put off, but they were hungry and in need of rest, for we had ridden hard from Kildrummy to Perth. And I much preferred to meet the English with spirited soldiers at my bidding.

LONG AFTER THE SUN had slipped from the sky, the pink glow of twilight lingered in the west. What little talk went on that night amongst my men was hushed. Unusual for a band comprised mostly of Highlanders who could not ask another to pass a cup of water without a shout and rumble of fists. It spoke of just how exhausted they truly were. I had pressed the march to Fife—a feat, given the unruly lot they were—before relenting so they could renew themselves.

From Perth, we went back the six miles to a place called Methven and set up camp just south of the Almond River. To the southeast sprawled a patch of woodland. It was there that Christopher, Neil Campbell and a small group went with their short bows in search of game to bring back and share. The rest of us sat about our cooking fires, as we boiled pottages and passed flasks of thin ale. Some, footsore, had already bedded down, too weary for dreams. Their packs were their pillows. The stars, their blankets.

For a time, I stood at the edge of camp with Edward and Thomas Randolph as we chewed over strategy.

"Not many options, as I see it." Edward unearthed a stone with the toe of his boot and with a swift kick sent it scuttling down a short slope. "By accounts, we'll be outnumbered two or three to our every one."

Randolph flinched beneath his suit of mail before casting a look around us at the lay of the land. "We can claim the higher ground, there—to the south of the river."

"He'll have anticipated that move of us," I said, uneasy, "but as you said, Edward, we've precious few options. It will at least draw Pembroke further from the city. A small advantage for us. Pass the order, then. Up and in position before sunrise."

Nodding, Thomas and Edward went off to relay my command. Nearby, young Douglas was perched in a tree, twirling a knife between his hands, his feet dangling on either side of the stout limb which he straddled.

"A bit too eager, wasn't he?" James said to me.

I stepped over a snoring soldier and stood directly below James. The toe of his boot swung in front of my eyes. I stopped it with the flat of my palm. "Who?"

"The Earl of Pembroke." He stabbed the point of the knife deep into the tree limb.

"Why do you say?"

His shoulders lifted. "I just don't ever trust any of them—Englishmen, that is."

"Ah." I folded my arms across my chest. "You said something like that before."

"No, I said I hated them then."

"Aye, well, at least I know what side he's on. It's the Scotsmen around me I worry about."

Pulling his knife free, he swung a leg over and dropped to the ground on quiet cat's feet.

"Do you trust me?" he asked directly.

"With my life."

"But you don't know me."

Ever since he joined us near Lanark I had watched him closely. If Longshanks had sent him as a spy, he was a damn good one. James was always there, always listening, and far sharper of mind than anyone would know of him because of his sparing words.

"I knew your father. Isn't that enough? Now, best steal a few hours rest, both of us, for tomor—"

His head snapped around. Looking wide-eyed toward the woods, he whispered, "Do y'hear?"

"Christopher and the others, hunting perhaps?" In truth, I could hear nothing but low conversation and the stirrings of men nodding off to sleep.

"Listen." His finger drifted up, pointing toward the black tangle of trees a few hundred feet away.

What came to my ears were sounds that made the heart go cold: the far-off clank of bits, the grating of metal on metal, the snap of fallen branches underfoot . . . and the muffled rattle of weapons held ready. I scanned the tree line and at the far northern end, closest to the river, a glimmer of starlight played off a shield painted with a red dragon.

"*Pembroke.*" I yanked my sword from its scabbard. "Tell everyone to arms. We're under attack."

Without faltering, he raced through the camp, yelling, "To arms! To arms! The English are upon us!"

The camp burst to life at his sharp cry. Men scrambled for their arms and horses. The sudden surge of bodies and black chaos made it near to impossible to find my own tent. As I spun around to get my bearings, I tripped over a pot of boiling water. The glowing coals of the fire scattered. Hot spray splattered over my legs.

Embers sizzled as the water hit them. I gasped at the pain, but in a moment the sting was forgotten with a greater terror. The English had parted from the forest's edge. The thunder of hooves shook the ground. Edward reached me as I scurried to find my horse.

"Where is Gerald?" I shouted. I forced myself not to limp. I could not have my men see me in distress. "Damn it. I need him now!"

"What orders?" Edward attempted to follow me without getting trampled underfoot.

"Tell them to hold back. No matter what, they are not to leave the camp."

He broke away into the darkness. All I could see around me was panic, disorientation and desperation. Damn! I had thought Pembroke a man of his word. Never expected this of him. *But I should have . . . should have known.* Where was Gerald?

Finally, I found my tent and burst inside. I searched for my axe, but could not find it in the near blackness. It should have been on top of the chest. I had seen Gerald lay it there an hour past after whetting the edge. I grabbed my shield and dug an arm beneath the straps. As I turned to go outside, tugging my hood of mail over my head, I plowed into Gerald with my shield. He stumbled backward, then jerked a weapon up to his shoulder in reflex. Moments later, he lowered it with a shaking hand as recognition swept over his face. His grip on my axe haft was like a set of irons. I had to wrench it from him.

"M-m-m'lord?" he stammered. "Your horse?"

"No time, Gerald. Arm yourself with swift prayers. There's a knighthood in it for you should we both live to tell of this." I pushed past him and raced back toward the edge of camp. A few dozen of the Highlanders who had kept their weapons at hand had broken into a run, their battle cries shrill as banshees in the frightful night air. English cavalry bore down on them, lances couched. Then they struck their marks with a mighty crash. Blades drew back and cut silver through the blackness. The suicidal fools before them toppled like wheat before the scythe.

I grabbed Edward by the elbow. "I told you to tell them to hold."

"I did!" He jerked his arm away. "Bloody, fucking Highlanders. They don't heed anyone but their own—not me, not even you."

There was no more time for debate. They fell upon us in an awful rush. Horsed knights rammed into our ragged lines. A lightly clad knight galloped at me. He swung his broadsword clumsily. I ducked, then spun and hacked open his calf with my axe. As a howl tore from his throat, I hooked the underside of my axe head in the crook of his arm and ripped him from his saddle, dashing him to the ground. My foot slammed down on his head, shoving it into the earth to expose his neck. I made merciful work of him and claimed his horse as my own.

In the midst of all the screams and grunts and curses, bodies fallen and blades arcing high, I caught sight of Pembroke's dragon surcoat. I tried to make my way to him, but there were fifty men between the two of us and most of those were not my own. I fought on and on until my arms and legs burned. I shouted to my commanders and men when I could discern them, told them to hold ground and gather round. Deaf to my commands, they fended off each blow that rained upon them. As I continued to fight for my own life, some of my bravest and ablest fell wounded and dead around me. In time, Christopher, who had somehow made it back from his hunt on horse, found me and held off more attackers than I could count. Twice, he saved my life. Together we fought our way to the center of camp, now a ruinous, blood-soaked battlefield, littered with bodies.

When I saw Edward with a small, but indomitable circle of Scotsmen, warding off the English that came after them, I took heart. Sword heavy in hand, with one thrust I laid low an English pikeman. As I lifted the reins of my newly acquired horse to turn and join my brother, something heavy and sharp snagged my right forearm. I heard a mocking laugh and jerked my head around. The iron points of a morning star were embedded in the links of my mail. Its chain rattled and I looked past its length to find myself staring straight into the triumphant eyes of a mounted English knight, one I recognized from the courts as Sir Philip Mowbray.

I struggled to free my sword arm. His laughter grew more heinous as he pulled me toward him. My left arm was wedged tight inside the straps of my shield. I sought leverage to pull my arm free. Finally, I loosened my shield and flung it to the ground. Before I could lift my axe from my belt, Mowbray yanked me from the back of my horse. Unbalanced, I tried to pull him down with me, but as his weapon ripped from my arm I fell backward, onto the ground. The air shot from my lungs. My head smacked against a stone.

"Help! Help!" Mowbray shouted over the clang and rumble. "I have their king!"

From where I lay dazed, I saw Christopher spur his horse hard, swing his whole torso forward and deal a forceful blow to Mowbray, who reeled in his saddle. Gulping air, I rolled away from the tangle of horses' legs and pushed myself to my knees. I picked up the sword that had fallen from my grasp. I do not know where I found the strength or purpose, but I latched onto the bridle of my horse, found the stirrup and pulled myself up.

Some fifty or sixty feet yet away, Gerald beat an Englishman to the ground with his sword, flailing back and forth with the last waning shreds of his strength. He glanced at me, grinned in a moment of pending victory, and pulled back his blade for the final plunge. Then, his eyes went wide. He fell to the ground in a lifeless heap. His head flopped forward at an odd angle—his neck severed by a throwing axe.

I wanted to go to him, to pick him up in my arms even as he lay there with the blood draining warm from the back of his head onto the trodden ground. But there was nothing I could do. Nothing. His eyes were fixed open, toward the stars. He jerked once, then went stiff. He was gone. Dead.

Then I cried a cry greater than any I had ever given. "For freedom and kingdom! Rally all to *me*!"

As the angels above received my plea, Scots drew around me. We battled our way to Edward's circle and those of us on horse then broke from the melee and made toward the woods. Men on foot straggled behind. Riding hard and fast, I had no chance to take account of who had made it free, but James and Gil de la Haye were there beside me, beating off the few determined English who tried to pursue us.

At last, we reached the edge of the wood, our breaths coming in bursts and our horses drenched with lather. The brightness of morning broke over the hills and shed its red, revealing light on Methven.

DEPLETED AND BATTERED, WE crossed the Almond and the Tay and made for the mountains of Atholl. Half the day we rode, urging our horses on until they would go no more. When at last one of my knights swayed and fell to the ground in exhaustion, we stopped and took tally. The day before we had numbered forty-five hundred; the next we were barely a tenth as many.

With aching arms, I pulled off my hood and sank to the ground. "Where is my nephew, Thomas Randolph? Where is he? Fraser? Inchmartin? Neil Campbell?" Name after name crowded my head until it pounded with the din.

Gil dropped beside me with a grunt. "Fraser and Somerville fell on the field, side by side. I saw Campbell bringing up our rear."

"Inchmartin fell, too," the Earl of Atholl said. A long cut marked his forehead and blood seeped from his left forearm just above the wrist. "But your nephew—they dragged him from his horse . . . alive. Took him prisoner. He lasted most of the fight."

"Roger Kirkpatrick?" I asked.

Solemnly, Atholl nodded. "Dead."

"Christopher?"

They all looked at each other and shrugged. No one answered.

We huddled silently. The afternoon sun beat down on the tops of our skulls, baking the sweat, dust and blood into thick, leathery hides on us.

Restless, James paced about. He had not a single scratch on him.

"Eighteen," he muttered, stopping to stare at the grass at his feet.

"Eighteen more coming?" Edward jammed his sword point into the rock-hard ground and pressed his weight upon the pommel for support.

"No," James answered. He raised his eyes and looked plainly at Edward. "I killed eighteen men."

"My compliments," Edward said, both cynical and sincere. "You beat my count by four."

I do not remember lying down, only that I felt the cool, damp grass against my cheek and the earth holding me up like a great, endless bed.

Ah, James, you were so very right about Pembroke. I cannot trust any of them. And I should keep an eye on those around me. There is a price on my head. Just like Wallace. They lied to him and lured him into a trap and then tortured him for sport.

I tried to rest, to gather my strength, but thoughts churned in my head like a water spout above a stormy sea. Around me, men moaned from their wounds. Atholl, James and Edward went around, tending to them, but without bandages or anything to cleanse the wounds there was pitiful little they could do. Vaguely, I heard Edward give orders to wait where we were for stragglers to catch up with us. Then he sent off a few of the haler men on horses to go seek out food and shelter for our wounded. I watched him through a fog, his lips moving, understanding the words slowly. He started toward me once, opened his mouth and then went off. My bones felt as though someone had scraped them clean with a knife. My head throbbed. I wanted to sleep, but I was too tired, too—

"You have lost some blood," James remarked above me, "from this wound, here, on your leg. We should get your mail off and wash it."

Then he knelt down and slipped the hood back from my head. "And a gash there, by your ear. Deep, but not too big."

I could not remember being struck in those places. As hard as it was, I pushed myself up and gripped his arm. "He will go to Kildrummy."

"Pembroke? Aye, but what can we do about it? Just look around you."

I nodded and felt myself sinking to the ground again. I touched the tender wound by my ear and pushed the skin closed. "We must go to Aberdeen. Leave here. Go to Norway."

Elizabeth, Marjorie . . . he would take them. I must get to them. Save them. Kildrummy. Aberdeen. Nor . . . Norway. Leave. Save . . . them.

28

<u>Edward, Prince of Wales – Carlisle, 1306</u>

I CARED NAUGHT FOR the place: the north or south of it, village or countryside, mountain or seaside. It was the apple spotted by blight and devoured by worms. And yet, my sire would not toss it aside. He would not let Scotland wriggle from his old, crooked fingers. When he learned of the sacrilegious murder of John Comyn of Badenoch and then Bruce's hasty crowning in Scone, the fury of it all propelled him from his sickbed.

The king summoned every squire in the land eligible for knighthood to Westminster Abbey. There at the Feast of the Pentecost in May, he would knight me and some three hundred others. Among those who answered the call were Hugh Despenser the Younger, the son of one of my advisors by that same name, and a promising young Marcher lord named Roger Mortimer. We kept our nightlong vigil at the altar, our hands folded in prayer and our lips moving as we confessed our copious sins to Our Heavenly Father. Beside me, Piers pressed between his palms three hornbeam leaves: three for the Holy Trinity. At first light, we bathed in holy water and dressed in gowns of white for purity and cloaks of red for our blood. On our knees, we heard Mass and then the Archbishop of Canterbury blessed our swords one by one. Next, my sire conferred our spurs upon us. It drained all his strength to stand for such duration. Twice, he swooned and caught the arm of the archbishop. That night at the feast, his face was blanched, dark crescents of blue hung beneath his eyes and he often closed them, submitting to the fatigue that vexed his aging body. But he was never at any loss for oaths of bloodshed against Robert the Bruce.

The dwarfish darkling Aymer de Valence, the Earl of Pembroke, had already been expeditiously dispatched across the border to trail and drag down the perfidious Bruce and anyone who had blood ties or dealings with him. After the knighting, I led a great train northward. My ailing sire journeyed at a slug's pace in a litter far behind us.

Cost what it may, with quick severity Gilbert de Clare, Piers and I purged the wild Scots from their lairs in Galloway and thereabouts. The smoke that rose from their villages laid a death shroud of soot and ashes over the land. We burnt their crops, slaughtered their cattle and my men took their pleasures in their women. I did nothing to restrain my army. The fewer Scots there were, the less chance I should ever be forced to come back to this pus-infested piss-hole.

As a leaf in autumn too long upon the branch that quavers and drifts to earth, Lochmaben fell into my eager hands. There were no Bruces cowering within. They had all run, scattered like mice in a hayfield. Small matter. What was a king without any subjects? A fugitive in his own country. Content with my prize, I went to Carlisle, where parliament was in session, to report to my sire of the swift justice my companions and I had dealt.

I searched the castle, but could not find him. Then Sir Hugh Despenser the Elder pointed him out to me from a window of the castle where we stood. The king had taken his supper on the banks of the river that evening, just upstream of the bridge outside the city gates. Servants had brought a table, linens and a comfortable chair for him and set it in the grass, beaten down by the commoners who often gathered there on the floodplain in the summertime. I thanked old Sir Hugh and, with Brother Perrot at my side, made my way toward the river. At the gatehouse, I stopped and turned to Piers.

"Wait here," I insisted.

"Why?" he asked. "I thought we were going to share the news of our wonderful triumph?"

"I know, I know, but," I touched him lightly on the shoulder, "I must fulfill a promise I once made to you and the time to do so is now. It will go more smoothly if I broach the subject directly . . . and alone."

Agitated, he nodded. "Very well."

I parted from the cool shade of the gatehouse and went out over the bridge, the sun so bright it nearly drove me back, to meet my sire.

Although the journey from Westminster had compromised the king's health even further, I had been told, a change in physicians since arriving in Carlisle had performed miracles. The previous physician had prescribed rigorous bloodletting; the current one favored herbal concoctions and generous doses of fresh air. The king had finished his meal and departed the riverbank. I cringed upon seeing him walking with renewed vigor, however stiltedly, along the bridge over the River Caldew. My greyhound, a most loyal fawn and white bitch given to me by my oldest sister Margaret, loped timidly at my heels as I approached him. A gaggle of counselors flocked behind him in their colored robes.

He sneered. I was accustomed to the tepid greeting. Before I could impart the news of my success, he drew a ragged, wheezing breath, then spoke, "Pembroke crushed Bruce at Methven . . . and what have you done?"

I took a step back and forced a smile, satisfied in my work. "We took Lochmaben from them and subdued all Galloway and Annandale. The whole southwest is in our hands now. Piers Gaveston was a courageous and astute commander—instrumental in our success. I should like to reward him with the Fife of Ponthieu, as it was my mother's and—"

His hand shot out and grabbed my hair. With surprising force, he shoved me to my knees so hard I thought my kneecaps would shatter on the cobbles. My hound whimpered and crept toward me. My sire kicked her in the ribs and she scuttled off with a yelp.

I, too, squealed. I could not help it. He twisted my hair, pulling it from the roots. My scalp stretched until my eyes bulged. *The pain, my God, the—*

"You, who have not won so much as a rod of ground by your own hand or head, would give away your inheritance?"

The rage in his voice increased with each syllable until I thought every vein in his body might burst from it. His advisors and barons looked on, wordless, judgmental.

"There was no one left to defend Lochmaben when you tripped over it! Instead of defeating a Scottish army or bringing me prisoners of worth, you and your odious playmate make a mockery of your vows of chivalry and commit acts of such abomination . . . Coward's work!" He gave my hair another twist. "And you ask to bestow favors on *him*?"

I reached up to his arm to free myself, but he yanked me up by the hair and dragged me to the wall of the bridge. He slammed my face into the stones. It felt as though a hole had been shot through my skull from cheekbone to cheekbone. Moaning, helpless, I stared down into the churning black water of the river.

"My hope for you is fast fading," the king said. Then he let go of me.

I lay draped over the wall, the stone edge pressing sharply into my ribs. Blood dripped over my upper lip and I licked it away. "And my love for you is long gone."

"You know *nothing* of love. You are possessed by a sickness and I shall cure you of it." My sire loomed above me. The lion sizing up his prey. "I hereby banish Piers Gaveston from the whole of this island—for life. Let him learn of humility elsewhere."

With his councilors bunched behind him, he left me there. I crumpled to the cobbles. Through the white, throbbing pain, I looked toward the gatehouse. Piers was not there. Blood poured from my nose. I raised my sleeve to sop it up.

Boots clicked on the stones before me. Piers unbelted his surcoat and lifted it over his head. Then he bent down and offered it in a wad. I took it and held it to my nose. On her belly, my greyhound crept to me and wedged her slender muzzle under my arm.

"You should not be here right now," I muttered into the soaked cloth.

"If you say go, I will go."

Surely, he did not mean those words? But what choice did we have? If not banishment, then a dungeon it would be. Darkness and rats. Lice and fouled meat. A long, slow, torturous death. And this for serving me with such blind devotion? The ache in my heart was ten times larger than the one in my head.

"How much longer will he curse the earth with his steps?" I wondered aloud.

My sire . . . he fancied himself a genius. And in the matter of laying low entire peoples, perhaps indeed he was. One man, however, had already once had him by the throat and he didn't even know it.

At the far end of the bridge, a crowd had gathered, waiting to enter through the heavily guarded gates, even though the confrontation between my sire and me had long since ended. A little child with a dirty face peered from behind his father's knee and pointed at me. I held out my hand and Piers pulled me gently to my feet. As I turned and began on my way with dreadful reluctance back to the castle, Piers stormed toward the onlookers.

"Be off, you pock-faced hogs! You sewer-slimed rats! Have you nothing better to do than gawk? Have you never seen a man fall? Off with you!" He shooed them all back with a flurry of his hands and then guided me carefully over the bridge and on into Carlisle Castle.

The very next day, he was escorted under guard to Berwick where he boarded a ship. They would not tell me to where. Unable to see my dear Brother Perrot one last time and share farewells, I was forced to attend parliament. The issue there was my much delayed, but now impending, marriage to the Princess Isabella of France. I had no say in it.

What had I done to incite my father's loathing except be born into the world? He would never take pride in me, never love me as I was. Yet he says *I* know nothing of love? It was he who brought Piers into my life and encouraged our bond. But now that he senses it is something more, something *immoral*, he bombards me with contempt? As if that punishment alone might incite me to change. I am not weak; nor am I incapable.

I am who I am—and it is as God made me.

Someday, though . . . someday, long after my sire was dust beneath my feet, I would prove him wrong. I would do what he had failed to. I would defeat the Bruce on the battlefield . . . or die in the trying.

Until then: Edward of Caernarvon, Prince of Wales; master of nothing.

29

<u>James Douglas – Atholl, 1306</u>

KING ROBERT SENT WORD to Kildrummy, urging Nigel to
bring the womenfolk and meet us at our place of retreat:
a rugged camp on Deeside deep within the woods, well upriver
of Aberdeen. To the north and west of us stood the tallest mountains in all of Britain, guardians of the heavens glowing pink with
campion at the edge of day. Along the glen were nestled red-barked
pines with twisting branches and in between were patches of deer-
grass. The lower hills bloomed with the bright yellow of tormentil
and the deep purple of heather. To our south stretched the far
reaches of the Forests of Atholl.

For weeks now, Robert had waited for them to come. Day
after day, rising before dawn, he climbed to the same high hill and
watched from his rocky eyrie. Every evening the same again. But
day after day went by and nothing. No one. He did not pace or fret
or fray away with worry. He simply waited, his eyes as hard and
fixed as chips of stone, gazing above the treetops, surveying along
the river's course.

Then, late one morning—they came.

He had stayed there on top of the hill longer than usual. When he came down it was at a dangerous sprint. Flakes of rock tumbled and flew beneath each footfall. He caught himself on the trunk of a pine at the base of the hill, breathless. Nervously, he tugged at the hem of his tunic and then briefly touched the scar in front of his ear. His beard nearly hid it, but not entirely.

"Edward went on up the path to meet them," I said.

Dumbly, he shook his head and paced ten feet, running both hands through his dark, full head of hair, then back again. He stopped, sidled up to me and said very low, "Should I change my shirt?"

I squinted at him. "Into what, sire? The wardrobe has not yet caught up with the royal train."

He laughed, or tried to. "Gerald used to remind me of such things."

We both went silent with grief. In three short months, Gerald had taught me much about the road to knighthood. Taught me how to look after the king and watch his backside for him. What he liked and disliked and what he would say or do in any situation—like trying to make a joke when his nerves were taut. Then Robert sighed from the bottom of his lungs and took off at a quick trot along the path that ran parallel to the river.

I claimed a seat on a fallen log amongst a group of men who sat about their noonday fire smoking salmon. John, the old Earl of Atholl, sat on the ground, tearing the moldy crust from a loaf of stale bread. The cut on his head had festered and swollen considerably, leaving him temporarily disfigured until Gil had cut into his cheek with a hot knife and drained the wound, then cleaned and dressed it. Atholl had spoken hardly a word since fleeing Methven. His son, David, had married into the Comyn family and the entire precipitation of events since before Robert's crowning had left Atholl alienated from him. Many families were split asunder now. I knew nothing of my own, nor would I be likely to find out anything about them anytime soon.

Fish and fowl were plentiful now, but come winter it would be a harsh living. Bundled warm in our wadmal, Hugh and I used to go out riding in the snow, laugh as we pelted each other hard with balls of ice, and slide down the hillside on scraps of old canvas. But at home, the hills were only a portion the size of those here. And there it was never so far to the next croft or manor or village. Here, you were lucky to see any hint of mankind after days of traveling. Neil Campbell sat down beside me, a quarter of a fish cupped in his palm. He plucked flakes of meat away from the bones and stuffed them into his mouth.

"Did you hear?" I said to Neil. "They're on the road up ahead. Almost here."

"Who?"

"Robert's close kin, from Kildrummy."

He trailed a dirty sleeve across his mouth, leaving bits of fish scattered in his beard. "My Mary? My boy Colin, too?"

"Aye."

Just as he leapt to his feet, Nigel Bruce came riding slowly along the road at the edge of camp. Neil rushed to his wife and helped her and his young son down from their horse and clutched both fiercely. From the mount behind them, Robert's other sister, Christina, slid down wearily into Edward's grasp. He steadied her and took her over to a log to sit. Although the sun was now high and hot, she had a lightweight blanket draped over her hunched shoulders. Nigel gave her a cup of water. She sipped sparingly, and then stared into it.

Slumped sideways, Queen Elizabeth nearly fell into Robert's waiting arms. His embrace was as much out of obvious relief as it was simply to hold her up. She murmured a few words to him and he obligingly escorted her over to sit beside Christina. Elizabeth placed an arm around her sister-in-law and they leaned against each other, succumbing to their fatigue.

Only Marjorie seemed not to suffer at all for their rough journey. She wandered about the camp, rife with curiosity and quite unaware that the men were beginning to cast looks at her. When last I saw her at Kildrummy, I had not noticed her changing shape: the burgeoning curve of her hips, the firm, apple-sized budding breasts. Yet there was still so much of her innocent manner—the idle chatter, the giggling—that betrayed her youth.

Boyd brought up the tail of the retinue, hailing every man who had ever shared a barrel of ale with him. Judging by his string of greetings, that included over half the camp.

The lines of concern were carved deeply into Robert's forehead. A circle of lords and knights quickly grew around him. They began to talk, low at first. Then their voices rose with vehemence. I went to them, anxious to hear news, although I suspected it was not the favorable kind.

Alexander Lindsay, who had been with Nigel in Kildrummy, spoke and hung his head. Then he shook it hard as they barraged him with questions.

Finally, Robert raised both hands. "From the beginning."

Lindsay rubbed at his neck and swallowed hard. "By the orders of King Edward of England, all who support the traitor Robert the Bruce are to be regarded as outlaws and denied ransom and trial when taken. Christopher Seton, captured at the Battle of Methven, was hanged, drawn and quartered at Berwick." Then he bowed his silver-white head and muttered, "God have mercy on his soul."

Neil's face went white and he staggered away, down toward the river.

"She knows?" Robert asked.

Nigel nodded, glancing at Christine. "Twice widowed and not yet thirty."

Then Lindsay rattled off an endless list: those dead on the field, those captured and executed, and those not accounted for, including the Earl of Lennox. Many of those I had come to know since springtime were now gone—their names fading to memory like wisps of smoke carried off by the wind. Survivors from the battle at Methven had trickled in during the month since. Many, too many, had died of their wounds even after escaping the English. For a while, it seemed we laid more bodies in graves every day than living folk came to join us. There was hardly one among us who did not have some scar or limp to remind him of the terror of it.

"Tell him about Randolph," Boyd urged with a sneer.

Robert looked at Nigel. "What happened to him?"

Nigel plainly did not want to have to say it. "Swore himself Longshanks' man in return for his life."

"Bloody traitor," Boyd mumbled, then spit at the ground. He kicked at the dirt and wandered off to beg for food.

Robert had nothing to say on the matter. He looked at me, knowing I understood, then began to walk away. A few strides later, he turned about and asked Lindsay directly, "What about Aberdeen? Can we take ship from there?"

Boyd broke in as he shuffled back to the group, an oatcake in each grubby hand. "You can't even get there. It was the first stinking place Pembroke went after Perth. We're bloody lucky we made it here. He's not far behind us, I wager."

"He's right," Edward said. "All routes east from here are blocked. The ports are held by the English."

If I thought Edward Bruce an arrogant bastard before Methven like the rest of the world did, I now had a wholly different appreciation of him. He was vain and impulsive, aye, but indispensable as well. If you wanted a man who would charge head first at the enemy and break their ranks, it was Edward you called upon.

"North then? To the Orkneys," Robert schemed. "The Bishop

of Moray was headed there."

Ever cautious, Nigel shook his head. "Ross and Sutherland are against you, Robert. You may as well march straight into England as go there. And the west is just as treacherous. John of Lorne there is a kinsman of Comyn's, don't forget."

"That leaves Lennox," Atholl said, breaking his long silence.

Neil came up from behind me. "If we can get to Kintyre," he said, a broad smile breaking over his sun burnt face, "I have lands there. It's not all that far from Ireland, where they hate the English more than anyone. And the MacDonalds of the Isles—they are your best friends, sire." He pounded his chest with pride.

Robert took reassurance in Neil's words. He had mentioned the younger MacDonald, Angus Og, before. The route was a narrow one, past wide lakes and over big mountains, with enemies teeming on either side. But if we could get to Lennox . . . that was not very far from Rothesay where Hugh and Archibald were with my uncle, James Stewart, who was an old man when I was a lad.

"Then south we will go," Robert announced, his voice tinged with resignation.

I imagined Pembroke and his vast army over the next hill, bearing down us. I envisioned hostile Scotsmen, still virulent with hatred over Red Comyn's murder, trailing us through the heather like lame and fading deer. And then I thought of Rothesay and my brothers and dreams of Ireland, green and bountiful, overtook me. I would find them and take them there and when it was time, I would come back and fight beside Robert.

I would win back my home. And I would make certain the English could never again take from me what was mine.

EPILOGUE

Robert the Bruce – Pass of Dalry, 1306

ABBOT MAURICE OF INCHAFRAY leads the way past Tyndrum, bobbing and sweating on his cantankerous, swayback mule. The mist has nearly lifted, revealing the thin trail ahead. Uneasy, I glance at the mountains around us. The closer we come to the sanctuary, the larger the mountains loom and the darker the glen becomes.

At first sight of the little church, clinging to the bare hillside, I send a rider on ahead to call James back, who has been riding in the vanguard with Edward. While I wait for him, I beckon to Nigel and he eases his horse up beside mine.

"Do you recall that castle, sitting out on the little island in Loch Dochart?"

"Aye." Nigel's forehead furrows. "Why?"

"If we are set upon, I want you to go there with the women. Take the Earl of Atholl. Lindsay as well. Half a dozen other men, no more. If you are pursued, then you can hold out there for some time. If you . . ." I cast a glance over my shoulder at Elizabeth, riding beside Marjorie, and smile placidly. They are too far back to hear our hushed conversation, but she returns the smile with haunt-

- 274 -

ed eyes. "If you are not, then you will go back to Kildrummy. It's a strong fortress—and further from England's border."

"What if Pembroke has already marked it? We could hold out for months, perhaps even into winter, but he would be back eventually."

"Go north to the Orkneys. The Bishop of Moray will find a way to Ulster for you. Elizabeth's family will take the women in, I pray."

"And you, Robert? What about you?"

I shrug. "I'll go wherever they'll have me. For the moment, I am putting my hopes on Angus Og."

"A divided family, the MacDonalds."

"I'm betting on that fact, Nigel. When I took Dumfries I emptied it of every sack and barrel in the buttery. Alexander sent those victuals and more on to Dunaverty, at the furthest edge of Kintyre. By the time we get there, if we do at all, Thomas and Alexander will be waiting with Angus Og. I told them to seek him out and swear whatever oaths needed to secure his allegiance. The men of the Western Isles, though they quarrel amongst themselves daily, would cling to their last sea-battered rock for dear life before they would ever prostrate themselves before an English king."

"But the English king has ships," Nigel argues. "A lot of them."

"No English king has ever brought the Isles under his thumb. Longshanks knows his limit."

Off to the side, James now sits quietly on his pony, waiting for the foot soldiers to pass by. As we come by, he falls in beside us.

"Do you see them, James?"

"See who?" Nigel swings his head from side to side, his brown eyes wide.

"Whoever it is who is watching us," I say.

"Here and there." James gazes into the distance, serene, one hand lightly on the reins and the other pulling the strap of his flask over his head for a swig of water. "They are like fleas. If you see one on your arm, there are a hundred more hiding in your mattress."

"Take Gil. Go up that crag." With a tilt of my head, I indicate a peak to our right, ahead of the church. "Come back and tell me what you see."

"As you wish. But it will be on foot. No horse could make that climb without breaking a leg."

James snaps his reins and rides off to collect Gil de la Haye. As our long, irregular column limps to a halt in the valley at the foot of the priory, I see James and Gil scramble deftly up the hillside and vanish behind a knife-like ridgeline. Everywhere, cliffs of iron gray fall away from broken precipices patched with green. The mountains thrust up so abruptly, it seems the sky is higher here than anywhere I have ever been. The sound of a rushing waterfall comes from some invisible place. A fast and narrow stream flows from that unseen source between two great horns of earth out into the first stretch of a small, bow-shaped loch. Scattered clouds creep across the sky, throwing the valleys into half shadow, half sunlight.

Abbot Maurice is halfway to the priory when I begin my climb alone. Several times he stops to gain breath and so I catch up with him before he reaches the little, dilapidated church on the naked hillside. Its roof is caved in from a hundred years of snow. Doors and windows stand gaping like the mouths of decomposing corpses. Beside it, in the tiny, rocky churchyard, is a grave-marker—a simple stone cross, half leaning over like it might topple at any moment, its carvings pitted and chipped. The shrine of St. Fillan.

As if some invisible hand has reached out and pushed me down, I kneel before the abbot next to the shrine. On the slopes below, my army waits, both tired and impatient. Abbot Maurice flourishes his hands above my head over and over and drones on in

Latin. I assume this will be a brief matter—I had sinned, terribly, in God's own house and was asking Him, through Father Maurice, to forgive me—but on and on the abbot mumbles, touching me on the head, dabbing me with water, waving a cross before me. My legs go numb below the knee. My neck begins to ache. I look up at the sky and see the sun dipping from its heights and heading toward the western edge of the world. My men, at first welcoming the brief respite after the morning's challenging trek, are growing restless and wary. I glance often at the place where I had last seen James and Gil, but when they finally reappear and begin to return, it is at quite a distance from there.

Father Maurice, fat as a pregnant sow, grunts as he reaches behind him. He turns back toward me. In his hands, a small, plain box rattles slightly. "These are the Holy Relics of St. Fillan's."

I place my hands upon the little wooden box and repeat a long chain of Latin at the broken prompting of the abbot. While we are so engaged, I hear the tramping of feet from further on up the hill. Finally, James Douglas drops to his knees beside me. Next to him, Gil sinks down, panting.

"This is not the time, James," I say as the abbot pauses to take a breath.

"Agreed, my lord," James utters apologetically. "It would have been better of me to tell you this a day ago."

I look at him sideways. James' countenance is ever the same. I cannot discern joy from anger there, concern from indifference. Always, the reticent lips are thin and firmly set in a straight line. Coal black, tightly curled hair contrasts against the clear pallor of his skin. The eyes, small and piercing, give the impression of watchfulness and constant thought, but never emotion, not a flicker of it. Except for early that morning, when he had knelt before Elizabeth—but that is neither here nor there right now.

He bows his head, as if to receive the abbot's blessing. "We are being watched this very moment. Further along, they line both sides of the pass—hiding, but not well enough."

I cast my eyes back down. My hands slip from the casket of relics. "Father Maurice . . . the short version? Half a blessing is better than none at this moment."

"Ah, but there is no such thing as half a sin, my king," the abbot protests in insult.

"Nor such a thing as half dead," I reply tersely. I feel the hairs stand up on the back of my neck and arms. I fold my hands in prayer.

The abbot grumbles and continues on, his words coming out faster, but no fewer.

I lean over toward James and whisper, "By whom?"

Gil snorts. "Macdougalls."

"John of Lorne," I say to myself. Red Comyn's son-in-law. But at the name, the abbot freezes in his ritual. I look up at him. "A problem, Father?"

"*Kyrie eleison.*" He gathers up his things: the little cross, the relics, his palm-sized bottle of holy water. Tucking them under the fleshy pocket of his arm, he wrings his hands. Perspiration trickles over his temples.

As he makes to leave, I grab the hem of his dusty frock. "Father?"

"We're done, my son. The Lord forgives us all. Even Macdougalls."

I let him go. At once, he slides down the hill with a great deal more energy than he had come up it and calls for his mule. I turn to James and Gil as I stand, dull pinpricks of pain shooting through my legs.

"An ill sign. I take it he has had his own troubles with John of Lorne." I pick my way down the incline, James and Gil close on my heels. I look at the high, broken summits to the south and the shadowy valley that dives between them.

Merciful God, if we are trapped in there, the only way out will be to fight our way through. I told her I would fight if I had to and it will too soon come to that.

"James, do you know how many?" We thread our way amongst the men, most sitting on the ground passing the last crumbs of bread between them, some napping, others playing dice to pass the time.

"Impossible to say, but I doubt they outnumber us. We dared not go too close. I don't think they saw either of us."

Nigel and a group of knights are grazing the remaining horses just off the path our little army has beaten down. As we near them, I turn to James and Gil. "I can't take the chance of going into the pass with the women."

"We turn back, then?" Gil squints. The top of his cheekbones and nose are raw and peeling from too many days in the sun. A thin man to begin with, he looks gaunt enough now to be blown into dust by a strong wind.

"No, we go forward."

"My lord?" James touches my arm and points toward a gap between two crowding mountains. "They're coming."

His eyes are those of a hawk's, for it is several heartbeats that I stare at the very place he has pointed to before I can see even the slightest hint of movement.

"Nigel!" I call. "Take the horses. Go now!"

Nigel starts toward me, gripping his sword hilt. He looks at me, then at Marjorie. She is clutching a soiled blanket to her chest as she leans forward in her saddle to lay her head upon the arch of her pony's neck. Her tangled yellow hair hangs across her cheeks.

He pulls his sword from its scabbard and shakes his head wildly. "We'll never make it free."

"You will." My fists become boulders, dangling at the ends of my arms, weighing me down. I unclench my fingers and slide my own sword from its sheath. "Take the horses. Godspeed, good brother."

With the burdens of a hundred lifetimes hovering over him, Nigel turns to go. Marjorie looks toward James, but he is already seeking out his men. With not enough time to string his bow, he pulls free his blade and casts out orders to some of the soldiers. Her forehead bunched in confusion, she cuts loose her gaze on him and tugs at the reins to join her Uncle Nigel. Nigel calls for Elizabeth, Christina and Mary. The men assigned to them quickly cover the rear. Frantic, Mary clutches young Colin up in her arms for a moment. Then, Nigel tosses him up on the back of a horse and helps Mary up.

I watch them leaving and share a glance . . . only a glance, no more, with Elizabeth before too many men scurry between us with a rising clamor. They gallop off, northward and away from the loch, back from where we had come. So many miles, so very long a way.

With every ring of their horse's hooves, I feel my heart drift further and further from me until there is nothing inside my chest but a hollow ache.

A cry of warning rips from Edward in the front. Argyll warriors, three hundred or more, armed with their axes and swords, race as agilely over the rock-littered ground as hill sheep. They swoop out from the hidden glen and howl their battle cries from haunting faces of blue, lime-white hair streaming behind them in fine plaits . . . their plaids streaking from their waists in a fury of color. Sparks of sun glint off the metal studs of their small, round shields. Spears flash above their heads, then fall toward earth as they eye their first marks.

Perched arrogantly on an outcrop, John Macdougall, Lord of Lorne, slams the tip of his long sword down before him and bears his weight upon it as he roars out his murderous orders.

Scots will die this day—brave Scots. God-fearing as I am, I wish it were not so, for I, too, will kill or die in the fighting. There is no gain in massacring our own, but today is not the day, nor here the place, to embrace in peace. The pitiless John of Lorne, who leads these Highlanders of Argyll, has but one end in mind—and that is to cut my beating heart from my chest and avenge the death of Comyn.

I raise my sword high above my head and with it my voice. "You'll not go from here today, Lorne, and say you left Robert the Bruce drowning in his own blood! Try if you're that big a fool. But I tell you this is *not* my day to rise to heaven. It'll be yours to go to hell! Red Comyn awaits you!"

My other hand moves down to find my axe, snug against my waist. With that as my courage, I take to my horse and go to the rear just as the first whooping wave of Highlanders crashes against our outer lines. I call out to my men. They hold valiantly, neither winning ground nor gaining it, their line unbroken. As time goes brutally by, the blood of Scotsmen soaking the ground, I know that Elizabeth and Marjorie are further from danger.

The fighting is long and fierce. Bodies are crammed so close in the narrow strip between slippery hill and glittering loch that long-hafted spears are rendered useless. I know not how many foes I alone dispatch—they come one after another so fast I can barely save my own skin, let alone see to my men.

Somehow, we endure, although I know not if it has been an hour or a day. They cannot break us and at last begin to fall back in broken waves, struggling up the hillside. The clamor and chaos of a fresh battle has given way to scattered patches of fighting: the random thud of a weapon lobbed at a shield, punctuated by the demonic howls of the dying.

I have but a moment to catch my breath, scrape the now cold and crusting blood from my brow, and call a retreat to spare what lives I can. Edward rushes by and I know he at least has survived this awful day. Then I see James waiting at the rear for me on his pony. His countenance bears evidence of both exhilaration and exhaustion. I follow close behind Edward.

Before we reach James, a riderless horse blocks our path momentarily. Then I hear a dull blow, the high bray of a horse going down, the snap of bones. With a curse, I guide my mount around the stray beast. There, on the dark, blood-wet grass, lies James, his eyes sinking back in his head. At first as I race toward him, it looks as if he has lost an arm entirely. But then I can see, halfway between wrist and elbow, his forearm bent oddly backward, his flopping hand pinned beneath his hipbone.

A wounded Highlander, lying nearby, pushes himself up on hands and knees and begins to crawl toward James, heaving himself along, as if determined that if he is to be left behind, he will bring down one more of his enemies to even the score. He clenches a knife in a mangled hand and creeps steadily closer. Now only feet from James, he raises his torso up. The knife jerks backward over his shoulder.

I let out a cry that startles him. He turns his head as my axe swings down upon his skull. I feel the jolt of metal shattering bone. Blood rains over me.

I bark at Edward to hold up and plunge from my horse to pull James up from the ground. A light load, I sling him over my horse's withers, then pull myself back into my saddle. Twisting my hand tightly in the tail of James' shirt, I spur my horse forward.

Balquhidder, 1306

OUR LOSSES ARE SEVERE. And at a time when we can ill afford them. Southward we straggle, slowed by our wounded and lack of horses. Clouds blot out the sun and an early chill invades the air as evening comes on.

Gil, who has been leading the way, circles back to tell me we are somewhere near Balquhidder. There is no indication we have been trailed, crippled quarry that we are. Around us, bare hillsides are giving way to swaths of forest and Gil points to a faint shadow tucked deep amongst the trees.

"There's a cave there," he says, his voice drawn with fatigue. "I don't know that it will hold us all, but we can at least lay our wounded within before the rain drowns us."

As we head up the slope, James stirs to consciousness, moaning. He slips to the side and I dig my hand deeper in the wad of his shirt, hanging on with a strength I would have thought would be long gone by now.

At the cave, I hand James down into Boyd's bearish grip and he takes him and lays him inside. The place reeks of mold and dampness and now the sharp tang of blood floods the air: the smell of life and of death. I leave my horse, go inside and sink down onto the cold, hard floor of the cave just within the entrance, pale gray light playing over rows of writhing bodies behind me.

Then the feeling washes over me—total and utter exhaustion so deep I feel I could sleep a hundred years. But there is too much to think on. Too much that has happened. And I know there will be no sleep tonight for me. Some of those we tried to save and have brought here suffer gravely. They will not see the sun rise.

Elizabeth and Marjorie have been whisked off under Nigel's keen guard. I know not when I will see them again, or where. They will be hunted, pursued, just as we are. I can only pray they get as far as Kildrummy. I dare not think otherwise. Wish as I may, I can do nothing to ensure their safety. They are in God's care, at His mercy.

Oh Lord, I beg you—keep them safe. Let no harm befall them.

Darkness invades. I feel the shadows creep upon my heart and I shiver, even as Edward sees to the lighting of a small fire near me. Gil squats before me, touches me on the shoulder, but even in that kind gesture I can gather little strength. The task I have embraced, the dream that has compelled me . . . foolish impossibilities.

James rouses, props himself weakly up on his good elbow, and glances fleetingly at his crooked arm. Then he rolls his head back and sinks down again, gritting his teeth.

Men will die, because of me. Because I would not bow to an English lord. Stubborn, stupid, fool!

The night wears on. My head buzzes with thoughts I cannot banish, fears I refuse to face. On the rim of my sight, a black, blurry dot sways from side to side—a spider dangling from an overhang in the cave. It lets out a length of silken thread and sails downward. But the thread is too short, the damp breeze blowing in from the mouth of the cave just enough to push it back, away from where the slanting wall juts out. For a long while it hangs there, its legs twitching in futility. And then it scampers back up its fine, shining rope and five more times it tries again to reach the wall. To me, the space it is trying to span is not so far, but to the wee spider it must be miles.

Dawn arrives, faint and cold. Still, I have not slept. Cries of agony come from the wounded. The fortunate ones have slipped beyond feeling pain. Gil is hard at work, tending to them, while Boyd gives boisterous words of encouragement. Outside, Edward swaggers about, flailing orders at those who yet have the strength to stand.

I look again at the spider, seeing it more clearly now in the growing light, and rise to my feet on numb, quivering legs as I stoop to avoid the low ceiling. I step toward it, thinking to reach out, squash it and spare it the effort. But as I do so, it lets out one more thread and the draft of my movements is enough, barely enough, to waft it to the wall. It clings there, momentarily stunned by its success. Then it anchors the first thread and climbs further up the wall, beginning from a new point. Raptly, I watch as it builds its gleaming web and I am humbled by the persistence of so simple a creature.

Like the spider, I will fail more times than I succeed. The cost will be dear. At times, as now, it will be unbearable. But giving up would be to have lived in vain. For as much as I doubt myself, these men, these broken and bleeding men around me . . . they believe in me for reasons I cannot myself understand.

I drag my feet to the mouth of the cave, my bones grinding with weariness. The sun's rays, growing stronger, fall upon my face. I close my eyes, inhale the damp morning air, and think of Elizabeth.

Author's Note

Folklore has a way of becoming its own truth—sometimes even larger than recorded history. I employed both the lore and the recorded annals in the telling of this tale. In the portrayal of detailed events in this book, I have made every attempt to maintain historical accuracy; however, it must be remembered that the Scottish struggle for independence spanned several decades. During this time, countless battles and sieges occurred and many, many people took part in the events of the era. Political entanglements were far more complex than what I have presented here. Therefore, some events have been condensed out of necessity.

In trying to bring the people on these pages to life—with all their inherent fears and dreams, flaws and ambitions—I have elected to use language familiar to our own era. My objective is to approach historical fiction as a storyteller, rather than a historian, so that the great stories of the past will be relatable to today's readers.

King Edward I of England was not referred to as 'Longshanks' until quite some time after this story took place. But I have chosen to call him by that name to eliminate confusion between him and his son, as well as Edward Bruce.

I have often felt as though I was born in the wrong century— or maybe that I have lived before. Given my Scottish roots on my maternal grandmother's side and my inexplicable attraction to the events of this time . . . perhaps I did.

Acknowledgments

While I revel in the solitary nature of the writer's life, this book could never have seen its way into print without a group effort.

I owe a great deal of gratitude to my fellow critique group members—Anita Davison, Mirella Patzer, Lisa Yarde and Julie Conner—all of them angels, who saved me from committing untold egregious errors. Their patience and attention to detail is beyond measure.

Boundless thanks also goes out to my small army of readers: Joni Johnson, Diana Robinson, Cheri Lasota, Paul Reid and Greta van der Rol, who generously offered to peruse the whole story during various stages in its metamorphosis. It was their brutal honesty that chiseled a crude manuscript into a book that I'm proud to share—and their encouragement that goaded me into doing so. Special mention goes to Ali Cooper, who held my hand through the final technical stages.

And to my husband, lifelong love and best friend Eric Brickson, I owe the existence of my dream. He, in his eternal support and tolerance, gave me the room to grow roots and the air to unfurl leaves.

About the Author

N. Gemini Sasson holds a M.S. in Biology from Wright State University where she ran cross country on athletic scholarship. She has worked as an aquatic toxicologist, an environmental engineer, a teacher and a cross country coach. A longtime breeder of Australian Shepherds, her articles on bobtail genetics have been translated into seven languages. She lives in rural Ohio with her husband, two nearly grown children and an ever-changing number of sheep and dogs.

www.ngeminisasson.com